Praise for *The Castle School for Troubled Girls*

"An achingly beautiful exploration of grief and relationships, parents and children, the ways we hurt, and the ways we heal. Gripped me from the first page and held me fast long after I finished reading."

—Gilly Segal, *New York Times* bestselling co-author of *I'm Not Dying with You Tonight*

"Hooked me from page one. I couldn't stop reading until I had every single answer."

—Francesca Zappia, author of *Eliza and Her Monsters*

"Beneath the trappings of a fast-paced mystery, this novel holds a heartrending exploration of adolescent grief... Memorable."

—*Booklist*

"Complex and layered...A heartfelt exploration of grief, guilt, and recovery."

—*School Library Journal*

"An effective exploration of mental illness, and it will share a coveted place on reading lists with Laurie Halse Anderson and Patricia McCormick."

—*The Bulletin of the Center for Children's Books*

"Mental health awareness wrapped in a captivating storyline."

—*Kirkus Reviews*

"Skillfully illustrates the weight of grief, the difference between adaptive and nonadaptive reactions to trauma, and the healing power of radical acceptance."

—*Publishers Weekly*

## Praise for *What Kind of Girl*

"Both timely and timeless, *What Kind of Girl* is a powerful exploration of abuse in its many forms, as well as the strength it takes to rise up and speak your truth."

—Amber Smith, *New York Times* bestselling author of *The Way I Used to Be, The Last to Let Go*, and *Something Like Gravity*

"I immediately saw myself in this book, which so thoroughly explains the thought process when coming to terms with victimhood and survivorship. I felt understood—*What Kind of Girl* is my new best friend."

—Chessy Prout, author of *I Have the Right To*

"Important, raw, timely, and ultimately hopeful."

—Shannon M. Parker, author of *The Girl Who Fell* and *The Rattled Bones*

Praise for *A Danger to Herself and Others*

"A thrilling page-turner."

—*School Library Journal*, Starred Review

"A compelling and beautifully told story."

—Kathleen Glasgow, *New York Times*
bestselling author of *Girl in Pieces*

"This compelling character study begins like a thriller—the mystery of what happened to her friend Agnes draws considerable suspense… It becomes a nuanced exploration of mental illness."

—*Booklist*

# THE
# CASTLE
# SCHOOL
## FOR
# TROUBLED
# GIRLS

## ALYSSA SHEINMEL

sourcebooks
fire

Published by Sourcebooks Fire, an imprint of Sourcebooks
P.O. Box 4410, Naperville, Illinois 60567-4410
(630) 961-3900
sourcebooks.com

The Library of Congress has cataloged the hardcover edition as follows:

Names: Sheinmel, Alyssa B., author.
Title: The Castle School (for troubled girls) / Alyssa Sheinmel.
Description: Naperville, Illinois: Sourcebooks Fire, [2021] | Audience:
    Ages 14. | Audience: Grades 10-12. | Summary: Paralyzed by grief, Moira
    feels punished when her parents send her to a therapeutic boarding
    school in Maine where she meets eleven other troubled girls and
    gradually begins to understand her parents' true intentions behind
    sending her there.
Identifiers: LCCN 2020044896
Subjects: CYAC: Grief--Fiction. | Mental illness--Fiction. | Therapeutic
    schools--Fiction. | Boarding schools--Fiction. | Schools--Fiction.
Classification: LCC PZ7.S54123 Cas 2021 | DDC [Fic]--dc23
LC record available at https://lccn.loc.gov/2020044896

Printed and bound in Canada.
MBP 10 9 8 7 6 5 4 3 2 1

# one

The first thing they tell me is that the school is called the Castle and the campus is called the Kingdom.

"Doesn't that sound nice?" my mother says, her voice maddeningly upbeat.

I roll my eyes. No matter what they call it, my parents aren't sending me to a fairy-tale charm school for aspiring princesses. Not when there are two enormous men waiting by our apartment's front door to take me there. I glance at my dad, but he won't meet my gaze. Mom must have told him that this is for the best. He always lets her take the lead.

A glossy brochure is spread out on the coffee table in front of me, a name printed in block letters across the top: THE CASTLE SCHOOL. The pictures show a building that looks like one of those medieval castles in the Black Forest in Germany, the kind you see on postcards and in tourism magazines and books.

They never tell you that the king who had those castles built was mad, that he tortured and enslaved people to make his pretty buildings.

Finally, I say, "You're sending me to reform school?"

King Ludwig II. That was his name, the German king who built the castles. Mad King Ludwig.

"It's not a *reform* school." Mom's voice shakes. "Teenagers get sent to reform school as an alternative to *prison*." She recites the words as though she practiced them. "*This* place is nothing like *that*. This isn't a jail, it's a castle!"

Technically, there are plenty of castles that served as prisons. Take the Tower of London. But I don't think Mom is in the mood for that kind of historical trivia. Nathan always loved my little factoids. If he were here, he'd say Mad King Ludwig's name out loud, exaggerating the *v* sound. *Lud-vvvvvig.*

"This is a school for girls going through a rough patch. Girls whose parents…" Mom pauses, then closes her mouth. Her dark brown eyes are bright with tears even though she's the one *choosing* to send me away.

In my head, I fill in the rest of Mom's sentence: girls whose parents can't handle them anymore. Girls whose parents can't stand them anymore. Girls whose parents are at their wits' end because their daughters might not graduate this spring. Girls whose parents are so disappointed with the way their daughters have turned out that they don't know what to do. Girls whose parents think there's something *wrong* with them, so they send them away, hoping for a fix.

That's not a rough patch. That's just rough.

I press my hands against the sofa, feeling the spot where the material is slightly scratchy from the time I spilled grape juice as a little kid, a stain Mom was never able to get rid of completely. An accident for which she still hasn't forgiven me.

I'm willing to bet that she's been thinking about sending me away for a while, but only made up her mind to go through with it last week, when—instead of doing the extra credit work my teachers so generously assigned me over winter break so I could maybe graduate with the rest of my class this spring—I came home after curfew with a tattoo on my arm.

Well, not that night *exactly*. I was able to hide the tattoo for the first few days.

I'd originally wanted to get a line from my left index finger to my heart, because my grandmother once told me that traditionally, Jewish women wear their wedding rings on their index fingers. She said she chose to wear hers on her left index finger because she believed that finger was the beginning of a direct line to her heart. The tattoo I'd imagined going up my arm and across my chest would have been a symbol of the space my best friend took up inside my heart.

But I knew a long line would have been impossible to hide, so I decided to get something smaller at the halfway point between my finger and my heart, on the inside of my upper arm. A little red arrow pointing in the right direction. Red for love; red for the blood beneath my skin. I'd kept it bandaged and dry for days, hidden beneath long sleeves.

And then my mother walked in on me in the bathroom. I'd taken my shirt off to check on the tattoo in the mirror, holding my arm up like a bodybuilder. She didn't even look at me, only at my reflection. She screamed like she'd seen a ghost.

It's not like I'd gotten a tattoo of Nathan's *name*. There was no need for that, since the word already felt written on my skin, into my heartbeat, coded into my DNA. But to Mom, a tattoo was a tattoo, no matter how small. As far as she was concerned, I'd branded myself.

Later, Mom assigned me chores to punish me for what I'd done. I said I didn't see why I should be disciplined for doing something to my own body, but she insisted, and my father kept quiet. So I checked the mail, took out the trash, washed the dishes. At the time, I thought Mom must have read some parenting magazine from the 1950s on how to discipline your rebellious teenage daughter.

Now, she tells me the school told her that assigning chores would help keep me from backsliding further. If I went too far into darkness, I wouldn't be eligible for the program anymore. It's not a hospital, Mom explains. Girls who are too sick can't go there.

I like the sound of that: *too far into darkness*. I wonder if it's in the brochure.

"They say he's the best." Mom brushes an invisible strand of hair away from her face. Mom always says we have the same hair—dark brown, straight, thick—but I've never believed it. My hair is always a mess. Mom never has a strand out of place.

"Who?"

"This teacher."

4

"No, I mean, who says he's the best?"

She reaches for the brochure on the coffee table. "It says so."

"Their own advertising materials say they're the best?"

My mother clutches the brochure like it'll protect her from my sarcasm. "The guidance counselor at your school suggested it," she says, like that makes it official. "The food is all organic. You'll be out of the city, breathing fresh air. You'll have space to recover there."

One of the men by the door tells me to pack a bag. He mispronounces my name.

"Moy-ra, not Moor-a," I correct him. If my parents had ever met this man before, they'd have told him my name. Which means they're about to send me off into the wilderness with a stranger, to a place they've never seen in real life.

I take a drink from the water bottle I keep close by at all times: hooked on to my backpack, my jeans, my wrist. I drink until the water pushes everything back down: the lump in my throat, any food working its way around my belly, the bile I taste in the back of my mouth.

Doesn't my mother realize there's not a shrink in the world (I know she called him a teacher, but let's face it—places like this are run by therapists) who can make time go backward, who can turn me into the sweet little girl she always wanted me to be? The shrink would have to turn back time all the way to before my birth. He'd have to switch things around in utero.

Maybe that's why they call them shrinks. Mom wants someone who'll shrink me down to nothing.

5

When I was little, like a lot of only children, I asked my parents for a sibling. Mom said she couldn't give me one, and I was too young to understand what that meant. For a while, I walked around with my belly sticking out, like I thought I could create my baby brother or sister, having no idea how those things were really done. By the time I met Nathan in eighth grade, I'd given up on having a sibling. After we became friends, I didn't feel like I needed one anymore.

"Moy-ra," the man by the door repeats, mocking me by overenunciating. I check Mom's face for a sign of hesitation about sending me away with a man who can't say my name properly, but she looks as determined as ever. And Dad's still avoiding eye contact. Once Mom makes up her mind about something, there's no changing it. And she's clearly made up her mind about me.

What kind of parents *punish* their daughter because her best friend died?

"Just Moira will do, thanks," I say, standing. The man and his companion bend their legs into a crouch, as if bracing themselves for impact.

"There's nothing to be gained by trying to run." One of the men holds up his hands to block me, even though I'm at least six feet away from him. He bends and straightens his fingers.

"You told me to pack my bag." I point to the hallway on his right. "My bedroom is that way."

I can't help but think, as I walk past him, that he's a little bit disappointed. Surely his job is a lot more interesting when someone tries to make a break for it.

Maybe I *should* try to escape. But how? There are two bodyguards between me and the front door, and we live on the seventh floor of our apartment building. It's not like I can climb out the window and shinny down the drainpipe.

And if Nathan were here, he'd reasonably point out that I'll either be under my mother's thumb here or under some quack's thumb at this special school. I can hear his voice saying, *what difference does it make?*

So I start packing.

Mom cries when I leave. Again, I'm tempted to point out that she's the one sending me away. Dad hangs back. For a second, I think he's going to shake my hand, like I'm a business associate or something, but he ends up sort of patting my back.

Mom presses her wet face against my dry one in lieu of an actual hug or kiss. Physical affection doesn't come easily to her. Even when I was little, she didn't like me to sit on her lap or bury my face in her neck, the way other little girls did with their moms. Mom is nothing like Nathan's parents. They hugged me the first time they met me.

"You'll see," Mom says, pulling her face away. "When you get back, you'll feel better. You haven't been yourself since Nathan." She doesn't say *since Nathan died.* She never does. She's big on euphemisms. Like calling the literal fortress you're sending your daughter to a *school.* "When you get back, all of this will feel completely different. You'll see."

*All of what,* I think but do not say.

# *two*

My two bodyguards won't tell me where the school is located, which is really stupid, because I could have easily seen it on the brochure if I'd bothered to look at it more closely. Plus, when we get to the airport, there are signs all over announcing the destination of our flight: Portland, Maine.

My companions wear black pants and tight black shirts, and they don't tell me their names. Both of them have their hair cropped short, and one puts on a charcoal-gray knit hat during the drive to the airport. They have to take their shoes off and empty their pockets at security, just like I do. One of them even gets a pat-down from a TSA agent. When he lifts his arms over his head, I see that he has a tattoo like a bracelet around his upper arm, much bigger than mine. I bet no one sent *him* away for getting it.

I've always thought Maine sounded like a nice place to visit: lobsters and pebbly sand between my toes, rocky jetties and crashing waves. If we were a different kind of family, maybe we'd have taken a road trip up there one August. Maybe we'd have stayed at a bed-and-breakfast on the ocean, though the water would be too cold, even in August, to do anything but dip your toes in. I would've worn jean shorts with warm sweaters at night, the ocean breeze forcing me to bundle up, and I would have watched from my room as local teens built bonfires on the beach. If I were a different kind of girl, I might've gone down to the beach to meet them, but even in my imagination, I stayed inside.

Something tells me that the Maine to which I'm heading will bear little resemblance to the Maine I imagined.

While we wait to board our flight, I look up facts about Maine on my phone. Maine is the only state in the country with a one-syllable name. Nearly 90 percent of the nation's lobster supply comes from the waters off the coast of Maine. Maine's earliest inhabitants were descendants of Ice Age hunters. Ninety percent of the country's toothpicks are produced in Maine. The black-capped chickadee is the official state bird. Maine lies farther northeast than any other state. The average low temperature in Portland, Maine in January—today is January seventh—is thirteen degrees Fahrenheit.

On the plane, I let my hair fall across my face and drink as much water as the flight attendants will give me. Maybe my companions think my parents sent me away because I'm on drugs, that I'm trying to flush all the chemicals out of my system before I get to the Castle School, where they'll make me take a drug test. These men don't know about the lump that took up residence in my throat a few months ago, back when the weather was still warm and the days were longer and the average low temperature in Portland, Maine was fifty-one degrees. I brought my water bottle from home, but they made me give it up when we went through security.

When we land in Portland, there's a sign with my name on it outside the baggage claim: *Moira Dreyfuss*, handwritten in black ink. The letters start out big but get small by the end because whoever made the sign ran out of space on the page. The person holding it is tall, but he looks young—not much older than I am. The boy with the sign wordlessly leads the way to a van, hefts my bag inside, and heads for the driver's seat. He has curly red hair that Nathan would say looks like a clown's wig. (It's not nearly that long or that bright, but Nathan would say it anyway to make me laugh.) On the side of the van is the name of the school and a picture of a castle. I can make out a few words beneath THE CASTLE SCHOOL that have been painted over: FOR TROUBLED GIRLS. I wonder when they shortened the name.

I blow on my hands, trying to keep warm. I have a wool hat on, but I don't think I remembered to pack gloves. My black-clad companions sign the papers the boy hands them and then nod in my direction. I wonder if other parents bring their daughters here themselves. Maybe my parents had to pay extra for a muscular escort.

"I'm Randy," the boy mumbles as I climb into the van. He's wearing a windbreaker rather than a real coat. He must be freezing, but maybe he's lived in Maine his whole life and he's used to the cold. Or maybe his curls are better at holding in warmth than my hat is.

I look at the sky as Randy pulls away from the airport. The incoming planes are lined up brightly in the dark sky, waiting for their turns to land like a very organized constellation. I try to guess which of the planes will take my escorts away. Will they head straight to the home of some other troubled girl? Maybe she'll rush for the door, providing them with more excitement than I did.

I wonder if my parents will get some kind of report regarding my behavior on the flight so they'll think the muscled escorts were money well spent. No matter what the report says, my mother will assume I behaved badly.

Maybe I should be glad she sent me away. At least it'll be a break from seeing the disappointed look on her face every day. The thing is, Mom's right about one thing: I deserve to be punished. She's just wrong about why.

Randy slouches in the driver's seat as though he only just had a growth spurt and hasn't gotten used to being tall yet. After a few minutes, I ask, "How long have you had your license, anyway?" I add, "I only have my learner's permit." Nathan and I got our permits together, though as it turned out, we never had a chance to practice driving.

"My dad taught me to drive when I was thirteen."

"But how long have you had your *license*?" I ask again. I'm not normally particularly chatty, but I'm not normally being driven down a nearly empty highway by a total stranger.

Randy glances at me briefly. He has light brown, almost

amber-colored eyes. "Six months." I think maybe he's blushing, but it's hard to tell in the dark. Randy returns his focus to the road, his hands in perfect ten-and-two position on the wheel like they teach in driver's ed.

I'm worried that I've offended him, so I try for what I think will be an inoffensive question. "Is Randy short for something?"

"Randy," he says. "Bertrand."

"Your name is Randy Bertrand?"

"No." He pushes his hair back from his forehead, revealing a patch of freckles just beneath his hairline, and squints at the road. "My name is Bertrand, but only my father calls me that."

The father who taught him how to drive at thirteen.

Nathan's father called him Nate sometimes.

"Why doesn't your father call you Randy?"

"He likes the sound of Bertrand."

I don't know quite know where to put my hands, so I slide them beneath my thighs.

"My dad likes old-fashioned things," Randy explains. "That's why he likes the Castle so much."

"Your father works at the school?"

Randy nods. "He runs the place."

I remember that Mom said they called the campus the Kingdom, so I ask, "Does that make you a prince?" It's supposed to be a joke, but Randy scowls.

"You're not supposed to be sitting up here, you know." He points to the rows of seats behind us. "You're supposed to sit back there. And you're not supposed to talk to me."

I unclick my seat belt and climb into the back seat.

I don't know how long we drive. I don't have a watch, and my phone is in my backpack, which I left up front. It feels like it's been hours since I've seen anything but trees along the side of the road. Even longer since we passed another car.

Finally, some light appears in front of us. I lean to the side, looking around Randy's head. I can make out the silhouette of a turret. Randy stops in front of twisted metal gates lit on either side by old-fashioned-looking streetlamps. He hops out of the car, keys jangling in his hands. He leaves his door open, and cold air fills the van as he unlocks the gates and pulls them open.

Flickering gas lamps line the driveway, which curves around the Castle like a moat. It's not *huge*, as castles go. (Not that I'm an expert on the subject.) But it's unmistakably a castle: three stories high, gray stone walls, arched windows, a single round turret. A flickering light hangs over an enormous wooden front door. Randy puts the car into park and jumps out.

I try to open my door, but it's locked, and I can't unlock it. It must have one of those safety locks they use for little kids. And in the back seats of police cars. Randy walks around the van and opens the door for me.

"Where are we?" I ask.

"At the Castle."

"But where in *Maine* are we?"

Randy grins and holds out his arms, gesturing to the woods around us. "This is all part of the campus."

"But we're still in the state of Maine, right?" I want the question to sound like a joke, no big deal, but my voice is shaking.

I've never felt air this cold. At home in Manhattan, the snow usually melts into slush almost as soon as it falls. Here, it looks frozen solid. And the stone walls rising up in front of me don't exactly look warm and inviting.

"Come on," Randy says. He sticks a key into the center of the enormous wooden door. It looks like it was built to accommodate horse-drawn carriages, rounded at the top, made of planks of wood so raw that I'm scared I'll get a splinter just from standing close to it. I half expect it to lower vertically like a drawbridge. But much to my surprise, the door Randy opens is regular-sized, cut into the wood of the bigger door. Under other circumstances, it might strike me as funny that the door is locked. Judging by the darkness around us and the distance we drove from the airport, this place is so far in the middle of nowhere that there's no need for locks and keys to keep people out. Or in.

Seriously, *where* have my parents sent me?

"Everyone else is asleep," Randy explains, closing the door behind me. He flips a switch, and the front hallway lights up. There are narrow fluorescents overhead, like the ones in my school back home, and they make the stone walls and floor look alternately blue and green. "What time is it?" I ask. It's dark enough outside that it could be the middle of the night. But I don't think it's been that many hours since I left New York. Because we're so far northeast, the sunset here is even earlier than it is in Manhattan.

14

From behind Randy, a voice says, "What do you need to know the time for?"

I turn around. The man must have been standing behind the door when we came in.

"Moira," he says, pronouncing my name correctly. "I'm Dr. Prince."

I almost laugh—his name is Dr. Prince, and he owns a castle? No wonder Randy scowled when I asked if he was a prince. Dr. Prince continues, "I've heard so much about you from your mother."

"I haven't heard anything about you," I say, "and I would like to know the time. It helps me, you know, get myself oriented."

"Whatever oriented you before you arrived clearly hasn't been working. Maybe you should try being disoriented for a change." Dr. Prince chuckles, but the laughter doesn't reach his eyes. He's wearing a tweed jacket over a vest and a flannel shirt, like he's a college professor rather than a therapist. Maybe he believes he can trick the girls here into forgetting that this is an institution for troubled teens if he dresses like it's a regular boarding school.

*Then again*, I think, shivering in the cold of the front hall, *maybe that's just how he keeps warm.*

"It must be late," I try. "Randy said everyone was asleep."

Dr. Prince nods. "Exactly. Here at the Castle, you do not need to know the time."

"What do you mean?"

"You need to know only when it is time to sleep and time to wake. Time to eat and time to work."

"How will I know when those times come and go?"

The doctor smiles another smile that doesn't reach his eyes. "I will tell you." I'm not sure I've ever heard anyone speak with so few contractions.

After a beat, he adds, "I think I will turn in. Bertrand, show our new guest to her room, will you?"

If there was any doubt in my mind that this was Randy's father, it disappears when he says his son's name, even though there's no resemblance between them. This man has straight black hair and light blue eyes. His skin is white and freckle-free.

I can't believe my parents shipped me off to the middle of nowhere with this weirdo in charge.

Actually, that's not true. That part is easy to believe.

Mom's probably glad to be rid of me.

# three

If Nathan were here, he'd be laughing about the fact that this place is a castle run by a guy named Dr. Prince. Is his wife Mrs. Prince or Ms. Princess? Joke after joke would spill out of his mouth. I'd look up the name and the etymology of the word *prince* until I found some piece of trivia interesting enough to stop him from making another bad joke.

I wish I still had my water bottle.

Randy leads me up a narrow stone staircase. He pulls my suitcase behind him easily. He's stronger than he looks, I think, eyeing his back. He's tall and thin but wiry, like he's all muscle. His sneaker-clad feet land softly on the stone floor.

"You a runner?" I ask. The question comes out louder than I intend, my voice bouncing off the walls.

"Yeah," Randy answers. "Every day unless the weather's too bad."

I picture him running through the grounds that were depicted so prettily in the brochure, weaving his way between the snowdrifts, sweat freezing along the edges of his hat and scarf.

By the time we reach the second-floor landing, it feels like we've been walking up the stairs forever. The first-floor ceiling must be ridiculously high. Randy leads me down a long, fluorescent-lit hall with several narrow wooden doors on either side. The wheels on my suitcase rattle over the stone. Randy heads for the last door on the left. Before he opens it, he flips a light switch beside the door, and I can see light coming from the other side.

Inside, there are two twin beds, one on each side of the room, with a tall window between them. Beige carpet covers the floor, maybe in an attempt to make the room feel warmer than the stone hallway. Randy hefts my suitcase onto the bed on the left side of the room.

"They'll go through your stuff in the morning," he explains.

"Go through my stuff?"

"They usually do it right away, but you're the first person to arrive after bedtime."

"Bedtime?" I echo. "What are we, eight-year-olds?"

Randy shrugs.

The covers on the bed on the other side of the room are thrown back messily, so I guess I must have a roommate. But if it's bedtime, shouldn't she be here?

"Where's my roommate?" I ask.

"Eleanor's in the infirmary."

"Why?"

Randy shrugs again.

"If they go through your stuff, don't they, like, take all the things you might be able to hurt yourself with?"

"What makes you think she hurt herself? She might have the stomach flu."

"Does she have the stomach flu?"

Randy heads for the door. "Bathroom's at the end of the hall."

"Got it." I don't want to be left alone in this strange place yet, so I ask, "Do you go to school close by?"

"Sort of." Randy hovers in the doorway. "Homeschooled."

"Oh." I wonder how far away the nearest regular school is. "Do you like homeschooling?"

Instead of answering, Randy says, "I'm not supposed to be alone with any of you girls."

"You were alone with me in the car."

He shrugs again. "Necessary evil."

I take a deep breath around the lump in my throat. "Is that what they tell you? That we're sent here because we're evil, or bad, or whatever?"

"No." He shakes his head. "That's not what they tell me." He runs his hands through his messy hair, glancing around the room. "I better go. I've already been here too long."

"How do you know when there's no time here? Maybe you've only been here thirty seconds."

Randy smiles—a real smile that reaches his eyes, unlike his father's—but then sets his mouth into a firm line.

"You should go to bed," he says.

◇◇◇◇

After Randy leaves, I stare at the unmade bed on the right side of the room. The closest I've ever come to sharing a room with another person was when I slept on the pull-out chair in Nathan's room. It wasn't the sort of thing that was normally allowed, but they made an exception for me.

I take my phone out of my bag. The battery's almost dead. I want to look up what time the sun sets here, but there's no service, and it's not like anyone offered me a Wi-Fi password. Plus, I still don't know exactly where *here* is. With Nathan gone and my parents having sent me away, it's not like I have anyone to call or text. I have the phone numbers of some of my other class-mates, but I've never really been on texting terms with anyone but Nathan, especially after I started skipping school to spend more time with him.

Maybe tomorrow, when I don't show up for the first day of the semester, my classmates will wonder where I am. Maybe they'll post on social media, #WhereInTheWorldIsMoiraDreyfuss. (I hear the joke in Nathan's voice.) But of course they won't wonder where I am. I've barely made it to class in months, even when I wasn't hundreds of miles away.

I look around for a socket to plug my charger into, but there isn't one. I head for the bathroom—surely there are girls here who use hair dryers, right?—but there aren't any sockets there, either.

I linger in the hallway, listening for sounds coming from behind the five other wooden doors. These must be the bedrooms of the girls I'm sharing this floor with, right? But it's silent. Guess that bedtime thing actually works.

I head back into my room and close the door. According to my almost-dead phone, it's nine p.m. There are heavy curtains on either side of the window, but there's no need to pull them shut; it's pitch-black outside. I can't even see the moon. In fact, with the lights on, I can't see anything through the window but my own reflection.

To have something to do, I unpack. At the foot of each bed is a dresser with three drawers, and a small closet is built into the wall on either side of the door, though I quickly discover that the hangers don't come off the rod. I glance at my roommate's side of the room. She put her face wash and shampoo on top of her dresser, so I do the same.

I change into pajamas, then climb into bed and close my eyes. The overhead light is still on, the same sort of fluorescent that's in the hallways. I wish there were a place for a small reading lamp by my bed. My cell phone has a flashlight, but that seems like a waste of what little battery I have left.

With a start, I remember I have a tiny flashlight on my key chain. My dad gave it me to when I started walking home from school by myself in sixth grade. I told him I didn't need it, but he insisted. I dig my keys out of my backpack and unclip the light. Is this the sort of thing they'll confiscate tomorrow? I need to find a good hiding place for it, just in case.

Under the mattress seems too obvious, as does inside a pillow-case. I get down on my hands and knees. The carpet is rough, like the industrial kind they have at airports. I crawl around the room, running my fingers along the seam where the floor meets the wall.

At the head of my bed, just under the window, I feel a snag. I grab it and pull, exposing the stone floor full of cracks and crevices, just right for hiding a pocket-sized flashlight.

I fit the light into a crack, then press the carpet back down, stomping on it with my socked foot. It looks just as smooth as it did before I pulled it up.

I go to the door and stick my arm out—my left arm, the one with the tattoo. I flip the light off and close the door, turning my eyes to the pitch-dark room.

I'm not tired enough to sleep, but it's so dark that I can't even stare at the ceiling. So I just listen. It's too cold out for crickets, too still for wind. If Nathan were in the opposite bed, he'd lament this whole bedtime situation.

*Seriously, Moira, a bedtime? When was the last time you had a bedtime?*

He wouldn't worry about wasting his phone battery. I imagine his hazel eyes lit up by his phone. I pretend I can smell the minty scent of the tea tree oil soap his mother made him use because she said it was a natural antiseptic.

Nathan would make up a scary story about a girl who was sent deep into the darkest woods at the northeasternmost point of her country, where the days are short and the nights are long. He'd say she went to live in an old stone fortress haunted by the ghosts who'd lived there centuries ago.

I'd point out that we don't know how old this building is. It probably hasn't existed for centuries; not much in this country has.

Nathan would say I was letting facts and figures get in the way of a good story, but he wouldn't make me feel like a loser for it, because he never did.

I roll over on my side and squeeze my eyes shut. How did I end up here?

Mom would probably say the path that led me here began in eighth grade, when I met Nathan. She decided he was a bad influence because I spent less time at home once he was in the picture. She never understood that I simply liked being at his apartment better than I liked being at ours. In Nathan's apartment, no one scolded me because my ponytail was messy or because I forgot to take off my boots the instant I stepped inside. I got my first period in his bathroom (and went to his mother for help, not to my own) and had my first kiss in his bedroom (though we quickly agreed we were better as friends).

I think the path that brought me here began before I met Nathan. Maybe in first grade, when I got my first (and only) bad mark on a report card for sloppy handwriting and Mom looked so disappointed. Or in fifth grade, when we found out I was allergic to hazelnuts, which meant Mom couldn't bake with them anymore. And Mom looked so disappointed.

Or maybe it began in seventh grade, when I started picking fights with my father at the dinner table, usually about politics, prompting yet more looks of disappointment from Mom—not because of my political beliefs, but because I didn't understand (what she considered) appropriate dinner-table conversation.

Maybe I unwittingly started walking on the path that brought me here the very first time I disappointed her, which probably happened when I was too young to remember it.

I hold my cell phone like a stuffed animal. My eyes begin to feel heavy at eleven forty-five; by eleven fifty-nine, I can't keep them open anymore.

For one second before I fall asleep, I think I hear music.

But maybe I'm already dreaming.

# *four*

It's still dark when the sound of footsteps wakes me. Maybe it's the middle of the night and one of the other girls is using the bathroom. The thought makes me realize that I could really use a trip to the bathroom, so I swing my legs over the edge of the bed and head to the door.

It takes my eyes a second to adjust to the bright lights in the hallway, like when Dorothy lands in Oz and opens the door of her black-and-white house to discover a world of Technicolor. Three girls are walking toward the bathroom—I guess it's morning after all. I glance back at the window in my room; the fog outside is so thick that the daylight hasn't broken through. I close the door behind me and follow the girls down the hall.

The bathroom looks like a bathroom in a college dorm—or at least what I imagine a college dorm would look like—four stalls with toilets, and four curtained shower stalls. There's a row of sinks with a long, narrow shelf and a cloudy mirror above them. It takes me a second to realize the mirror is made of polished metal, not glass. There are girls coming out of the shower, girls brushing their teeth at the sinks. The room is steamy, the tiles slick beneath my feet. The sinks are yellow, the shower curtains are yellow, and the tiles on the floor and walls are yellow. Maybe someone thought the color would look cheerful. Instead, now that they're fading to gray and clogged with steam, it looks like someone painted the room with rancid butter.

"Oh my god, it's number twelve," a girl standing near me squeals, toothpaste foam spraying from her mouth. Her short, tawny hair is damp. She's wearing a pink bathrobe, but I can see that her arms and legs are long and coltish, like she hasn't finished growing yet.

"The twelfth girl," says another, startling me as she comes up behind me.

"Twelfth?" I ask, blinking.

The girl behind me explains, "There were eleven of us. You're the twelfth."

I take inventory of the girls in the room, counting one girl I can hear in the shower. "There are only ten of you."

"Eleanor's in the infirmary."

My roommate. "Right."

"I'm Virginia," says the girl brushing her teeth, the one who squealed when she saw me.

The other girl moves to face me. "Virginia's our resident ADHD."

I've never heard of anyone being sent away for having

ADHD. I try to imagine how severe her disorder must be to make her parents send her here. Maybe they decided they needed a break from her energy. I wonder if she's as angry with her parents as I am with mine. She doesn't look particularly angry. In fact, she's smiling.

Virginia says, "And that's Cassandra Owens. Cass. Truant."

"Which one—Cassandra or Cass?" I ask.

Cass grins. "Funny, aren't you?" Cass is taller than I am, her black hair in tight braids piled into a bun on top of her head. (Later she tells me they're not braids; they're called Senegalese twists.) She's already fully dressed in jeans and a sweater, though she has fuzzy slippers on her feet.

She points to a dark-haired girl wrapped in a towel, rubbing cream into her skin. "That's Reva Narang. Flight risk."

"Flight risk?" I echo.

"Ran away from home so many times that her parents figured it was safer to send her away before she did it again."

"Got it." I nod. "Will there be a quiz later?"

Cass doesn't laugh. "And that girl?" She points to a skinny girl in loose-fitting pajamas who's pulling her dirty-blond hair into a tight ponytail. "Beth Bryant."

"Let me guess," I say, "Anorexic."

Virginia shakes her head. "No. Heroin addict. Alice Li is the anorexic."

Cass breaks in, "Don't be so melodramatic. Beth did heroin *once*." She looks at me and explains, "Really, she got hooked on opioids."

27

"It's the same thing," Virginia insists, "and it was the heroin that got her sent here."

"Actually," Cass corrects, "she volunteered to come, remember? She only tried heroin when she couldn't get any more pills, and it freaked her out enough that she asked her parents for help."

I can't imagine *asking* to be sent to a place like this.

"Do you always introduce everyone with both their name and their reason for being here?"

Virginia laughs.

"No point in keeping up pretenses, is there?" Cass says. "We're all neatly categorized in the good doctor's files. Anyhow, Alice is in the shower. Just don't call her that."

"Don't call her Alice?"

"Don't call her *anorexic.*"

"Why?"

"She thinks she's perfectly healthy. She should probably be at a place that specializes in eating disorders, but she got kicked out last summer."

"They kicked her out of treatment?"

Virginia taps her hands against the tile wall as Cass explains, "Those places have rules. Break them enough times, and they'll say you're disrupting the experience for the other girls. Dr. Prince and Alice have some kind of deal that she can't stay if she loses a certain amount of weight or something."

I narrow my eyes. "Yeah, but doctors are supposed to treat you. It's in the Hippocratic oath."

"Even doctors have their limits," Cass says, like it's no big deal.

"Dr. Prince is real strict about not taking girls who need more help than he can give." She reaches out and laces her fingers through Virginia's so she'll stop tapping. Or maybe out of affection. Maybe both. "So, what'd you do to get sent here?"

I cut too many classes. I snuck out to visit my best friend's grave in the middle of the night even though I had to take two subways and walk a mile to get to the cemetery in Queens. I didn't grow into the daughter my mother wanted me to be, and she'd finally had enough.

But I don't say any of that. Instead, I say, "I got a tattoo without my parents' permission."

"Tattoo?" Virginia says. "Lemme see!" She reaches out like she's going to search my skin until she finds what she's looking for.

Cass grabs Virginia's arm before she gets close enough to touch me. She pulls Virginia close and kisses the top of her head. Virginia leans into Cass's embrace as though she's already forgotten that she wants to look at my tattoo.

"Aren't you under eighteen? How'd you manage to convince someone to give you a tattoo?" Cass asks.

"Fake ID," I say simply. Nathan got them for us halfway through our junior year. We never had a chance to use them together.

"Well, don't worry," Cass says. "The doc will come up with a better reason for you being here than having a tattoo. Like me—I'm a high school dropout—"

"Truant," Virginia corrects, but Cass shakes her head and says firmly, "Dropout. *Truant* is what my parents called it, but I'm not a fan of euphemisms."

Unlike my mother. Nathan hated them, too. He said they were just a fancy way of lying.

Cass continues, "Anyway, Dr. Prince said that being a dropout was just my *presenting problem*."

"Presenting problem?" I echo.

"Yeah, you know, therapist-speak for the catalyst that brought you to therapy, but deep down, you have bigger issues. Like, me dropping out of high school is a symptom of my issue with a authority, which goes back to growing up with an alcoholic father, which goes back to, which goes back, which goes back to..." Cass rolls her eyes, and Virginia giggles. "The Prince says I have to resolve all of those *go-back-to*s in order to move forward."

"And go back to school," I quip. Another go-back-to, but Cass shakes her head.

"Not necessarily."

But isn't that the point of therapy to *fix* the presenting problem? (I don't know much about therapy etiquette, but I'm pretty sure it'd be rude to ask this question out loud.)

Then again, if my presenting problems are that I got a tattoo and that my mom doesn't like me all that much, I guess it's too late to do anything about them.

"You call him *the* Prince?" I ask instead.

"Didn't you meet Dr. Prince when you got here?" Virginia asks.

"Yeah, but you called him *the* Prince."

"So will you, before long," Cass says.

Virginia twists herself out of Cass's arms. "You better get dressed. It's almost time for group."

"Group?"

She nods. "We start every day with breakfast and group therapy. Then we have class till lunch. Then we have individual therapy with the Prince in the afternoon."

"What do the rest of us do while one of us is having therapy?"

"Private study."

"What's that?"

"Whatever we want to do, really, as long as we're in the classroom or in our dorm rooms. Shelly does checks, so we're not technically unsupervised."

"Checks?"

"You know, she sits with us in the classroom for a little while or surprises us by poking her head in our bedrooms to make sure we're not up to no good. That kind of thing."

"How long is individual therapy?" I ask. "Dr. Prince can't possibly see all the students here for an hour every afternoon."

"Forty-five minutes. We do every other day."

"Yeah, but how many students are there?"

"Twelve, now."

"Twelve on this *floor*, but how many students total?"

"*Twelve*," Cass repeats, sighing heavily.

"There are only twelve students in the whole school?" I ask. I know this isn't the biggest castle in the world—a distinction I read is claimed by multiple countries—but it's still a *castle*. It can fit more than twelve students.

31

"Didn't you read the brochure before your parents shipped you off?"

I shrug. "Not that carefully." Not at all, really. I mostly looked at the pictures.

Cass snorts. "Well, none of us looked at it *carefully*."

A pale girl with very light blond hair stops brushing her teeth to say softly, "I did." Virginia whispers to me that her name is Grey and that she's "Depressed with a capital *d*."

Cass says, "Like Virginia said, you should get dressed. Group starts soon."

"How many minutes do I have?"

Virginia shrugs. "I don't know, not that many."

Cass adds, "And you'll get to meet your roommate."

Eleanor. Right.

"How long have you guys been here?" I ask. Cass makes it sound like everyone already knows each other so well. Can I possibly be the only new girl this semester?

Cass explains, "Most of us got here in September. But the new semester started a week ago, that's when Reva arrived—"

"And Beth came two days ago," Virginia adds, and Cass nods.

"Since there are only twelve spots, they fill up fast."

"What happened to the girls who used to be here? The ones Reva and Beth and I replaced?"

Cass shrugs. "Dana—she was a dropout like me—and Carmen—drugs—went back to their regular schools, I think. Astrid—she was Eleanor's roommate before you got here,

PTSD—she was supposed to come back, but she ended up at inpatient."

"Impatient?"

"*Inpatient,*" Cass corrects. "She was too sick to stay here. Like I said, the Prince is real strict about that. He said she needed the sort of care he can't provide here."

I don't know if that makes me feel better, because my parents didn't think I was so much trouble that they sent me someplace with even more care, or worse, because apparently Dr. Prince is so strict that he stopped treating a patient because she got sicker.

All doctors have to take the Hippocratic oath before they start practicing. I've practically got it memorized, even though I have no interest in becoming a doctor. I'm not convinced that all—or maybe even most—doctors take the oath seriously.

Rumor has it there's this one hospital in New York where they turn away patients if they don't think they can cure them, because too many patients dying would threaten the hospital's ranking as the best. So they deny care to people who are long shots, because statistics are more important to them than actual humans. All the other reasons sick people can't get the care they need are bad enough—not having the right insurance, not living in close proximity to the best doctors. But having a doctor refuse to treat you because you're too sick—what the hell kind of doctor is that?

The worst kind of doctor.

And now I know Dr. Prince is *that* kind of doctor.

"But that's how there ended up being an opening for you," Cass says. "Because Astrid dropped out at the last minute."

"Lucky me," I mutter, and Cass grins.

"What's your name, anyhow?" Cass asks as she and Virginia leave the bathroom hand in hand.

"Moira," I say.

"Welcome to Castle, Moira." Cass makes my name sound like a punch line.

# ELEANOR

Eleanor always liked the edges of things. She slept on the edge of the bed, so close to the side that her parents were scared she'd fall off, but she never did. When they visited the Grand Canyon, her older sister was too scared to step up to the fence and look down into the gap, but Eleanor couldn't get close enough. She'd have climbed over the fence if her parents hadn't been holding her hands. At Niagara Falls, Eleanor leaned so far over the barrier that she could feel the spray of water on her face and a security guard told her to step back. She walked close to the curb on sidewalks and always took the aisle seats on planes. She ran her fingers along the sides of books, from the picture books she read as a child to the novels she read now. It was from a picture book that she received the first cut she can remember; as she ran her finger along the edge of a page, the paper sliced her skin.

She was sitting on her mother's lap at the time. Beneath her,

Eleanor felt her mother jump when she saw blood coming out of her daughter's right pointer finger. Her mother put a Band-Aid on the finger and kissed it. She told Eleanor how brave she was for not crying.

Eleanor's interest in edges only increased after that. It wasn't only sharp things: sometimes it was the smooth line of a silver picture frame or the velvety tips of her cat's ears. At school, she could press her skin into the corners of desks and chairs.

The first time she pierced her skin on purpose, Eleanor gasped in surprise. It hurt, but it also felt like letting something go. It felt *better*.

She thought there must be something wrong with her skin. It fit too tightly over her muscles, bones, arteries, and veins. The cutting was the only way she could loosen the tension, relieve the pressure. She knew it wasn't normal, what she did, and she knew it wasn't healthy—at least, she knew that other people wouldn't consider it healthy. But no one else had any idea how it felt to live inside her body.

For years, her family thought she was merely accident-prone. She tended to hurt herself when she set the table, did the dishes, opened up soup cans, or put away the groceries. If there were a dozen roses in the house, Eleanor was sure to be pricked by a thorn. If a button needed to be sewn on, Eleanor was sure to lose track of the needle.

It was her sister who finally found the collection in Eleanor's bedside drawer. The knives and the razor blades, the shards of glass and tips of pencils. It was her sister who brought the entire drawer to dinner one night, emptying its contents onto the table. Eleanor watched all those edges scattering among her family's plates, knives, and forks. Then her sister pulled up Eleanor's skirt and pointed. Her parents couldn't see all of the scars—not the one between two of her toes or the one under her left arm. No one, Eleanor thought, would ever look closely enough to see those secrets. But still, they saw enough: enough to be frightened, enough to believe that their little girl needed help. They didn't want to talk about it among themselves; Eleanor's was not a family who asked each other for help.

The brochure for the Castle School arrived at their house two weeks later, which Eleanor supposed was as close as her parents would come to talking about it.

# *five*

Virginia links her arm through mine on the way to group therapy. I feel the sharpness of her elbow against my rib cage, even through her sweatshirt and my sweater. I haven't walked like this with another girl since kindergarten, when the teacher required us to pair up to go to and from the lunchroom, to and from recess, to and from the bathroom.

The girls at my (old) high school walk like this sometimes. Some of them tried to hold my hand in the days after Nathan's funeral. But I stiffened at their touch, and they were quick to let go.

After Nathan died, I tried to go to school—I really did, no matter what my mom says about it—but I couldn't stand being there, where everything and nothing had changed. The school held a special assembly in Nathan's honor, a chance to remember him and process our grief, as though that could be done in the space of a forty-minute class period. (Though I guess for most of the kids there, who didn't know him well, forty minutes was probably more than enough.) And there were those girls, being nice to me, trying to offer comfort, and the boys, throwing sad looks my way. But the rest of the time, they still laughed in the hallways and snuck outside to vape or whatever they did during free periods.

They had no idea that this was an emergency, that every day without Nathan was an emergency. I hated how it didn't feel like that for my classmates, but I also hated when they acted sad, because they didn't know him and love him like I did. They had never noticed that the iris of his left eye had a dark brown fleck on one side so that in the right light, it looked like he had two different-colored eyes. They didn't know that his fingers were thicker than mine but not longer, so that when we held our hands up to each other, our fingertips lined up perfectly.

So I cut class. And I avoided going home as much as possible, because my mom was just as bad as the kids at school: feigning sympathy while insisting that other things were still important—grades, college admissions, household chores.

Out in the world, there was still traffic, still red and green lights, still people rushing to work and to the supermarket, still moms pushing babies in strollers and people eating at restaurants, all of them oblivious to the emergency of Nathan's absence. But I couldn't blame those people, because unlike the kids and teachers at school, they were strangers. They didn't *know* what had happened.

Just like the girls here.

Ahead of Virginia and me, Alice and Reva walk together, their heads so close that their dark hair touches. Beth reaches out to catch Alice's wrist from behind like there's something she has to tell her; Alice spins on her heel to face her. These girls, like the ones back home, know how to *girl* better than I ever have.

Group therapy/breakfast is in what can only be described as a dining room. Instead of a bunch of tables like a cafeteria at a regular school, there's one long table with six chairs on each side, one at the head, and one at the foot. The table is made of dark wood about six inches thick, and the chairs are intricately carved and heavy. The paneling on the walls is dark wood, and the floors are wood, too, but a lighter shade than the rest. The room is long and narrow, and there's an enormous chandelier hanging from the ceiling. There are double doors on each side but no windows. We must be in the center of the building.

Virginia and Cass grab plates and silverware, cereal and eggs from a long sideboard against the wall before they sit down, so I serve myself, too. The forks and knives are metal, not flimsy plastic like you sometimes see at places like this in the movies, but I think the prongs on the forks are duller than the forks at home, the edge of the knives less sharp.

A woman sits at the head of the table. Her long dark hair is pulled into a neat ponytail at the nape of her neck, and she's wearing a cable-knit turtleneck sweater with slacks. She doesn't look particularly different from other teachers I've had. Virginia, in the chair next to me, leans so close I can smell her coconut-scented shampoo and whispers that Carol is the therapist who runs group.

Across from me is a girl with patchy, thin black hair. Even her eyelashes and eyebrows are mostly gone. She's dressed plainly, in gray sweatpants and a dull green sweatshirt, but despite her hair and her outfit, I think she's probably the most beautiful girl I've ever seen in real life.

"That's Mei," Virginia whispers, and I nod. Maybe Mei is sick. Maybe she had to undergo chemotherapy and lost her hair; maybe she's here to deal with the trauma of her illness. Maybe she's dressed in soft, baggy clothes because the chemo has made her skin dry and itchy. The thought of chemo makes me shiver: the bag of poison hanging from a cold metal stand, the drip of liquid down a narrow tube, through an IV, and into your bloodstream. Thick, dirty hair falling out until you finally decide to shave your head, like you can beat the chemo to the punch.

But then Virginia says, "Mei pulls her hair out."

"She pulls her hair out?" I echo, looking up.

"It's on the obsessive spectrum, like OCD. It's called trichotillomania."

Another girl walks in and takes a seat at the end of the table.

"Eleanor Edwards," Virginia whispers helpfully, loud enough that Cass—sitting on Virginia's other side—shushes her.

Nothing about Eleanor appearance gives her problems away. Her long, light brown hair falls into her face the same way mine does—though hers is thick and wavy, unlike my stick-straight curtain—and the sleeves of her bulky sweater hang past her wrists. She's wearing black leggings and brown duck boots. I smile at her hopefully, but her face is set in a blank stare. I realize she probably has no idea who I am, no idea that I arrived last night and took over half of her room.

For a while, there's only the sounds of spoons scraping the bottoms of cereal bowls and of chewing. It smells like milk and scrambled eggs. I eat my piece of plain toast absently; food hasn't exactly been interesting to me since Nathan died. Carol gives a couple of pills to Virginia and to Grey. She puts plastic containers in front of Beth and another girl ("Halsey," Virginia whispers, "alcoholic"), the kind with a label and a top that they give you in the doctor's office to pee in.

"Now that we're all here," Carol says, "let's ask our new student to introduce herself."

All eyes turn to me, and I nod. I've given presentations in class before. I'm a straight-A student. Or I used to be, anyway.

"I'm Moira," I say. "I'm from New York." I tuck my brown hair behind my ears. I half expect everyone to say *Hi, Moira* the way they do in movies about AA. But they all just stare like they expect me to keep going.

I don't.

Eventually, Carol smiles and says, "Nice to meet you, Moira," then lifts her gaze to look at the whole table. "Who'd like to start today?" she asks.

Cass raises her hand and starts speaking. She got a letter from her parents yesterday; her brother's graduating a semester early, and they're so proud. "The letter never actually mentioned, you know, my status as a high school dropout, but I could tell that's what my parents were thinking when they wrote it. Like, they thought they could convince me to be more like my brother by telling me how well he's doing."

"How can you be so sure, Cassandra?" Carol asks. "You're not a mind reader. Perhaps your parents were simply expressing their pride in your brother, independent of you."

Cass snorts. "I know my parents."

When group breaks up, Carol takes me aside to tell me that she's going to escort me upstairs to go through my things.

"Isn't it time for class?" I ask. I wish I'd thought to hide my cell phone and power cord the way I hid that tiny flashlight. Maybe I could find an outlet somewhere if I searched long and hard enough.

Carol smiles. "This is more important than class today. Don't worry, you won't miss much."

I nod, glancing back at Eleanor as Carol leads me away. My roommate has yet to make eye contact with me.

◇◇◇◇

"So how does this work, exactly?" I ask as Carol opens the door to my room. I try not to stare at the edge of carpet I lifted last night. I don't want my gaze to lead Carol there.

"What do you mean?" Carol asks, her back to me.

"What's the curriculum? Is it like regular school?" I don't see how it can be when it's only half days. "Will there be tests?"

Carol shakes her head. "No, dear. Classes here aren't structured like your school back home."

I don't actually care how classes are structured. It's not like I studied for a single test at my regular school last semester. Another time, another place, I'd be frantic that I might fall behind the kids at my school back home. I'd worry about how it would reflect on my record, whether I'd ever catch up. Two or three years ago, if you'd told me I'd be one semester shy of graduation and unlikely to actually graduate, I'd have said you didn't know what you were talking about. I've been preparing for the end of high school for practically my whole life. By the end of freshman year, Nathan and I had already started studying for the SAT. He was better at the math, and I was better at the verbal, so on practice tests, our total scores were usually about the same. We planned to apply to the same colleges, or at least colleges close to each other. I couldn't wait to move into the dorms, to get away from my mom.

But of course, Nathan never filled out a single college application, and neither did I. I couldn't remember where I wanted to apply without Nathan to guide me. By then, my grades had slipped so low that no one would have accepted me, anyway.

Maybe if I'd maintained my grade point average, my mother wouldn't have sent me away.

Carol confiscates my cell phone, and she takes most of my makeup—mascara, eyeliner, and concealer, though she leaves my lip gloss behind. I don't know why I bothered packing any of it. Carol doesn't confiscate any of my clothes, which is a relief, though she rifles through the pockets and runs her hands along the seams. After seeing the girls at breakfast this morning—half were in jeans or leggings and sweaters like me, the other half still in their pajamas or sweats—I'd guessed that this wasn't the sort of place with a super strict dress code, but you never know.

Carol digs into the corners of my suitcase, then shifts her focus to the bed. While she runs her hands along the mattress, I turn to look out the window.

It's huge, almost floor to ceiling, made up of at least a dozen squares of glass and held closed with a handle that latches. There's no lock keeping it shut, but just outside the window are a set of crisscrossing and heavy-looking black metal bars held in place by a padlock. Beyond the bars, the trees are so thick that even if we weren't in the middle of nowhere, I wouldn't be able to see a single building or light nearby.

It reminds me of some trivia I read about Alcatraz, the island in the San Francisco Bay that used to be a prison. Even though the island was nearly impossible to escape from, the prisoners were still kept locked in their cells, their movements closely restricted.

In American History last year, my class had a long conversation about criminal justice reform. The teacher asked the class whether we believed that prison should be a punishment or an opportunity for rehabilitation. My classmates debated as vociferously as candidates running for office, but I mostly tuned them out. I was thinking about Nathan, wondering how much longer I'd have to sit there before I could visit him.

My mother said this place was nothing like a prison.

The bars across the window suggest otherwise.

# six

I have my first session with Dr. Prince in the afternoon. Cass has designated herself my first-day-of-school guide, so she leads the way up a winding set of narrow stairs to his office. The stairs are wooden and so steep that I hold on tightly to the handrail.

"Moira," Dr. Prince begins, gesturing me toward a large wingback chair. I sit, pressing my hands into the velvety brown fabric beneath me. Dr. Prince perches in an identical chair across from me, far enough away that we're not touching but close enough that if I straightened my legs, I could touch his knees with my feet.

Dr. Prince's office has a stone floor and wood-paneled walls like the dining room. But instead of a chandelier or fluorescent lights overhead, there are sconces that look like candlesticks mounted along the bookshelves, complete with fake drips of wax molded into the plastic. The walls of the room are curved because this office is the castle's turret.

My loose jeans and scuffed boots don't look like they belong in this room. Dr. Prince, however, fits perfectly. He's wearing another tweed jacket with patches on the elbows and glasses that perch on the edge of his nose so he can look over them. He looks positively out of place in the twenty-first century, certainly completely unable to relate to a bunch of teen girls. The air is musty and heavy with the scent of paper.

"Moira," he repeats.

"Yes?"

"Moira." He makes the word sound longer than it really is. I read somewhere that calling a person by their name is supposed to establish trust, but the way Dr. Prince says *Moira* makes my skin crawl. I fold my hands in my lap, interlacing my fingers.

"Moira Dreyfuss," he says finally, like he's just finished a meal. "It's an interesting name."

I shrug. It's difficult to avoid eye contact, the way these chairs are lined up. He must have done that on purpose. Maybe he thinks eye contact will help him categorize his patients, label them with problems for his files like Cassandra said. Problems he can claim he cured because his school won't admit anyone too sick.

Does he think I should be *grateful* that he let me in? Does he think of it like getting into a top-tier college instead of a safety school?

Well, I'm not about to be grateful that my parents sent me away.

I look at my knees and at the thick carpet on the floor. "Is it an unusual name?"

"You hardly see it anymore. You get your Mauras and your Maureens, but *Moira* is rare."

I'm not sure if he's making small talk or if this is actually interesting to him. I've never actually met a Maura or a Maureen, so from where I sit (inches away from where he's sitting), Moira is the less-unusual name.

Mom made me see the school guidance counselor back in September. Her office was about a third of the size of this one, just a desk with a chair beside it for students to sit in. She said I could call her by her first name, Cary. Her desk was crowded with papers and a stack of books and a framed picture of her family—she and her husband and their baby boy. She acted all sympathetic and sorry for what I'd gone through, but then a few months later, she apparently suggested that my parents send me here, so clearly she thought there was something wrong with me that needed fixing. I guess I could blame her for the fact that I'm here, but the truth is that Mom never needed anyone to convince her there was something wrong with me.

In Dr. Prince's office, there are no books stacked absentmindedly—they're all arranged carefully on wooden shelves built into the walls. There are no pictures on his desk across the room, not even a snapshot of his son.

I tuck my hair behind my ears. "Randy said his first name is really Bertrand. Bertrand is an unusual name."

"You wouldn't think the two names would go together, but they actually sound quite nice alongside one another."

"Bertrand Prince?"

"Moira Dreyfuss."

I lean back in my chair. It's wide enough that I can sit cross-legged without hitting the arms. I'm warmer than I've been since I arrived here. I wonder if Dr. Prince heats this room specially to make us more comfortable during therapy. Or maybe it's warm in here simply because this room is the castle's highest point and heat rises.

"Now, Moira," Dr. Prince says, "why do you think you're here?"

I drink some water from the glass I took from the dining room this morning. In the movies, places like this don't let their patients drink from glasses or cut their food with metal knives. In the movies, patients aren't allowed to wear shoes with laces or pants with zippers.

"You're the doctor," I answer. "You tell me why I'm here."

I'm certain my mom filled him in on everything: my school absences, my slipping grades, my late-night disappearances.

"Come, now, Moira." Dr. Prince shakes his head. "You can do better than that." I can see why my mother liked him over the phone. His voice is deep but not intimidating. Older and wiser, like an uncle's voice.

"I got a tattoo," I say finally.

"You think your parents sent you here because you got a tattoo?"

"What do you think?"

"It seems an extreme response."

"I certainly thought so."

"What I mean to say, Moira"—he emphasizes my name again. Maybe they taught him to do that in medical school because they thought using a patient's name over and over again created a bond. If he even went to medical school. Dr. Prince seems more like the PhD sort of doctor than the MD kind of doctor— "is that your parents seemed like perfectly reasonable people when I spoke with them. I can't imagine they'd send you here only because you got a tattoo."

"Well, I don't know, Dr. Prince," I counter. "It seems to me that it's in your best interests to fill all twelve slots here. So maybe when you found yourself with a few openings this semester, you took it upon yourself to fill one of them with me."

Maybe the guidance counselor at my school gets some kind of kickback for referring students. Like, maybe a third of my tuition goes to her or something.

Dr. Prince smiles another one of his strange fake smiles that don't reach his eyes. There's a gap between his bottom teeth. "Moira, believe me, I've never had trouble filling all twelve openings. In truth, I turn away many more girls than I admit."

I fold my arms across my chest. "Well, what did they say?"

"I'm sorry?"

"What did my parents say that sounded so reasonable to you?"

"They said a lot of things, Moira, but I'd prefer that you tell me yourself about what was happening at home."

"And I'd prefer to know their *perfectly reasonable* criteria for sending me away."

Dr. Prince keeps his calm gaze trained on me, his fingers

tented beneath his chin. Maybe he thinks I want to go home. Surely he's had plenty of patients who beg to be sent home from the minute they arrive.

But I don't particularly want to go home.

I don't particularly want to go anywhere.

"Let me guess," I begin. "They said I'd missed too much school."

The cutting class started before Nathan died. I missed half of junior year, too. After Nathan was gone, I guess Mom thought I'd go back to being a model student—the one thing I ever did right, in her eyes—but I kept on cutting, even more than before.

Dr. Prince nods. "They did."

"And they said that I'd stopped talking to my mother."

Dr. Prince smiles. "Almost. They said you only talked to her when you were yelling about something."

That didn't happen often. Mostly it was the silent treatment.

"They said I'd stopped eating." I haven't had much of an appetite since Nathan died, or for a while before that. Hence the loose jeans, the plain toast at breakfast.

Dr. Prince nods. "They did."

I roll my eyes. You try eating with a lump in your throat the size of Texas. "So, what, they think I'm on drugs? That I have an eating disorder?"

He shakes his head. "They do not think that."

"And they told you about the tattoo, didn't they?"

"Yes, they did."

"Was my mother crying when she told you about it?"

51

"I'd rather not discuss—"

"Don't bother," I interrupt. "I'm sure she was. I bet she said something like 'The tattoo was the last straw.'" I can hear my mother's voice saying it. When she saw the tattoo, she cried because it meant I couldn't be buried in a Jewish cemetery. I said that didn't matter, because I wanted to be cremated anyway. Seeing Nathan's coffin lowered into the ground turned me off to the whole burial thing.

"Do you know why I can't be buried in a Jewish cemetery?" I ask suddenly. If I hadn't been so angry at my mom, I probably would have looked it up as soon as she'd said it. It's the sort of fact that normally would've interested me.

"I believe that in your religion—"

"My family's religion," I correct. Technically, I'm Jewish. I had a bat mitzvah in seventh grade and everything. But I'm not sure how I feel about it at the moment.

"Well, in the Jewish religion," Dr. Prince continues, "one is forbidden from cutting oneself, whether in service of an idol or in a fit of grief."

My tattoo hadn't been a fit. I planned for weeks before I did it, researched tattoo parlors and artists, looked at different pictures of arrows until I found the right one.

Here's something I read Jewish people *are* supposed to do in grief: tear their clothes. At Nathan's funeral and again at his shiva, I noticed that his parents' and grandparents' clothes were torn. Nothing over the top: Nathan's mom had cut a hole in her black cardigan, and his father had ripped the lapel of his blazer.

Maybe hundreds, thousands of years ago, that tradition began *in a fit of grief.*

When they told me Nathan died, I didn't have a fit. Having a fit was Mom's territory: when I missed school, or Thanksgiving, or the first night of Hanukkah. Even when we fought, I yelled back at her, but I didn't have fits. Not like her—tears in her eyes, her throat hoarse, the vein in her neck throbbing.

"How do you know that?" I ask. "About tattoos and Jewish cemeteries?"

"I read about it," he answers. "One comes across many such traditions in my line of work. And I can understand that your mother was distressed that you did something at odds with the religion she practices."

"What kind of doctor are you, exactly?" I ask. "Because it seems to me that you're not supposed to alienate your patient in the very first session by taking her parents' side over hers."

"I am not taking sides," Dr. Prince insists. "In fact, I very much want you tell me your side of the story. But in any event, you are not my patient, Moira."

"Then what am I doing here?"

"You're my student."

I'm beginning to see why the other girls call him *the* Prince. He hasn't slouched—not once, not for a second—during this entire session. He keeps his chin held so high that I have to lean back to see into his eyes. He speaks slowly and carefully, enunciating each syllable so that even when he does use contractions, it sounds like he's saying the full words.

It occurs to me that his PhD might not even be in psychology. If he thinks of himself as a teacher, he could have gotten his doctorate in anything, I suppose. Literature. European history. Animal husbandry.

"Student of what?" I ask.

"I'm sorry?"

"What is it exactly that you teach? I mean, seriously, your methods—new age organic food and time deprivation—what's the point? How are those things supposed to help anyone?"

Dr. Prince smiles. A real smile this time.

"What's so funny?"

"No one has ever described my methods as new age before."

I cross and uncross my legs. It's impossible to get comfortable.

Dr. Prince keeps his feet firmly planted on the floor. "In any event, my dear, you are absolutely right. I should begin our time together by telling you a little something about myself, about what we do here." His knees look like they're bent at perfect right angles. Nathan would say that maybe he's not a man at all, but a robot.

"I think there's value in getting you girls away from the environments that so clearly weren't working for you."

I interrupt, "How do you know they weren't working for us?" I'm not sure why I feel the need to defend not just myself but the other girls as well.

"My dear, if they had been working, then my students' parents, teachers, and doctors would never have called me."

Okay. Fair enough.

"And I think the value of getting away is amplified when you are among your peers—when you know you are not alone. When you know that there are other people in the world who have problems just like you do."

I let my hair fall across my face and mutter, "None of these girls have problems just like I do," but I don't think Dr. Prince hears me. More loudly, I say, "Seems a little counterintuitive, dragging us out to the middle of nowhere so we'll feel less alone."

"Perhaps," Dr. Prince concedes. "But you'd be surprised how quickly my students become close. Perhaps that has something to do with living together, as you say, in the middle of nowhere."

I shake my head. I've only ever been close to one person.

I can't think of any reason to change that now.

# seven

When I get back to our room, Eleanor is there, laying out clothes on her unmade bed. Before I can ask, she explains, "I have one more night in the infirmary. Just getting a fresh set of pajamas ready to bring downstairs."

Maybe if Eleanor had been in the bathroom this morning, Cass and Virginia would've told me why she's here the way they did with the others. It feels like it would be rude to ask now.

Eleanor moves carefully, tucking her wavy hair behind her ears and then letting it fall forward again, biting her lower lip and standing on her tiptoes as she concentrates. She's not tall—probably an inch or two shorter than I am—and even though it's hard to tell with her bulky clothes, I think she's slim, maybe even skinny. The kind of girl my mom would describe as *slight*. Her skin is pale, and her eyes are blue, surrounded by light eyelashes. After laying her pajamas flat on the bed, she lifts and folds them.

First her pants, tight like long underwear. Then a turtleneck, then a pair of socks. Maybe she's on the obsessive spectrum, like Mei. I find myself glancing at her hairline.

I tug at the neckline of the T-shirt under my cardigan sweater and lie down on my bed. The mattress is thinner than my mattress at home, and I can tell that beneath the sheets, it's covered in some kind of plasticky waterproof material—I guess that makes it easier to clean between students. It's cold here, but I don't think I could sleep in a turtleneck. I'd dream of choking to death. But high necklines must not bother Eleanor. She's wearing a turtleneck under her sweater now. She pulls its sleeves over her wrists.

Without looking at me, she asks, "How'd your first session with the Prince go?"

"I don't know. How's it supposed to go?"

Eleanor snorts. "Good question."

I'm kind of relieved that my roommate's going to be in the infirmary again tonight. One more night with the room to myself—a night to stay up past bedtime and use my flashlight to read if I want to. Carol didn't confiscate the books I packed.

One more night when I can still say the last person I shared a room with was Nathan.

◇◇◇◇

Dinner is supervised, like breakfast and lunch before it. Shelly—the woman Virginia said does room checks—sits in the doorway of the dining room and watches us eat rather than sitting with us like Carol did. Shelly watches Alice most carefully. Alice lets her straight black hair fall across her face as if trying to hide every bite she takes. Eleanor sits clear on the other side of the table, as far from me as possible.

"At least it's not a Dr. Prince night," Virginia says in between bites. I eat my food slowly, careful to chew until each bite is small enough to make it past the lump in my throat. So far, the food here is actually delicious. I wonder how Dr. Prince gets fresh (or at least fresh-tasting) vegetables in the dead of winter.

"What's a Dr. Prince night?" I ask.

"Some nights, the Prince eats with us."

"Is it bad when he does?"

Virginia shrugs and starts talking to Reva across the table. Cass picks up the thread of our conversation. "I wouldn't say bad. Just… heavier."

"Heavier?" I repeat.

"Heavier," Halsey agrees from across the table. She has a Southern accent; later, I find out she's from Georgia. Alice is sitting next to Halsey and looks up with alarm at the word, as though just being in the same room where it was spoken might cause her to gain a pound. Halsey rests her hand on Alice's arm.

Cass explains, "It's like having therapy while you eat."

I nod in Shelly's direction. "Doesn't *she* make things… heavier?"

Cass shakes her head, and Virginia leans in close to me to whisper, "Shelly's technically a teacher, but mostly she just keeps an eye on us."

I remember what Carol said this morning—that classes here aren't like the ones I'm used to.

"What does Shelly teach?" I ask.

"Little of this, little of that. Emphasis on little." Cass speaks as though Shelly can't hear us.

Virginia giggles, rejoining the conversation. "Moira hasn't been to class yet." She leans her head on Cass's shoulder. Cass kisses her hair. I take a long gulp of water. Nathan and I weren't a couple, but we sat close like that sometimes.

"You'll see tomorrow," Cass says. "It's not exactly college prep."

I wonder how long it'll be before I'll start making jokes about this place, before I'll know all there is to know about it like they do.

Maybe Mom will send me back here next fall. Maybe I'll never graduate high school. Instead, I'll be trapped in an endless loop of therapy with Dr. Prince, semester after semester, year after year. At least it'll give Mom something interesting to say when people ask why her only child's not starting college next fall like the rest of her peers—something that will make people feel sorry for her but not judge her like they would if she had to explain that I simply cut too many classes to graduate on time.

"You going to eat that?" Halsey asks. I shake my head, and she stabs a green bean on my plate with her fork.

"Is there a cook here or something?" I ask.

Halsey nods, chewing. "She comes in the mornings. Cleans up the mess from the night before. Sets up lunch and dinner."

From my right, Beth adds, "There's a carriage house on the

other side of the driveway where the staff lives. Did you notice it when you drove in?"

"I guess I missed it." I don't even know what a carriage house is.

"Carol lives there. And the cook. Shelly lives here in the building somewhere."

"Why doesn't she live in the carriage house with the others?" If they can talk about her like she's not here, I guess I can, too.

Beth shrugs. "I think there's a rule about needing two adults in the building for this many girls in a place like this?"

Eleanor breaks in. "Shelly's rooms are near the infirmary." There's a beat of silence as everyone remembers where Eleanor is sleeping tonight.

"The janitor lives off campus," Cass continues. "I've never seen him do anything but change the light bulbs."

Our conversation is interrupted as Shelly puts a can of Ensure directly into Alice's hand.

Beth's plate is loaded with desserts. "Sweet tooth?" I ask her, though I'm watching Alice struggle to lift the drink to her mouth. She looks like she's about to cry, but Shelly doesn't leave her side.

Beth shrugs. "Trying to regain the weight I lost when I was using. Anyway, I need some kind of vice to replace the one I've given up, right?"

"Right," I say, as though I know anything about addiction.

My mother would probably say I was addicted to Nathan. Which is absurd. I just loved him.

Maybe staying here for another few semesters wouldn't be that bad. At least then I wouldn't have to see the look on my mother's face every day.

By the time everyone's plates are empty, Alice is still working on her can of Ensure. "I'm finished," she says finally. Shelly reaches down for the can and shakes it.

"There's still some in here." Shelly's voice is flat.

"I'm finished," Alice repeats.

"You can't get up until the can is empty." Shelly recites the words like she's said them a dozen times. I wonder what makes her qualified to force-feed an anorexic. "The rest of you can go," she adds without looking at us. No one leaves.

"I drank it all," Alice says, her voice splitting.

Shelly puts the can down on the table. "Finish." Alice reaches for it, but her movements are in slow motion, as though her brain is having trouble telling her muscles what to do.

"Oh, for crying out loud," says a voice to my left. Before Shelly can stop her, Mei grabs the can and chugs what's left. A dark-haired girl sitting beside Mei opens up her mouth as if to gasp, but no sound comes out.

"That's Raina Alvarez," Virginia whispers when she sees me looking. "She can't talk."

"She's a selective mute," Cass clarifies. "She *can* talk, but she just also *can't*, if you know what I mean."

I nod. Some part of me knows exactly what she means. The day after Nathan died, and maybe for a day or two after that, I don't think I said a single word. It wasn't just that the words

61

wouldn't fit around the lump in my throat. It was that talking seemed like so much effort and so pointless as to be impossible. Why talk when there was no Nathan to talk to anymore? I wasn't *choosing* to be quiet, though Mom still got impatient with me when I didn't answer her inane questions. (How was I doing? What did I want for dinner?)

Mei slams the can onto the table with a satisfying smack. "Finished," she announces.

Immediately, every girl stands up, and I follow suit, gathering my plate and piling it with the others on the dark polished sideboard next to the table. It looks as though it's meant to display rows and rows of delectable desserts for glamorous dinner parties, not the dirty plates of a bunch of troubled schoolgirls.

"Does that happen a lot?" I whisper to Cass, who shrugs. I glance back at the nearly bald girl across the room. "Wouldn't have guessed she had it in her."

"I get the feeling Mei's a lot stronger than she looks," Cass says. "Imagine how strong you'd have to be to pull that much of your own hair out."

I shiver, but I can't help thinking that Nathan would have approved of Mei finishing Alice's drink. He'd have winked at me from across the table, grinning like everything that was happening was part of an elaborate inside joke between the two of us.

For so long, that's how it felt. Everything that happened, boring or exciting, unfair or hilarious, happened to *us*—the two of us, as a team.

It's not like I was *completely* isolated before Nathan came along. But when I went to someone else's apartment after school, it was mostly because our parents had arranged it. For years, Mom eagerly scheduled my playdates, like she thought that if she managed my social life, eventually I'd catch on and be, you know, social. Or occasionally someone would come over to our apartment because the teacher had assigned a school project that we were supposed to work on together. In sixth grade—the first year they didn't make the whole class sit together at lunch—I didn't exactly sit alone in the cafeteria, but I always rushed through lunch so I could spend time in the library instead of lingering and laughing with the other kids. I couldn't imagine that any other *person* could be more interesting than all the stories and facts in the books and articles I read.

And then, when I was thirteen, Nathan showed up, and we started speeding off to the library together.

And we'd groan together when the bell announced it was time for fifth period.

Now, Shelly counts the forks and knives to make sure they're all present and accounted for. When she's done, it's clear that we're allowed to leave the dining room. Some of the girls leave arm in arm, some chatting with each other excitedly, some quietly.

I stay behind to refill my water glass before heading upstairs.

# MEI

She was born beautiful. That's what her parents always said. When guests came to her house, they always commented on her beauty, and her parents would say, *Our Mei was born beautiful.* Mei wondered how other people were born.

She wondered if other parents loved their children less than her parents loved her, because her parents often said, *Mei, you are so beautiful. We love you so much.*

That was why they'd named her Mei—Mandarin for beautiful, to honor her mother's side of the family. (Her dad was Jewish, with Eastern European ancestry. Hence her slightly incongruous full name: Mei Leah Stern.)

A natural beauty—that's what they called her. Mei didn't much care for nature. She preferred neatly stacked paper. Freshly sharpened pencils in a row. Books on a shelf arranged by height, by color, by subject, by author. She liked right angles and straight lines. *Natural* beauty was merely a trick of genetics. She'd read somewhere that scientists were perfecting beauty. Someday, it might be engineered at the embryonic stage. That wasn't natural beauty, though she supposed it would still lead to being born beautiful.

Natural beauty, Mei decided, was not a straight thing, not a right-angled thing. Beauty was alphabetization and carefully laid plans. Beauty was counting each bristle on a toothbrush, each slat in the blinds hanging above the living room windows. What was beautiful about something as random as the looks she'd been born with? Something over which she had no control, over which her parents had no control?

Mei decided to take control of her beauty, just as she had taken control over the forks in the silverware drawer, stacking them neatly on top of one another, marking them so she could tell which one had been used most recently and move that one to the bottom of the pile.

She began with her hair. Her whole life, her parents had insisted that she keep her straight, shiny hair long. Now Mei cut it short. She did it herself, more carefully than any hairdresser would have. A hairdresser would have wanted to cut in layers, to style it. But Mei cut blunt ends: straight lines, right angles.

Mei's mother screamed when she saw it. She ran into the bathroom, as though she thought Mei's long hair might still be on the floor and she could somehow reattach it. But Mei had flushed every last strand. She didn't leave a trace of her long hair strewn across the sink, on the floor, in the crevices between the bathroom tiles.

Mei loved having short hair. She wrapped the ends of it around her fingers. It occurred to her that shorter hair might feel even cleaner. She used her father's electric razor. She even shaved her eyebrows.

Not long after that, her mother started hiding everything sharp. When Mei's hair grew back, she found herself pulling it out with her hands. It didn't look nearly as neat as when she'd done it with scissors and clippers, but it was even more thorough. One day, she sat in front of the mirror at the vanity her parents had given her and realized she had pulled out all that remained of her eyebrows.

Within a few months, the brochures for the Castle School arrived at her house.

# *eight*

Here's the thing about staying up after everyone else is asleep: it's boring. I'm bored. Yes, I have my flashlight, and yes, I'm flipping through one of my books—*Wuthering Heights*, which I've read more times than I can count. Nathan never understood why I loved it so much, but he never interrupted once I started rattling off trivia about the book. (Like: *Wuthering Heights* was published in 1847 under the pseudonym Ellis Bell, and it was the only novel Emily Brontë ever finished. The book was banned at some point in Quebec, Canada—I can't remember when, and I can't look it up, which, come to think of it, is the most annoying thing about being without a phone here.)

I'm beginning to understand why Dr. Prince keeps everyone on the same schedule. Being awake while everyone else is asleep in a place as big as this kind of gives me the creeps. The light switch outside the door apparently stops working after a certain hour. Cass explained that Dr. Prince keeps the lights on a timer—he must have made an exception for me on my first night here.

I wonder if that was in the brochure. Not the exception, but the enforced bedtime. It would have appealed to my parents. They'd gotten sick and tired of my sneaking out at all hours.

Mom probably wouldn't have minded if I'd been up that late to study instead of visiting my best friend's grave.

Mom and I have different ideas about what's important.

I should try to sleep. May as well conserve the flashlight's battery for a night when I have something to do that requires it. Though I can't imagine what that *something to do* would be.

I drop to my hands and knees and crawl across the carpet. I lift the corner and reach under, searching for the groove into which the flashlight fit so well. Without thinking, I press my other hand flat against the floor to look for it, dropping the flashlight, which goes out.

I blink in the darkness, half out of disbelief at my own stupidity for dropping the light and half hoping that blinking will make me able to see more clearly. But it's too dark to see anything.

*Nice one, Moira*, I imagine Nathan saying. In my head, his voice is mocking, but not unkind. Nathan never lost his patience with me, never got angry at me.

Almost never.

I remind myself that I should be focusing on the task at hand: the flashlight, the floor, the carpet. There are so many catches and grooves in the floor that the light can't have gone far. I stretch my fingers out, searching.

Then I hear it: *music*. I stand and—holding my hands out in front of me—find the door to the hallway. I open it, peek my head outside, look toward the bathroom down the hall (at least Dr. Prince keeps *those* lights on all night), but it's quiet.

I close the door behind me and lean against it. It must have been my imagination. I drop back to my hands and knees and crawl toward the back of the room, feeling for the flashlight as I move.

But then, as I get closer to the window, I hear it again. Not exactly music, but a sort of bass rhythm that makes me think there's music out there somewhere far away.

I'm scrambling to find the flashlight now. When my hand finally lands on it, I have to stop myself from shouting in triumph. I turn it on and point it at the glass, but of course I can't see anything but my own reflection.

I reach out and open the window. The burst of air that rushes in is so cold that I almost slam the window shut again. But then I hear it again, a little bit louder now through the open window—an unmistakable bass beat.

I reach out into the darkness, my fingers curling around the cold metal bars. I lean forward.

I'm so surprised when the bars start to give that I almost fall out the window.

I spring back, pointing my flashlight at the bars. They're designed like a cage over the window, sealed shut with a padlock.

But when I look closely, I see the padlock is broken, barely hanging on to the metal bars. It must have rusted open over the years, thanks to the cold and the snow and the wind and the rain.

I point the flashlight at the ground beneath me. It's way too high to jump from here. And anyway, if I did jump, where would I go? This place is in the middle of nowhere, and it's the dead of winter. I'd probably freeze to death before I got very far.

But then comes that low *thump* again.

Maybe this place isn't in the middle of nowhere after all.

# *nine*

I dream of a ballroom alight with candles. The music is loud, and the room is crowded, hot from the press of bodies on the dance floor. The women are dressed in Cinderella ball gowns, and the men all look like Prince Charming. The women dance until their shoes are worn clean through.

◇◇◇◇

The actual *school* part of the Castle School is something of a joke. After breakfast/group therapy, Shelly leads us to a room that looks like the kind of place servants in old movies might refer to as "the blue room," or "the sitting room," or "the drawing room."

Instead of chairs and desks, there are two long couches with a coffee table between them, plus a couple of leather chairs with matching ottomans. Pastel curtains are shut tight over a wall of windows. The floor is hardwood, like in the dining room, but much of it is covered by a light gray rug. There's no blackboard, no computers, no overhead projector. The only thing that looks at all educational is the stuffed bookshelf at the far end of the room. Beth says we're allowed to take as many books as we want.

Cass sits on one of the couches, and Virginia sits on the floor at her feet, her back against Cass's legs. I sit next to Cass as Reva settles beside Virginia. I curl my legs up beneath me so that when Reva leans back, she won't hit my legs. Shelly arranges herself in one of the leather chairs, a notebook on her lap and a pen in her hand, and asks us to take turns discussing the last book we read. As we speak, she doesn't make a single note.

I always hated it that teachers got to choose what books we read during the school year—I firmly believe that what you read is a deeply personal choice—but I quickly realize why our English classes were structured that way. It's very dull—not to mention confusing—to listen to eleven girls talk about books I've never even heard of. (The lone exception is Cass, who talks about a book I've always wanted to read but gives away the ending. Now I'll probably never read it.)

After "English," Shelly distributes math worksheets. Reva moves aside so I can place my paper on the coffee table in front of me. It's calculus, which I started last semester—or, more accurately, which I mostly missed last semester. I look around, trying to gauge whether anyone else is struggling as much as I am with the assignment, and realize I'm the only one who's actually working. Shelly is flipping through a magazine, and Beth has folded her worksheet into a paper hat that she balances on Mei's nearly bald head.

"What's going on?" I whisper.

A girl named Ryan pulls my worksheet out from under my pencil. "You don't have to actually do the work," she explains. "It's not like we get grades."

"Then what's the point of having class?"

"Dr. Prince thinks it's important that we feel engaged with the outside world. You know, normal teenage things—books, math, science. Of course, he doesn't know that half of us haven't read a book in years."

"So how was everyone able to talk about books when Shelly asked?"

Cass laughs. I glance at Shelly, but she's still engrossed in her magazine. "We make up our books," Cass says. "Invent the plots, the authors' names, the titles."

"Oh," I say again. I don't let on that I know her book was real.

"Wait till tomorrow," Cass says with a grin, "when Shelly tries to teach P.E."

◇◇◇◇

I don't have one-on-one therapy today, so I have time to go upstairs before dinner, planning to unlatch the window, open the cage, and see the woods in the daylight. But when I get to my room, Eleanor is there.

*Our* room, I correct myself, closing the door behind me.

Once again, my roommate is laying out clothes on her bed.

"You staying in the infirmary again tonight?" I rub my hands together. Every room in this castle is cold, except for Dr. Prince's office.

Eleanor shakes her head.

"Then why are you laying out your pajamas already?"

"Can you think of anything better to do?"

I can't tell if she's bitter or just bored.

I glance out the window. Snow is curling down languidly. The flakes are far apart, as though they can't be bothered with hurrying to the ground.

I move closer to the glass and look down. There's another metal cage over the tall window below ours. Even with the first floor's high ceilings, a person could probably climb down the cages like a ladder.

The music I heard last night could have been from a car parked close by—local kids staying out late, drinking, doing drugs, having sex. Doing all the things teenagers retreat to the middle of nowhere to do so their parents won't find out.

Can I possibly be the only one who heard something? Then again, I may have been the only one who was awake at that hour, the only one not yet acclimated to Dr. Prince's schedule. I don't think the sound was loud enough to wake anyone.

"How was class today?" Eleanor asks. I don't ask why she wasn't there.

"Not like any class I've ever had before." I lie down on my bed.

"Can you even call it class when it's not in an actual classroom?" I mean my question literally: what's the etymology of the word *class*, and which came first, *class* or *classroom*? And why do we use the same word to talk about taking lessons that we use to describe socioeconomic status? But without internet access, I can't look up the answers to my questions.

It's really stupid that my parents spent months worrying that I was falling behind and wouldn't graduate on time, then decided to send me to a school that doesn't do much actual schooling. Yesterday, as she went through my stuff, Carol suggested that I might have to attend summer school to make up for lost time, if not repeat my senior year altogether.

"Cass says that technically, the 'classroom'"—Eleanor makes air quotes with her fingers—"is a drawing room."

I smile a little, because that was one of my guesses. "Did you know that drawing room is short for withdrawing room because that's where the women at a dinner party withdrew to after the meal in England in the seventeenth century?"

Eleanor looks at me like *of course* she didn't know that, because why on earth would *anyone* know that?

Not everyone is as interested in my trivia as Nathan was.

She turns back to her clothes. "It's our night to cook dinner."

I sit up. "They make the students do the cooking in this place?"

"Only sometimes. It's a therapeutic exercise, apparently."

"How is making dinner therapeutic?"

Eleanor shrugs. "You know, twelve girls working together is

supposed to be team building, problem solving. That kind of thing."

"Which night is it? Like, do we have to cook every Friday night or something?"

"Is today Friday?" She shrugs again. "We do whichever night the Prince says."

Eleanor opens the door and leads the way downstairs.

# ten

The kitchen here is huge, at least three times the size of any kitchen I've seen back home in Manhattan. There are modern appliances—two stoves and refrigerators, plus a toaster and a microwave oven. There are also two enormous brick-framed fireplaces taking up one wall. There isn't any soot around their edges, like they haven't been used in years, or maybe ever.

A long, wide, stained butcher block island takes up the center of the room. A few of the girls gather around it, not showing the least bit of interest in cooking. Cass tells them to move so she can open a cabinet, from which she pulls a large steel pot. Beth and Halsey float in and out of a door to the left of the stoves, bringing out first jars of tomato sauce, then cans of soup. There must be a pantry back there.

Other than the stone hearths, the floors are made of wide wooden planks. I read once that in colonial America, the widest pieces of wood were called king's wood and were supposed to be held in reserve for the king rather than used by local settlers for their own homes and ships. The biggest and tallest pines in New England were shipped back to Britain on special vessels that could hold fifty trunks at a time. There was even a Pine Tree Riot when settlers in New Hampshire milled pines that had been claimed by the British Navy. The first colonial flag had an eastern white pine tree on it. The planks at my feet might be wide enough to be king's wood.

I look up. None of the other girls are staring at the floor. They're walking across the hardwood like they've barely noticed it's there at all.

Randy is leaning against the wall near the fireplaces. He's wearing flannel pajama pants and a faded navy-blue sweatshirt, the hood pulled up over his curls. I head toward him.

"Your night to cook dinner, too?" I ask.

Randy smiles ruefully. "Boy's gotta eat."

"Yeah, but don't you and your dad have a regular kitchen of your own or something?"

"What, you think this place has multiple kitchens?"

"It's big enough to hold a few." I try to imagine where in this castle Randy and his father live. Maybe they've managed to carve something homey out of all this wood and stone. A place where they know the time and the day of the week and the Wi-Fi password.

Randy shakes his head. "Believe me, the empty space around here stays empty."

78

He probably knows this building better than anybody. I imagine a miniature version of Randy exploring the castle from attic to basement, kitchen to root cellar. (Where people stored root vegetables back before there was refrigeration.) Maybe Randy's not on Dr. Prince's sleep schedule. Maybe he heard the music, too. Maybe he knows this place so well that he doesn't have to wonder where the sounds were coming from. "How long have you lived here?" I ask.

"Long enough."

"Long enough for what?" Randy doesn't answer. "I mean, have you lived here all your life, or did you move here as a kid or something?"

Randy shrugs. I wonder what he thinks of his father's methods—bedtimes and no phones or internet—and whether his father is as strict a parent as he is a doctor.

None of the other girls join Randy and me in the corner. They ignore him the way they ignore Shelly, who's standing next to the sink on the far side of the room. Shelly's curly gray-streaked hair is tucked behind her shoulders, and her dark eyes bounce from girl to girl, probably making sure no one tucks a knife up her sleeve or tries to bring unauthorized food back to her room.

Maybe Randy's gotten used to going unnoticed among his father's students (patients?) after living with them for so long. I'm probably not supposed to be talking to him. Not just because it's against his dad's rules, but because it's one of those girl rules I never quite figured out.

Finally, Randy asks, "So what're you all cooking tonight?"

I look over at the other girls, crowded around the stove. You'd think it would be warm in here with the oven on, but it's just as cold as the rest of this place. By now, there are at least four separate pots on the huge range. Virginia flips through a cookbook, apparently incapable of choosing a single recipe. Cass says pasta is easiest, and Alice shudders.

"I literally have no idea what they're cooking," I answer.

Randy grins. He steps closer to me, so close I can feel the warmth of his body. He's tall enough that his head hovers just above mine.

The last time anyone was this close to me, it was Nathan. Even Virginia, when she looped her arm through mine yesterday, wasn't quite *this* close. I used to squeeze onto Nathan's bed, and we'd watch movies on his laptop until he fell asleep. I kept perfectly still, frightened to wake him. It left me with sleepless nights and neck aches, but I told myself I didn't need sleep as much as Nathan did.

The lump in my throat rises so high that I think it'll choke me. I left my glass of water on the other side of the kitchen. I hold my breath.

Randy reaches up behind me, where there's a stack of shelves. Then he steps away from me holding a cereal box, opens it, and sticks his long arm inside.

"Seems safer than anything your crew could throw together," he says, shoving a handful of cereal in his mouth before walking away.

*My* crew. Right. *They're* not cooking. *We're* cooking. I'm one of them. No matter that I'm only here because my mother was sick and tired of me, because I got a tattoo that was the last straw. As far as Randy's concerned, I'm just another one of his dad's troubled girls.

# VIRGINIA

No one understood that Virginia *wanted* to concentrate. She *wanted* to focus.

But how could anyone focus on one thing at a time? It got so boring so quickly.

Virginia's older brother was straight-A student with the attention span of a hawk stalking its prey. Or an owl. Or an eagle. And honestly, the poor little mice and rabbits probably would prefer it if the big birds got distracted once in a while.

Whatever—the point was that Virginia's brother could focus on one thing so singularly that Virginia sometimes thought his eyes might actually explode from going so long without blinking.

"It's called *concentrating*, kid," her brother would say, ruffling her hair.

Evan—that was her older brother, Evan—was twelve when

Virginia was born. Her parents would never admit it, but Virginia knew she must have been a mistake.

An accident.

A hiccup.

A slip.

*Slip-sliding away*, like the lyrics from a song by a band her dad liked.

Wait, no. That wasn't the kind of slip she'd been thinking about.

Right.

Her birth. Or really, her conception.

By the time she came along, Virginia's parents weren't exactly interested in toilet training and the alphabet and one plus one equals two. So she went undiagnosed through kindergarten and elementary school. Her teachers called her boisterous and said she wasn't living up to her potential. After all, they'd taught Evan; surely Evan Spier's little sister was a powder keg of potential just waiting to go off.

What *was* a powder keg, anyway?

Virginia was a thorn in the side of the teachers who'd adored her brother all the way up until sixth grade, when her teacher—a new, young teacher who'd never met Evan—suggested that there might be something more to Virginia's troubles than living in her brother's shadow. (Evan hadn't lived at home for years, by then. There was no shadow left for Virginia to struggle out from under.)

The teacher's name was Ms. Carpenter, and she was Virginia's hero. When Virginia's parents insisted that her distractibility was just a phase, Ms. Carpenter stood up to them, reviewing Virginia's transcripts and pointing out the comment every single teacher since kindergarten had made: "Virginia refuses to focus."

Maybe, Ms. Carpenter said, Virginia wasn't refusing to do anything; maybe she *couldn't* focus.

When her parents finally took her to see a specialist, Virginia knew it was more to prove Ms. Carpenter wrong than anything else. But when the doctor gave her a diagnosis, Virginia was elated. They tried Ritalin first. Then Ritalin SR. Then Adderall. Then something called Focalin that Virginia liked because its named sounded like "focus." Then Intuniv. Then a combination of all (or at least a few—she couldn't keep track) of the above.

The medicines helped, but it still took Virginia a week to do a reading assignment her classmates could finish in a day. Her parents told her to watch the movie of *Jane Eyre* so she wouldn't fail her exams, but she failed anyway; it was just as easy to lose track of a three-hour movie as a six-hundred-page book. Her parents hired a tutor to get her through biology, the class Virginia most wanted to do well in, hoping it might reveal the secrets behind her own health problems.

By the end of tenth grade, the charitable Cs that had dotted her report cards had turned into Fs.

It was Ms. Carpenter who read about the success Dr. Prince had been having with alternate forms of education that didn't involve testing or deadlines, Ms. Carpenter who sent them brochures for the Castle School. Virginia knew her parents were sending her to Castle for her own good, but she also knew that wasn't their only reason. They wanted some peace and quiet, the peace and quiet they thought they would have by now, back when Evan was their only child. Evan was hard at work on his PhD in American history, writing a dissertation longer than any book Virginia had ever managed to read. Evan hadn't lived at home in more than a decade.

Virginia didn't care why they sent her. She wanted out of the house, too.

# *eleven*

I can't sleep. Not because I'm thinking of Nathan. Not because this is my first night sharing a room with someone other than him. And not because I'm remembering the last few weeks with my parents: the note from the school guidance counselor; the call from the principal; the letter from Nathan's parents, thanking my parents for sharing me with them. A letter that did not prompt the reaction Nathan's parents must have expected. My mother yelled at me for being a better daughter to the Kaplans—"a couple of strangers," she shouted—than I was to her.

How could she call them strangers? Didn't she know that however *she* might feel about them, I loved them?

Of course she knew. She just didn't care.

Maybe I *should* climb out the window and run away.

Because seriously, what am I doing here? These other girls have *real* problems—selective mutism, ADHD, anorexia, trichotillomania (which I had never even heard of before), substance abuse, whatever Eleanor's here for. Dr. Prince probably thought I'd be an easy case compared to them. A nice success story to lure more parents into sending their daughters here next year.

But there's nothing he can do to make my mother like me.

I may be the most hopeless case he's got.

I roll over. Again. I can't sleep because I'm waiting to hear whether the music starts. If it doesn't, it could mean whoever was playing it isn't nearby anymore, that it was someone just passing through. But if the music does start, maybe there's still something out there—something permanent, something (relatively) close.

Nathan would understand why I want to find the source of the music. It's like a piece of trivia, a question that needs answering. Except this time, the answer can't be found with an internet search or a trip to the library. Not that I have access to either.

And Nathan would understand how helpless I feel without internet or library access. *Tough luck, Moy*, he'd say.

But he doesn't know I'm here. He'll never *know* anything ever again. When he died, he was frozen in time with whatever knowledge he'd built up by then, whatever personality he'd grown into by the age of seventeen.

I'll never know what he might have grown up to say.

I take a sip of water from the glass beside my bed.

My body won't lie flat, my fingers won't keep still, my legs won't stay under the covers. Is this how Virginia feels all the time? I pull the covers up and kick them off a dozen times. I try to be quiet; I don't know if Eleanor is a light sleeper.

Eventually, I get up and lean my head against the window, press my ear against the glass.

And there it is.

*Thump, thump, thump.* The rhythm is steady, like a heartbeat. Although heartbeats aren't steady, are they? They shift and change all the time, depending on whether a person is excited, or anxious, or scared, or sick. If heartbeats were steady, doctors wouldn't need to check them all the time.

I open the window. The cold shocks my skin, but I lean forward and reach out. The cage moves easily, thanks to the broken lock, which falls to the ground with a dull thud.

"What are you doing?" I jump back like I've touched something hot. Eleanor is standing behind me. "How long have you been watching?"

"A while." She steps closer so that we're side by side, looking out into the darkness. "What's that sound?" The *thump* is louder with the window open.

"Music, I think."

"Duh," Eleanor answers. "But where's it coming from?"

"I don't know."

I can't see my roommate's face in the darkness.

"Hang on," I say. I crouch down and dig my flashlight out of its hiding place. I point it out the window in the direction of the sound.

"Where'd you get that?" Eleanor reaches for the light, and I see marks on her wrist. They're angry and red, too fresh to have faded into scars.

Eleanor pulls her sleeve down and shrugs. "Like you got sent here because you're so well adjusted." She slides the flashlight from my fingers and points it through the open window again, taking in the broken padlock and the metal bars beneath us. I can see her breath, but she doesn't seem bothered by the cold.

She turns back to me and grins. "Shall we?" she says, like she's formally asking me to dance.

"Shall we what?"

Eleanor rolls her eyes. "C'mon, don't tell me you haven't been thinking about it."

"Thinking about what?"

"Otherwise, why would you have opened the window in the first place?"

"I was curious."

"Curious enough to make a run for it?"

"There's nowhere to run to. We're in the middle of nowhere."

Eleanor cocks her head in the direction of the sound and raises her eyebrows. "Apparently," she says reasonably, "we're not."

# twelve

*Curiosity killed the cat; satisfaction brought him back.* I wish I could look up the origin of that phrase. Instead, I'm watching my roommate climb out the window, the flashlight clamped between her teeth. Eleanor holds on to the metal bars like she's descending a ladder, then lands on a patch of snow between the trees. She points the light up at me so I can follow.

I've never been particularly adventurous. Nathan's and my idea of a wild Friday night was skipping studying to watch a movie—provided we could catch up on our schoolwork the next morning. But Eleanor expects me to climb out that window after her. She's taken the lead even though I'm the one who heard the music and found the broken lock.

What would Nathan do if he were here? For the first time since he died, I don't know the answer to that question, and not knowing makes the lump in my throat so big I feel like I can't breathe.

I'm not exactly graceful as I climb down in the freezing cold darkness, bundled in my puffy coat and winter boots, the metal bars frigid against my hands. The bare trees are so close to the Castle that if I leaned back, I could touch their branches.

I realize that if Nathan were here, he'd be making good-natured fun of me for taking so long to reach the ground: *Hurry up, Dreyfuss, while I'm young!* He'd push his hair out of his eyes so he wouldn't lose track of me as I moved from one metal bar to the next. His dirty-blond hair was so short in the end, but before that, it used to fall over his hazel eyes just so.

When I finally hit the ground, Eleanor shifts the light to the woods in front of us and starts walking toward the trees. "C'mon," she says, reaching back to take my hand. We walk side by side, the flashlight pointed at our feet. The woods are so thick that with one misstep, we could trip over a root and fall flat on our faces. Eleanor sets the pace. Despite her enthusiasm, she moves slowly, carefully.

"I can't get scratched," she explains as she ducks to avoid a low-hanging branch. "Not after my infirmary stay."

Her words answer the question I haven't asked. Not why was she in the infirmary or why her parents sent her here—I guessed as much when I saw her wrists—but *are we going back to the Castle later?* If Eleanor's worried about how she'll look to Shelly and Carol and Dr. Prince in the morning, she has every intention of returning.

Not that it's entirely up to her. I heard the music alone, saw the broken lock alone, hid the flashlight alone.

I could decide—alone—to leave.

If my mother found out that I snuck through the woods in the middle of the night, would she be angrier at Dr. Prince for not keeping me contained or at me for leaving?

She wouldn't be surprised, that's for sure. She called it *running away* when I went to visit Nathan's grave, even though I always came back. I had someplace to go, but nowhere to stay. So I always came home.

And I'll go back to the Castle School tonight. I just want to find out where the music is coming from first.

I'm not quite the hellion Mom and Dad think I am.

"It's freezing," I say needlessly. My teeth are chattering, and my breath is shallow. I felt like this the first time I visited Nathan's grave in the dark. I don't believe in ghosts or anything—I wasn't scared to be in a cemetery all by myself. The nerves came from breaking the rules, from being somewhere I wasn't supposed to be.

The flashlight only allows us to see a few feet in front of us. But the farther we walk, the louder the music gets.

Eleanor stops and points the flashlight ahead. "I think I see something."

Lights.

And not, like, headlights from a passing car. No, this is bright, warm light coming from a series of tall, skinny windows. Eleanor and I keep walking, arm in arm. The woods thin as we walk, nothing like the thick trees that surround the Castle School.

"Holy crap," Eleanor says. "It's *another* castle."

I nod, taking in the stone walls, the round turret, the floor-to-ceiling windows on the first floor, the smaller windows upstairs.

The music coming from inside is so loud I can hear every lyric. It's an old rock song from the eighties, a song I've heard a thousand times before. My dad always liked this song. If Nathan were here, he'd sing along. He'd take my hands and make me dance with him. He wouldn't worry about looking foolish.

I take a deep breath and swallow. The air is so cold and so thin that it hurts to breathe.

Eleanor lowers the flashlight. It's not nearly as bright as the lights coming from the windows ahead of us. We get close enough that we can see the driveway and the wooden front door-within-a-door that's identical to the one Randy led me through a few nights ago.

Well, except for one difference.

*This* door is wide open.

# thirteen

"We should go," I breathe, backing away slowly. I don't know why the open door frightens me, but Eleanor must feel the same way, because she turns and starts running. Toward our castle. *The* Castle. The *other* Castle. I don't know what to call it.

"Eleanor, wait!" I hiss, rushing to catch up with her. I'm scared to yell. What if someone hears us? Someone from either castle. I'm not sure which would be worse.

As the trees get thicker, we walk slowly and carefully again, arm in arm, our heads almost touching. We're even closer than Randy and I were in the kitchen tonight—not counting the layers of coats and sweaters between us.

"What was that place?" Eleanor asks finally.

"I don't know."

"Is there *another* Castle School?"

"I don't know," I say again. I shake my head, and my hair gets caught on a tree branch. I stop walking, and Eleanor redirects the flashlight to untangle me. As she works, I say, "But that castle had lights on and music playing. If it's a school, it's not like ours."

Eleanor snorts. "No kidding."

If these were real castles like the ruins that dot parts of Europe, there might be a reason why they were so close to each other. Back in the day, ancient walls—like Hadrian's Wall in what became the United Kingdom—were fortified with castles every few miles, stations where they could keep food, supplies, weapons, people.

I consider explaining all of this to Eleanor, then remember her reaction to my last piece of trivia. (The origins of the drawing room.) I don't think she'll be interested.

Even Nathan wasn't always interested. But he always at least pretended to be.

"So our best guess is that maybe it's another school, but one where the students are allowed to play music and stay up late?" Eleanor suggests tentatively.

I sigh. "If that's true, why couldn't our parents have sent us to *that* Castle School?"

For some reason, this makes Eleanor laugh, and then I start laughing, too. We laugh the rest of the way back, the light on the ground bouncing in time with Eleanor's giggles. We climb up the metal bars and into our room; this time I go first, Eleanor shining the light from the ground to show the way. Again, Eleanor climbs with the flashlight gripped between her teeth. When we're both inside, I close the window behind us and put the light back in its hiding place.

Eleanor yawns as she gets into bed. "It makes you wonder, though."

"Makes you wonder what?" How there could be another castle so close that no one here seems to know about? Why our parents sent us to the drab, depressing castle instead of the bright and cheery one? How sequestering twelve girls in this dark, cold castle is supposed to make anyone feel better about anything? Some of the girls here are really sick. This place could be seriously dangerous for them. Didn't their parents do any research beyond looking at the glossy pages of the brochure? I hear Nathan's voice saying, *I do more research than that before buying a pair of sneakers.*

I burrow beneath my covers and close my eyes. Even with the window closed and the covers pulled up to my chin, I'm still cold. I bet *that* castle is warmer than this one. I bet *that* castle's fireplaces are filled with roaring fires, unlike the ones here, empty and clean.

Finally, Eleanor answers, "It makes you wonder if they left that door open because they knew we were coming."

# *fourteen*

In group the next morning, no one answers when Carol requests a volunteer to start, so she turns and faces Alice, who's combing her straight, dark hair with her painfully thin fingers.

"Alice, I hear you spoke with your parents yesterday."

No one offered to let me talk to my parents. Maybe it's a privilege I haven't earned. I have nothing to say to them, anyway.

Alice nods.

"How did the conversation go?" Carol asks.

Alice keeps fingering her hair. "Fine, whatever."

"What did you talk about?"

"I don't know. How are you? What are you eating? I miss you. That kind of thing."

Virginia speaks up. "I miss my mom." Her lower lip is quivering like she's trying not to cry.

Carol nods. "I know you all miss your parents very much."

Without meaning to, I shake my head.

"Moira?" Carol prompts. I didn't realize she was looking at me. "Do you have something you'd like to say, Moira?" She pronounces my name correctly—with the *oy* sound instead of an *ah*—and with the slightest bit of an accent I don't recognize. (Later, Cass tells me Carol is from Brazil.)

Quickly, I say, "No."

"That's okay." Carol smiles knowingly, as if she's certain I do miss my parents and I'm just not ready to admit it.

Well, Carol doesn't know as much as she thinks she does.

I know what it feels like to truly miss someone. It's a constant ache, a hum inside my rib cage. In ninth-grade biology, we learned about a condition called a heart murmur, and I think missing Nathan is like a metaphorical heart murmur. A tiny disruption in my heartbeat, a nearly imperceptible buzz distorting the whole system.

Alice stops playing with her hair and clasps her hands on the table in front of her, blue knuckle over blue knuckle. She gazes at Beth—her sharp collarbones, her slim wrists—thoughtfully, like she's considering the pros and cons of opioid addiction as an alternative to starving herself.

Is any of this—talking to Carol, eating organic food, breathing Maine air—helping her?

Would Alice be better off at the other castle, the one with the bright lights and loud music?

◇◇◇◇

"Do we have therapy on weekends?" I ask Dr. Prince during my afternoon private session.

"You have private therapy every other day," he says.

"Including weekends?"

"Every other day."

I adjust in the chair, crossing my legs beneath me. "What if I were, like, religious and wanted to go to temple on Saturdays? Then you'd have to tell me what day of the week it was, right?"

"Do you want to go to temple for the Sabbath?"

I shrug and finger my hair like I'm examining it for split ends. "My parents weren't so religious that we observed Shabbat every week. And even if we had, I wouldn't want to go now."

"Why not?"

"I don't believe in God."

"Well, then, let's discuss that."

I push my hair away from my face. "I'd rather discuss the days of the week."

"Didn't God invent the days of the week?"

I squint at him.

His voice drops an octave as he quotes the Bible. "On the seventh day, He rested."

I say, "The Romans invented the days of the week."

"Really?"

I nod. "We still follow the Roman calendar."

"How interesting," Dr. Prince says, but I think he already knew. He seems like the type who would.

Maybe at the other castle they know what day it is.

"When can I talk to my parents?" I ask, changing the subject.

"Would you like to talk to your parents?" I wonder if Carol told him what happened in group this morning. Maybe they've decided that I secretly miss my parents desperately. Maybe he thinks he can get me to reveal some deep dark secret by answering my questions with questions. Maybe he's the world's most ineffective therapist, but he still manages to hoodwink twelve sets of parents into sending him their daughters every semester.

I say, "Alice talked to her parents."

"You can talk to your parents whenever you would like to talk to them."

The way he says it irks me, like my asking to talk to my parents marks some sort of step in his therapeutic process.

"Shouldn't *they* want to talk to *me*? They go to the trouble of sending me here, but they don't even care enough to check in."

"They check in all the time."

I narrow my eyes. "Define *all the time*."

"Your mother called the night you arrived as well as the next morning, and I have phone calls scheduled with both your parents twice a week going forward. Moreover, I've told them they're welcome to call or email with questions anytime."

I look around the office. No computer on the desk, no cell phone bulge in his pocket. I wonder how Dr. Prince receives emails.

"What will you talk about with them?"

The question seems to surprise Dr. Prince.

"Your progress, of course."

I almost laugh. They want me to *regress*, not *progress*. Mom doesn't like the person I've turned out to be. Or the person I chose to attach myself to when I was thirteen.

I still remember the first time I saw Nathan—the first day of eighth grade. It's not like he was the coolest kid in class. (I would never have been best friends with the coolest kid in class.) He just seemed entirely at ease with being there, with being the new kid, with having hair that fell into his eyes and a nose with a bump in the middle. (I learned later that he'd broken it at six years old.) He was the shortest boy in our class—most of the girls were taller than he was, too, including me—but that never seemed to bother him, either.

"Tell me about your parents." Dr. Prince doesn't fidget in his seat, doesn't uncross and recross his legs. I don't like the habit he has of shifting the center of a conversation halfway through it.

"What do you want to know?" I ask, folding my arms across my chest and planting my feet on the floor to mirror his. The floor of Dr. Prince's office is covered with a rug so thick I can feel its softness through my shoes.

"Do you think they're good parents?"

I shrug.

"Do you think sending you here makes them bad parents?"

"They were bad parents long before they sent me here."

"When did it start?"

I don't answer. Mom thought Nathan was a bad influence because I came home a lot less once he was in the picture. It wasn't like we were going out and getting into trouble. We were doing homework, watching movies, studying for the SAT. Mom never believed that we were just friends. She was so convinced our relationship was romantic that at the beginning of sophomore year, she gave me a box of condoms and made me promise to be safe.

She didn't understand the way we loved each other. Or maybe she was jealous because she knew deep down that I loved him so much more than I loved her.

Dr. Prince asks, "How did it start, your parents being bad?"

Halfway through ninth grade, Mom tried to put her foot down about how much time I was spending at the Kaplans'.

It became a daily battle. *Where are you having dinner tonight? What are you doing after school?*

My answers were always the same: *Nathan's parents invited me for dinner. I'll be at Nathan's house, studying.*

Then, closer to the end, the questions changed: *Where were you last night? Why weren't you in school today?*

But my answers were always the same: *I was with Nathan. Nathan needed me. I couldn't leave Nathan alone.*

Always *Nathan.*

*Nathan.*

*Nathan.*

I wonder how many times I said his name, over the years.

I drink some water from the glass I took from the dining room this morning.

"What was it like in your home in the months before they sent you here?"

For a while, it was quiet. After the funeral, the arguments stopped, like my parents were tiptoeing around me. It was almost peaceful. They never complained that I spent too much time in my room with the door closed, that I went out without telling them where I was headed, that I didn't eat. Even when I cut school, Mom didn't shout about it at first. They were careful, for a little while. Maybe even gentle.

Dr. Prince responds to my silence with another question. "Did you fight?"

I nod. Apparently, there was a grace period in which I was allowed closed doors, late nights, and skipped meals. And eventually, the grace period ended.

"What did you fight about?"

I sigh heavily and fold my legs beneath me again. "What didn't we fight about? I never did what they wanted me to do."

"How so?"

"I don't know." Maybe they expected me to go back to the way I was before Nathan came into my life. But Nathan had been there so long that I didn't even remember what I was like before him.

"What kind of things would your parents say when you fought?"

I close my eyes. Mom yelled at me to come home earlier. She yelled at me for cutting class. She yelled at me for missing dinner. All the same things she'd yelled at me for when Nathan was still alive. The only new argument was over the fact that I stopped taking the lunches she packed for me to school.

It would have been a waste of food if I'd taken them. My stomach was too full of water to fit anything else.

In one of our last fights before they sent me away, she said, *Don't let what happened change your whole life.* Dad was in the background, nodding along, always on her side.

As though losing Nathan hadn't already changed everything.

She said, *You still have your whole life ahead of you.*

As though that might be comforting, knowing that so much of my life was still to come when Nathan's life was over.

There were plenty of accusations that I was out of control. I'd cut too many classes for too long—first to be with Nathan, and then because it was impossible to sit in a classroom like nothing had changed when nothing would ever be the same. It was impossible to watch my classmates send sympathetic looks in my direction when I knew I didn't deserve their sympathy after Nathan died the way he did.

But none of *them* knew that.

My eyes are still closed when Dr. Prince asks, "Did they ever suggest that you see a therapist before sending you here?"

At least by sending me here, my parents aren't forcing me to go back to school, to walk through the hallways that I used to walk through with Nathan, to smile at the classmates and teachers who knew him but don't have to miss him.

I wasn't there the day he died.

Mom insisted I go to school that day.

*The first day of your senior year,* she said. *You can't miss it. It's too important.*

104

Like she had any idea what was actually important.

Finally, I answer, "I went to see the school guidance counselor once."

Dr. Prince nods. "People usually don't send their daughters here unless the options closer to home don't work."

I shrug. I've been taller than my mother for at least a year now. She couldn't have forced me to go to therapy, and she knew it; that's why she hired those black-clad men to escort me here.

Dr. Prince says, "Tell me a memory about your mother. A nice memory. Your favorite memory."

I look down. The rug is dark, dark green, nothing like the thin carpet in our dorm room. I'm tempted to take off my shoes and socks to feel the soft texture beneath my bare feet.

"She bakes." I'm surprised I'm able to think of something so quickly.

"Your mother bakes?"

I nod. I can see her in our kitchen, flour on her sweater, in her hair. I can smell the vanilla on her fingertips.

"Anytime she goes anywhere, she brings a cake, a pie, cookies."

"Do you have a favorite thing she baked?"

The edges of my mouth curl up, almost smiling. "Strawberry shortcake."

"And did she make it for you often?"

"On my birthday. Every year." My birthday is in late June, peak strawberry season.

"Any other times?"

I shrug.

"Did she ever bake it for anyone else, or was it just for you?"

"Once. She made it for—" I pause, the word *Nathan* getting lost somewhere in my throat. "For my friend's parents. Once."

She brought it to shiva at the Kaplans'. Even though Nathan died in September and strawberries weren't in season anymore. Even though, in a fight a few weeks later, she'd refer to the Kaplans as *strangers*.

Dr. Prince is looking at me intently. I blink, trying to break eye contact with him, but he keeps his gaze steady.

"Why did she bake it for your friend's parents, do you think?"

"Oh, you know. She thinks food is comforting or whatever. That it's rude to show up empty-handed. That kind of thing."

"Do you think she bakes because it helps her?"

"Helps her with what?"

Dr. Prince smiles his strange smile. "Do you like baking?"

I shake my head. "There's too much math. You have to get the measurements just so. All that precision is no fun."

When I was little, Mom asked me to help her bake, but I never got it quite right. She always corrected my mistakes before anything went in the oven.

"Perhaps that's what your mother likes about it," Dr. Prince says.

"What?"

"She likes precision rather than chaos."

I don't answer.

"Is it a happy memory? Her strawberry shortcake on your birthday every year? A joyful thing?"

"I guess," I say, but I know it for sure. My oldest memories are of strawberry shortcake: whipped cream on my nose, cheerful pink stains on the party dress I wore for my third birthday.

"Maybe that's why she baked it for your friend's parents," Dr. Prince says.

"Why?"

"Perhaps it was a happy thing for her, too. Maybe she thought it could transcend sadness."

"It's just a cake," I say. "Not magic."

"Maybe it was magic to her."

"There's no such thing as magic."

"Would you like to talk to your parents?" Dr. Prince asks again. I don't answer. I'm trying to remember what my point was before he ran circles around it. What kind of doctor is he, anyway? Shouldn't a therapist let a patient make her own point?

After a few moments of silence, Dr. Prince says, "Time's up." I walk to the door without looking at him.

"Would you please find Grey and tell her I'm ready for her now?" he asks my back, and I nod, though it takes me a second to remember which girl Grey is. Her name is a bit of a cheat sheet, though; find the girl with the saddest eyes, and it's bound to be her.

# GREY

Her parents had named her Grey. Really, what kind of life did they imagine she would have with a name like that? When she was diagnosed with chronic depression, Grey felt a little bit satisfied at the look on her parents' faces. The look that said perhaps this was their fault. Perhaps they'd sealed her fate when they wrote the word *Grey* on her birth certificate. Her sister's name was Alexandra.

Of course, there were other factors. Her parents fought constantly but stayed together "for the sake of the children," which made Grey feel at once relieved and guilty. There was a family history of mental illness on both sides, so there might have been a genetic component, though there was no way to know for certain.

When she was first diagnosed, Grey assumed she would go on antidepressants and start to feel better. The idea of medication gave her hope; it was the first time in a long time that she could remember feeling hopeful. That was the thing about depression—it didn't leave Grey feeling *sad*, necessarily. It was more that she felt hopeless, like—what was the point?

The point of *what*, she couldn't quite say.

They began with Prozac, but after a few months, Grey was still having trouble getting out of bed. She still went days without bathing or washing her hair; she sometimes refused to eat. Food seemed far too complicated, far too much of an effort.

*Besides*, she thought, *I lie in bed all day. I hardly do anything that works up an appetite.*

They switched to Zoloft. She thought she felt better. She put on makeup and went back to school. But eventually, she ended up back in bed. Wellbutrin was next. Then Paxil. And Cymbalta. Finally, they tried a combination of several different drugs, which the doctors called a cocktail. Whenever anything began to work, Grey's parents were so pleased, so proud, as if she'd put some kind of effort into it other than swallowing a pill (or several) every day.

Perhaps the pills only worked as long as she believed in them, a placebo effect. Or maybe they really did manipulate the neurotransmitters and receptors in her brain, but somehow, once her body figured out what the pills were doing, it fought back, rendering the pills useless. Her body and her brain seemed determined to stay Depressed.

Sometimes—when the meds were working, when she felt up to it—Grey read about depression: memoirs and textbooks and articles from medical journals. She read about people who were sicker than she was and about people whose depression was milder than hers. She read about patients who struggled with suicidal ideation and about people who required inpatient care.

During one of those effective periods when the chemicals in her brain allowed her to feel hopeful, Grey did the research that led her to the Castle School's website. Not quite inpatient care or a treatment facility, but a school with treatment. It was a low-chemical environment, she read. A place where pills were used as needed but medical intervention was accompanied by immersive talk therapy.

Grey ordered the brochure. When it arrived, she handed it, shyly, to her parents. Dr. Prince would help them. Dr. Prince was a genius.

Dr. Prince would help Grey overcome her body.

Overcome her brain.

Even overcome her name.

# fifteen

When I get back to our room, Eleanor is sitting cross-legged on the floor, running her fingertips across the rough carpet.

"I'm beginning to hate Dr. Prince," I say, standing in the doorway.

Eleanor leans back against her bed. "Nobody actually *likes* him."

"Does he ask annoying questions in your private sessions?"

"Of course," Eleanor says. "That's what therapists do."

I shrug. "I wouldn't know."

Eleanor cocks her head to the side, her wavy hair falling across her shoulder. "Don't tell me you've never been to therapy before."

I don't answer.

"I mean, seriously," Eleanor continues, "we were all sent to every therapist in town before our parents resorted to shipping us here."

The lump in my throat expands. The glass I brought to

therapy is empty, so I reach for the one next to my bed and drink even though the liquid is tepid, leftover from last night.

"Not my parents," I say finally.

"You *really* must have been trouble." Eleanor grins, but I don't smile back. "What'd you do?"

I got a tattoo. That's the only thing I actually *chose* to do.

I stopped going to school because I *couldn't* be there.

I stopped coming home for dinner because I *couldn't* eat.

I disappointed my mother because I *couldn't* be the daughter she wanted me to be.

I avoid Eleanor's gaze. She seems to understand I'm not going to answer her.

"So"—she nods in the direction of the window—"ready to go back out there?"

"Keep it down," I protest, closing the door behind me. I remind myself that it's Dr. Prince I'm irritated with, not Eleanor. But it feels strange to be talking about the other castle in the middle of the day. I don't believe in magic, but something about that other castle feels not quite real, like maybe it doesn't exist when the sun is shining.

Not that there's any sunlight shining through the fog outside.

Maybe it's sunny around that other castle.

Eleanor stands and opens the window. "Hey!" I protest, crossing the room and grabbing her wrist to pull the window shut. As usual, she's wearing long sleeves, so my hand wraps around her bulky sweater rather than her skin. "Shelly could check on us any time."

Eleanor disentangles her arm from my grasp. I hang on to her sweater as she pulls away, and I catch a glimpse of a white scar on the back of her hand.

"Do you really think that place is a school, too?" I ask.

"I thought you didn't want to talk about it when Shelly could come in at any time."

"I don't."

"So then why are you asking?" Eleanor says reasonably. "It's not like I know the answer, anyway."

I nod.

"There's only one way to find out," she says.

She doesn't seem to notice that I never answered when she asked if I was ready to go back.

She doesn't ask if I *want* to go back.

She's going either way.

◇◇◇◇

"We'll go right after lights-out," Eleanor whispers later, when we're brushing our teeth side by side, sharing a sink.

"We should wait a little longer than that," I counter. "Not everyone will fall asleep right away. They might hear us."

"They won't hear anything. The walls in this place are extremely thick."

"You heard me opening the window last night." Swish, swish, spit.

"Yeah, but I was literally in the room with you."

113

"What are you two talking about?" Virginia asks, joining us with her toothbrush.

"Nothing," Eleanor and I mutter, almost in unison.

Alice comes out of the shower, pulling her towel down over her legs self-consciously, trying to cover the tops of her thighs. The bathroom hasn't steamed up at all, so I ask, "Isn't the hot water working?"

Cass answers before Alice can. "Alice keeps her showers cold. Takes them twice a day." I shiver as Cass continues, "She thinks if she can just get it cold enough, it'll freeze the fat right off her."

"A really, really hot shower could melt it off," Virginia offers helpfully.

"I don't think the cold water will freeze the fat off," Alice corrects. "It burns calories, keeping yourself warm in the cold."

I put my hand to my throat, as though I can touch the lump there. With a start, I realize that it was gone last night when Eleanor and I rushed back from the other castle, climbed up the metal bars and into our room. Instead of a lump, there was my pounding heart, butterflies of adrenaline in my belly.

Just thinking about the other castle now makes the lump shrink ever so slightly.

I'm *excited* to go back.

I'm excited to find out what that place is.

Excited to figure out why Dr. Prince is keeping it a secret from us.

I haven't been excited about anything in months.

I turn my gaze away from Alice and follow Cass to the shower. She seems to know the ins and outs of this place.

"Hey, Cass," I say, "can I ask you something?"

Cass pulls her robe around herself. "Do you have to ask me *now*?" She nods in the direction of the showers. Each of the four showers has its own stall with a door in front of it so you can get out of the shower and put your robe on or wrap your towel around yourself before stepping into the main bathroom. I follow Cass into one of the stalls.

"I'm curious about something," I say.

"What?"

"Do you know why your parents picked this place? I mean, what if there were somewhere else—someplace, I don't know, brighter—close by?"

"*Brighter?*" Cass echoes, her voice dripping with sarcasm. "My parents didn't send me away because they wanted me to be happy."

"Sending you away seems like an extreme reaction to dropping out of school." Like my parents and my tattoo.

"Guess they figured I couldn't drop out of this place. You know, nowhere to go."

That settles it. Cass definitely doesn't know there's another castle nearby.

After lights-out, I insist on waiting at least an hour (or what we guess is an hour) before sneaking out. Eleanor and I talk to keep from falling asleep. We agree not to use the flashlight until we leave—we don't want to use up the battery.

"Do you think any of the girls who were here before us found the other castle?" I ask.

I hear Eleanor shift in her bed. "Maybe. We don't know when the padlock broke."

"How about your roommate before me?"

"Astrid," Eleanor supplies. "If she saw the broken lock, she didn't tell me."

"I was only here a day before I saw it."

"Maybe it wasn't broken last semester."

I sit on the edge of my bed and drink water, holding each sip in my mouth for a moment longer than necessary. "Do you think it's been an hour yet?"

Eleanor sighs. "You're the one who wanted to wait."

I nod even though I know she can't see me in the darkness. "Can you believe how much it snowed today?" I imagine us slipping and sliding across the woods.

"You're seriously asking me about the weather?"

"I'm just trying to keep you awake."

I talked to Nathan for hours when he couldn't sleep. Anything to keep his mind off the pain.

*Don't think about that*, I tell myself, feeling the lump start to swell. *Think about the other castle. Concentrate on figuring out what it is and why it's there.*

"Don't worry," Eleanor says. "I'm not sleepy."

"I wasn't worried."

◇◇◇◇

I'm not sure how much time goes by before I feel Eleanor shaking me awake.

"Listen," she says.

"I don't hear anything," I say groggily, and she shushes me. I can't believe I fell asleep. I hear Nathan's voice calling me a party pooper. I sit up and listen. It's faint, but I can just make out the notes of the song that was playing last night.

"You ready to go?" Eleanor asks. An icy breeze comes in from the open window. She's already bundled up in her coat and boots. I get dressed—we changed into our pajamas to brush our teeth, since it would've looked suspicious otherwise. I try not to wonder what will happen if Shelly does a midnight check.

In stories, things always go wrong at midnight. That's when Cinderella's coach turned back into a pumpkin, when she was exposed for who she really was.

I shake myself. This isn't a fairy tale. We're not princesses in disguise. Shelly isn't suddenly going to do a room check in the middle of the night.

"I'm ready."

# sixteen

*Over the river and through the woods, to Grandmother's house we go…*

I can't remember what those words are from (and I can't look it up), but they're stuck in my head, even though we're definitely not crossing a river or heading to Grandmother's house. Still, the line repeats on a mental loop as I clutch Eleanor's hand, following the sound of the music and the faint beam of light from my flashlight until we're standing in front of the other castle.

The door is wide open again.

I look up at the brightly lit windows. "What do you think?"

"Should we go inside?" Eleanor asks.

"What else did we come all this way for?"

"A leisurely middle-of-the-night walk in the woods in subzero temperatures?"

I burst out laughing, even though I'm tempted to point out

that it's not the middle of the night and we don't technically know the temperature. I can hear Nathan saying, *Don't ruin the moment*, though I know he wouldn't have minded my logic.

Eleanor is laughing, too, so hard the dim light from the flashlight in her hands dances across the ground.

"Shhh," I say through my giggles. "They'll hear us."

"Who'll hear us?" Eleanor counters. "We have no idea who's inside that place. Maybe no one."

"There's got to be someone in there—the lights, the music, the open door." Nathan always said I was very pragmatic and had good deductive reasoning skills. It came up during our practice SATs.

Suddenly, the music stops, and a voice cries out, "Are you guys coming in or what?" It sounds like a boy's voice.

We stop laughing abruptly.

"Guess they heard us," I whisper.

"Guess so," Eleanor agrees.

I give her a questioning look. She shrugs as if to say, *What's the worst that could happen?* We can always make a run for it, right?

I'm pretty sure the worst thing that's ever going to happen to me has already happened—my best friend died, and my parents sent me away.

By that logic, I shouldn't fear anything anymore.

I hear Nathan saying, *Very pragmatic, Moy.*

"Let's go," I say. Our footsteps crunch across the ice and snow and leaves beneath our feet.

◇◇◇◇

"It's about time," the voice says as we cross the threshold. "We were getting worried that you girls were gonna stand out there giggling all night."

We're in an entrance hall that looks exactly like the one in the Castle, but instead of fluorescents overhead, these walls are lined with bright, cheerful sconces.

The boy closes the door behind us. He's taller than I am but seems about my age. His hair is almost black, and there's a sparkle in his eye. Immediately, I know what kind of guy he is: the sort who makes trouble in class, exasperating the teacher, but who's so charming that she can't help laughing at his disruptions. "Christ, it's cold out there," he says. "Can't keep that door open for another night."

"How many nights have you kept it open?" I ask.

"A few." The boy shrugs. "So, what can I get you ladies to drink?"

The way he says it, I expect him to offer us champagne.

Champagne smells like butter. The last time I had it—Nathan's birthday last spring—Nathan and I discussed the smell at length. We still believed, back then, that he'd have other birthdays. We got caught taking swigs from the bottle, but no one seemed to care. Maybe we should have known then—when no one lectured us about underage drinking—how bad things were, but we were still full of hope.

The boy continues, "Honestly, the options are limited. We have water, hot chocolate, and I'm pretty sure Henry's got some soda hiding under the bed. Care package from his parents."

120

*Care package?* I feel like I'm in a foreign country. I understand the words, but they have no meaning.

"Undecided?" the boy asks. "No rush. Maybe you wanna warm up before you pick your poison. Come on in." He turns on his heel and heads down the long hallway, gesturing for us to follow.

"I don't think we should drink anything they give us," I whisper to Eleanor.

"Why not? You're the one who's always thirsty."

I blink in surprise; I didn't realize Eleanor noticed my constant water glass. "Okay, but didn't anyone ever warn you about taking drinks from strange boys?" Halfway through freshman year, my school had a special assembly just for the girls where they warned us about the things boys might try. (Nathan told me the boys spent the period goofing off. Apparently, no one planned a special assembly to teach them not to do those things.)

"You think this guy left the door open just to roofie us?"

"No, but in fairy tales, girls always get into trouble when they eat or drink anything. Alice grew and shrank in Wonderland. Snow White got put to sleep. Gretel almost got baked and served on a platter. Persephone got trapped in hell."

Eleanor rolls her eyes. Nathan would point out that while they're interesting trivia, fairy tales are hardly pragmatic.

"Those are all just stories," Eleanor says reasonably. "The last one's not even technically a fairy tale." She pauses, then adds, "We should tell Alice, though. She'd like that."

"Tell her what?"

"That girls are indoctrinated from a young age with the notion that food is dangerous."

"I'm sure she'd get a kick out of it," I say. "A new argument in defense of eating disorders."

We start giggling again. I know we shouldn't—none of this is funny. We're being led by a strange boy into a strange building. No one knows we're here.

"What is this place?" Eleanor asks the boy's back.

"The Castle School," he answers without turning around.

Eleanor and I exchange a look.

"Not to burst your bubble or anything," I say, "but we just came from the Castle School."

"You're not bursting my bubble," the boy says agreeably. "I know where you came from."

The way he says it makes me think he knows a whole lot more than Eleanor and I do.

I whisper to Eleanor, "What if we stepped through a portal or something back there?"

"Back where?" Eleanor asks.

"In the woods. In physics class last year, we discussed the idea that there are endless parallel universes. Maybe we accidentally crossed into a parallel universe." It's literally the only thing I remember from last year's physics lessons, most of which I missed.

"Someplace where the Castle School is warm and cozy instead of cold and foreboding?" she suggests.

"And full of boys instead of girls."

"We don't know that there are only boys here. We don't even know if there are *other* boys here." She nods in the direction of the boy's back.

"He said *they* were getting worried. And he mentioned someone named Henry."

Eleanor's voice makes me jump when she calls out, "Hey, you!" I realize we don't know this boy's name. "Are there other students here?"

He stops and turns to face us. "Yup," he shouts down the long hall.

"How many?"

"'Bout a dozen."

"All boys like you?" Eleanor asks.

"All boys," he answers. "But none quite like me, I'm afraid."

Eleanor rolls her eyes again. I'm glad to see that something other than my trivia that exasperates her. "Okay, but why are you here? All of you?"

The boy walks back down the hall and stops right beside us. In a low voice, he says, "Our parents sent us here. You know, to work out our problems." He makes air quotes around the word *problems.*

Eleanor looks at me. "Score one for an alternate universe."

The boy laughs. "Not quite an alternate universe," he counters, then turns and starts walking again.

Eleanor and I exchange a look. How much does he know that we don't? We follow him, the sound of the music getting louder with each step. We pass the turn that leads—in our castle, anyway—to the stairwell for the dorms. At the end of the hall, there's a set of double doors. In our castle, the doors are dark wood and always closed. Here, they're painted bright white, and they're open wide.

"By the way," the boy says as he leads us through them, "my name's Daniel Chu."

We follow Daniel into the biggest room I've ever seen. It's—there's no other way to describe it—a ballroom. Not that it's set up for dancing. There's an enormous stone fireplace against the wall directly opposite us, a roaring fire in its grate and a set of several soft-looking chairs in front of it, a group of boys slouching across them. There's a turntable—a real old-fashioned record player—to one side of the fireplace, but there's no record spinning. Instead, there's an iPhone spinning needlessly on top of it. Music blasts from several speakers set up around the room.

"Guess this place has Wi-Fi," I mutter.

To my left is a long wooden table with six chairs on each side, and at the other end of the room are floor-to-ceiling windows, through which I can see stars in the sky instead of the constant fog that surrounds our castle.

*Our* castle—I can't think of another way to distinguish it. I haven't thought of anything that way since Nathan. Haven't considered myself part of an *us*, a *we*, a team who had something that was *ours*.

Daniel spreads his arms wide. "Welcome," he says, sounding more like a butler in an old movie than a teenage boy, "to Castle South."

# seventeen

"Castle South?" Eleanor and I echo in unison.

"That's right," Daniel says. He unbuttons his sweater and flings it over the back of a nearby chair. He looks warm enough in just a T-shirt and jeans, but Eleanor and I keep our layers on, though I unzip my coat and unwind my scarf. "I offered you drinks." Daniel crosses the room to the table and comes back with glasses filled with water. Instinctively, I take a sip.

"Hey!" Eleanor protests. "You said we shouldn't drink anything."

I pause mid-swallow and glance at Daniel. He's grinning, that same sparkle in his eye.

"I'm not trying to poison you or anything." He holds up his hand like a Boy Scout. Then he takes the water glass right out of my hand and drinks a long gulp. "See?" he says, passing the glass back to me.

Slowly, I swallow.

I take another sip.

The lump in my throat is gone. Not like it's shrunk so the water can pass it more easily, but really and truly gone.

I hold my glass toward Eleanor. "Bottoms up," I say.

"Cheers." She taps her glass against mine. You'd think it wouldn't be that loud, not in a huge room where music is playing. But the sound rings out: *ding*.

The other boys all turn to face us. Some of them are in pajamas, others in jeans and T-shirts like Daniel. None of them look worried that they might get into trouble for inviting two strange girls into the building.

One of them gets up from one of the cozy-looking chairs by the fireplace and walks toward us. He's dressed impeccably but casually, in jeans that fit like they were made for him and a plaid flannel shirt with the sleeves rolled up. He's smiling, and as he gets closer, I see that he has friendly dark brown eyes. They don't have the same mischievous twinkle as Daniel's.

"I'm Henry Gordon," he says warmly. His black hair is cropped close at the sides with short twists on top.

"The guy with the smuggled soda," Eleanor replies.

"Strictly against doctor's orders." Henry grins. "Not organic or sugar-free, and chock-full of preservatives." Eleanor and I exchange a look. Soda is forbidden at our Castle School, too.

"We were hoping you'd come back," Henry says.

"Come back?" I echo. "You saw us last night?"

Daniel breaks in. "Who do you think left the door open?"

126

Henry adds, "Who do you think broke the lock on your window?"

"*You* broke the lock on our window?" I ask, incredulous.

"Yeah, we were going to have A.J. pick it. He's an expert at that kind of thing." Daniel nods at a blond boy across the room who wouldn't look out of place in a fraternity scene from one of Nathan's eighties movies. I wonder if picking locks has anything to do with why A.J. was sent here.

"But we didn't even need A.J. in the end," Henry continues. "That lock was on its last legs, between the cold and the salt in the air. Easy enough just to break open."

"The salt?" I echo.

"Yeah," Henry explains. "Your castle is even closer to the water than ours."

Maine is a coastal state. For all I know, the Castle School is perched on a cliff overlooking the ocean. Well, not exactly over*looking*, since the fog makes it impossible to see much of anything.

"Weren't you worried about getting in trouble?" I ask.

Henry shrugs. "Dr. Prince doesn't exactly run a tight ship."

Eleanor and I laugh. "Are you kidding?" she says. "Dr. Prince is so strict! Moira and I could get in trouble just for being *awake* at this hour, let alone sneaking out into the woods."

"So that's Moira," Henry says. "Who're you?"

"Eleanor Edwards," my roommate supplies immediately, shaking Henry's hand. "And come to think of it, I'd really love that soda."

Henry kind of half bows, gesturing to a staircase across the room. "Follow me."

They head toward the stairs, but I stay put and turn to Daniel. "We can't possibly be talking about the same Dr. Prince."

Daniel shakes his head. "I guess not."

I'm warmer than I've been in days and breathing more easily than I have in months. Maybe this *is* an alternate universe, one in which Dr. Prince is easygoing and my best friend never died.

"So if this place is Castle South, does that make our castle Castle North?"

"Bingo," Daniel says. He speaks into an imaginary microphone. "Tell the lady what she's won."

"Okay, but what are the odds that there'd be two schools that look exactly alike, run by two people with the same name?" Prince isn't an uncommon name, but still.

"I don't think it's a coincidence," Daniel concedes.

"What's your Dr. Prince's first name?" I ask. Only then do I realize I don't know our Dr. Prince's first name.

"Maura," Daniel answers.

They must be related. Sister and brother, maybe. Or husband and wife.

Which means Daniel's Dr. Prince—Dr. Maura Prince—might be Randy's mom.

At the very least, it explains why Dr. Prince thinks Maura is a more common name than Moira.

"So these two doctors built identical castles in the middle of nowhere for—" I pause, unable to imagine why anyone would do such a thing.

Daniel shakes his head. "Not exactly. There are two castles because some robber baron was trying to screw his ex-wife."

"What do you mean?"

Daniel explains that the first castle (Castle South) was built in the 1920s by a wealthy businessman as a country home. Then, when he and his wife divorced, he built a second castle rather than letting her have the first one in their settlement. (And, I guess, in a fit of spite, he made sure her castle was closer to the water and therefore colder, damper, and foggier.) Both castles stood vacant for years until the Princes bought them for a song and turned them into schools for kids like us, though Daniel doesn't specify what *like us* means, exactly.

It's obvious that the gender of the students—and the doctors—is hardly the only difference between the two castles. The boys are lounging around comfortably, and some of them are holding laptops or cell phones. I bet they're allowed to call and text their friends and parents back home anytime. They can probably do real schoolwork so they don't fall behind.

Not that I care about falling behind.

And it's not like I want to talk to my parents or have any friends to text back home.

If these boys are, as Daniel put it, *like us*, then where is *their* Dr. Prince, *their* Shelly, *their* Carol? How come they're allowed to sit around unsupervised?

Suddenly, I know exactly which question I want to ask first.

"Hey, Daniel, can you tell me what time it is?"

"Sure," he says, pulling a phone from his pocket. "Eleven thirty-nine."

I sigh. "Thank you."

Eleven thirty-nine. If we leave now, we can probably make it back to Castle North by midnight, before we turn into pumpkins like Cinderella's coach.

Even if that means I won't have time to ask the rest of my questions.

"I think we should get going," I say. "Don't want the other Dr. Prince to notice we're gone."

Daniel nods. "I'll get Henry and Eleanor," he offers, and jogs across the room. I stand awkwardly against the wall, waiting.

This is what school was like when Nathan stopped coming. Everyone felt like a stranger, even though we'd been classmates for years. The actual school *building* felt strange, even though I'd been inside it countless times.

Except this place actually *is* strange. These boys actually *are* strangers.

After a few minutes, Eleanor hops down the stairs, a can of Coke in her hand. "What's up?" she asks.

"It's almost midnight. We should get back." I expect her to refuse, to say that midnight doesn't matter, but instead she nods.

"Okay," she says. "Let's go."

Henry comes up from behind her. "You left your coat in my room." He holds it out, and I notice that Eleanor's sleeves are rolled up. There are two lines on her left forearm—the fresh red one, and one that's white, long since faded into a scar. The older one is smooth, as though she used a knife or a razor blade to make it. The new one, the one that got her sent to the infirmary, is rougher, as though she had to improvise, use something with jagged edges.

I read once that self-harm—the kind of cutting Eleanor does—releases endorphins and adrenaline so that even though it hurts, the chemicals in your body also tell you it feels good. So it can be addictive, like getting high or drunk.

"Thanks, Hank," she says, handing him her can of Coke. They're already on a nickname basis?

Henry—I'm not calling him Hank just because she did—nods. "You'll come back, won't you?"

"Of course," Eleanor promises. "Tomorrow."

Daniel walks us down the long hall and opens the heavy wooden door. I flick on the flashlight.

"See you soon," he calls out as Eleanor and I make our way back into the woods.

Eleanor loops her arm through mine. "That place," she breathes, "is awesome."

"It is." The lump in my throat is still gone. I breathe the thin, cold air deeply.

"Tomorrow night can't come soon enough."

"How can that castle feel so good when ours feels so terrible?"

"Better climate?" Eleanor suggests. "You know, farther from the water and all that?"

"I don't just mean the weather," I say, though with every step we take away from Castle South, I feel colder.

"Maybe it *is* an alternate universe, like you said."

"Yeah, a universe where parents actually care about sending their kids to a nice place to"—what was it my mother said?—"get to the other side of their rough patches."

Eleanor laughs. "They don't send you to a place like this because of a rough *patch*," she counters. "They send you here because of a rough life."

That's exactly what I thought when my mom said they were sending me here. I'm so surprised to learn Eleanor thinks the same thing that I almost stop walking.

"C'mon." Eleanor picks up the pace. "I'm so cold I can barely feel my toes."

"I know," I agree, rushing as Castle North comes into view. "It's like being truly warm for a few minutes in there made the cold out here even worse."

"Right?" Eleanor laughs. She puts the flashlight in her mouth and starts climbing up the metal cages over the windows.

Nathan would say that doesn't make any sense.

Nathan would also say that a few minutes of warmth is worth suffering from the cold.

I take another deep breath, but this time, it hurts.

The lump in my throat is back.

It's like I imagined it ever left at all.

# ALICE

Alice appreciated the space between things. She liked the space between her legs and the space between a waistband and her skin. That's what no one understood. She wasn't trying to lose weight; she simply needed more *space*.

People didn't know what it was like to take up too much space. To sit on a bus and feel your thighs spreading beneath your torso, edging toward the strangers in the seats on either side of you. To wait in line at the pharmacy and know that even as you stood there, your body was swelling and you were in danger of touching the person ahead of you and the person behind you. People said Alice was already thin, but *people* didn't know what they were talking about. Alice needed more air between her and everything around her. She needed breathing room.

She tried to explain this to her parents, but they didn't listen. They sent her to doctors and treatment centers, where she sat in group therapy sessions with skeletal girls who cried when faced with a cup of coffee. Alice tried to convince her parents that she was different, but every time she broached the subject, her mother burst into tears.

Three weeks before her parents sent her to the Castle School, Alice's family had dinner at her aunt's house, and her aunt served chicken in a cream sauce. Alice hated eating in someone else's home. She preferred restaurants, where it wasn't impolite to ask for the sauce on the side or to say *no dessert for me, thanks* or *I'm not hungry.*

Alice looked from her plate to her aunt, who was cluelessly spooning empty calories into her mouth.

Alice tried to scrape the sauce off her chicken. Chicken breast, she thought, really wasn't all that bad. Without the sauce, she could eat it. But no matter how diligently she scraped at the food, no matter how hard she pressed the back of her knife to the meat, still some sauce hung on.

*I wish I were a vegetarian*, Alice thought. Maybe she could become one all of a sudden: spontaneous vegetarianism. Anything to give her an excuse not to eat the sauce-covered chicken. She felt her family watching her: her aunt and her cousins, her parents. They were so busy focusing on her that none of them were paying attention to what they were eating. They all kept slicing their food, spearing it with their forks, and bringing it to their mouths without ever taking their eyes off her. Alice wasn't sure which bothered her more—the staring or the eating.

Finally, she stood, grabbing the chicken breast off her plate. She stuffed it in her jeans pocket. If they saw her pick up her whole plate, they'd tell her she had to come back. But maybe, she thought, if she left her plate but took the chicken, they wouldn't notice.

"I have to go to the bathroom," she said. She could feel their eyes on her as she walked away, could hear them whispering after she closed the door. The bathroom felt so small, so tight.

Alice pulled the chicken from her pocket and dropped it into the sink. She turned on the faucet and watched the water run over it, watched bits of sauce dislodge from the meat and swirl down the drain. She wiped the chicken with toilet paper until it was dry, clean and sauce-free.

She put the chicken in her left pocket, since there was still sauce detritus on the right side, where the chicken had been before. But when she got back to her place at the table, she realized she couldn't possibly put her chicken back on her plate; there was still cream all over it and on her fork and her knife. She fingered the chicken in her pocket.

All eyes were on her, boring their way into her space. Her family would make her sit there, crowding around her, until she ate.

She pulled the chicken from her pocket and brought it to her mouth. She tore at the meat with her teeth and her fingers. Surely everyone would stop looking soon, once they were satisfied that she'd eaten enough.

Her aunt was still watching Alice when she silently slid the Castle brochure across the table to Alice's mother.

# eighteen

"I can't find my shampoo," I whisper to Eleanor across our dark room the next night. We're both sitting on the floor, leaning against our beds, facing each other. I pull the blanket off my bed and drape it across my lap to keep warm.

"Look in Ryan's room."

"Why would it be in Ryan's room?"

"Kleptomaniac," Eleanor explains. "But she always gives things back if you ask her."

"Doesn't seem like there's much point in stealing anything, then."

Eleanor shrugs. "I think it's just the *taking* part she's interested in. Not the keeping part."

I nod. I'm getting better at remembering the reason each girl was sent here. Ryan: kleptomania. Alice: anorexia. Cass: dropping out of school. Raina: selective mutism. Halsey: alcoholism.

That last one, at least, is easy to remember. Halsey's name *sounds* like her reason.

And Eleanor: self-harm. I saw a small scar on her belly earlier when she lifted her arms over her head and her shirt moved to expose her stomach. I find myself wondering, if Eleanor were Jewish—I don't think she is, but let's just say—would they refuse to bury her in a Jewish cemetery because she cut herself?

Tonight, we're both fully dressed. We're wearing the little makeup that was left behind after Carol's purge. I lent Eleanor lip gloss; she let me borrow her blush. It felt like we were two regular roommates in a regular dorm—one with locks and light switches inside the rooms—getting ready for a double date, instead of two girls in a school where parents send their daughters to *recover*, getting ready to walk through the cold, dark woods to a bright and shiny castle in the middle of the night.

I've pulled my hair back into a ponytail. When Nathan was still alive, I got into the habit of keeping my hair pulled back— less chance of it getting caught on anything when I climbed onto his bed. After a while, I stopped wearing my hair down altogether. After he died, I had to get used to the feeling of my hair falling on my shoulders, into my eyes, down my back.

I woke up this morning thinking about Castle South. My thoughts drifted during group and again when I was supposed to be reading for our history lesson. ("Lesson" is generous for the discussion Shelley led. Come to think of it, "led" is generous, too.)

"Do you really think it's as simple as the boys get one place, the girls get another, and that's that?"

Eleanor leans her head back against her bed. "Maybe."

"Okay, but why is the boys' place so much nicer?"

"Maybe one Dr. Prince's philosophies are really different from the other's."

"If they were married, maybe that's why they split up?" I suggest. "If they're not together anymore, I mean."

"Splitting up over teaching methods seems unlikely," Eleanor says. "Though my parents aren't divorced, so I don't know how that kind of thing goes. They fight all the time, but I've never even heard them mention divorce."

"Mine either," I agree. "Not the fighting part. Just the not mentioning divorce part." My parents don't fight. Mom makes decisions, and Dad goes along with them.

"It's hard to imagine Dr. Prince fighting with anyone," Eleanor adds, cocking her head to the side so her hair falls over her shoulder. "He's always so calm."

I nod, but I'm thinking about something else entirely. "Maybe it's all an elaborate experiment. You know, try two different methods and see which gets better results."

Eleanor shakes her head. "They're *doctors*. They're not allowed to experiment on their patients like that. Especially kids."

Eleanor has probably never had to research clinical trials and experimental treatments. She doesn't know that desperate people beg to be experimented on. That desperate parents beg doctors to experiment on their kids, calling hospital after hospital, research scientist after research scientist, poring over medical journals for the latest breakthrough that might change everything.

Doctors experiment on people all the time.

And with a chill, I realize *that's* why the Doctors Prince chose these castles for their schools. Not because they came cheap, like Daniel said, but because in the middle of nowhere, there's no one to question what they're up to.

Mom would be furious if she found out. For half a second, I consider calling her. It would be nice to see her anger aimed at someone else for a change. But then I realize she wouldn't believe me. She'd think I was lying to get out of here. She'd think I was making trouble just like I did back home, sneaking out to Castle South the same way I snuck out to the cemetery.

Actually, the Princes are kind of brilliant, when you think about it. (Like my mom said, he's the best, right?) They've set things up so that if any of their students figure out what's going on and object to being experimented on, none of our parents will believe us. We've already proven ourselves to be so much trouble—liars and thieves and addicts—that our parents shipped us off to be someone else's problem.

Well, fine. It's not like I want to talk to my mother, anyway.

But what are the Princes planning on doing with their research? They can't publish it without letting the world know they've been experimenting on children without consent. Maybe there's something in the fine print on the applications so that parents give permission without realizing it.

Or maybe the parents all gave their consent willingly, even my mother. Maybe that's how desperate she was for someone to take me off her hands. It sounds like the plot of a horror movie—parents signing away their rights so a mad scientist can experiment on their kids—but in real life, desperate people do desperate things every day.

Nathan's mom... well, I don't want to think about that.

Finally, I say, "I guess we could ask Randy." The other night he said he'd lived here *long enough*. Was he talking about Castle North alone, or the entire property—both castles?

"Randy?" Eleanor echoes.

"Dr. Prince's son."

"Does that kid even talk?"

"Sure, he talks." I feel surprisingly defensive on his behalf. "Didn't he drive you from the airport?"

"My parents drove me here. It's not that long of a drive from Boston."

"Okay, but he must have picked up some of the other girls, right?"

"Yeah, but no one else who rode with him actually *talked* to him. It's not like being sent away makes you particularly chatty. Virginia told me she cried the whole ride, and she *wanted* to come."

"Oh," I say. Apparently, talking to Randy is another symptom of my inability to *girl* correctly. "Do you think he chose to live here with his dad in Castle North instead of with Maura Prince in Castle South?"

"Maybe it wasn't his choice. Maybe Maura Prince didn't want him."

I don't argue. We both know what it's like to have someone—even a parent—not want you.

# nineteen

Once again, the door to Castle South is open. Henry greets Eleanor like they're old friends. She follows him to one of the chairs by the fireplace. Henry whips out his phone, and Eleanor nods enthusiastically. The music changes abruptly; he must have let her pick out a song.

It's so warm. Not the false kind of warmth that comes from hissing radiators and heaters, but really warm, like there's heat coming from *inside* this place, from the bodies in the room, from the lights on the walls. I think of the musty smell in the air at Castle North, the industrial carpet on the floor of our room. Unlike Eleanor, I haven't been upstairs to the boys' dormitories, but I bet they have gleaming hardwood floors rather than rough carpet over stone. Maybe even the furnishings are part of the Princes' experiment.

I pull off my knit hat, tuck my hair behind my ears, and walk toward the enormous picture window at the end of the room. The glass is surprisingly warm to the touch, as if there isn't an icy Maine night just on the other side of it.

Suddenly, I wish I could stay here in this warmth forever.

"And you're back," an already-familiar voice says from behind me.

"Hey, Daniel." I turn to face him.

"Would you believe the stained glass in that window is from the sixteenth century?" he asks.

I shake my head. "I wouldn't, actually. There weren't any castles in America in the fifteen hundreds."

"Apparently, the rich people who built this house had the glass shipped over from Europe in the nineteen twenties. Can you imagine? It wouldn't even *occur* to me to do that."

I shrug. "The rich are different from you and me," I say, though for all I know, Daniel's family is loaded.

Daniel grins. "Nice Fitzgerald reference. Glad to see they're teaching you girls something up at Castle North."

I laugh. "I didn't learn it at Castle North." Nathan and I used to speak in quotes sometimes, though it usually wasn't anything as impressive as F. Scott Fitzgerald. He liked to quote the movies he grew up with: Disney fairy tales, Mel Brooks comedies, John Hughes movies, as if he'd been born thirty years earlier than he actually was. He said he had an old soul.

"Well, what *do* you do there?"

I'm about to answer—I want to compare notes on how differently the students at the two schools spend their time—when a new song comes on. A song I know well. I swallow, but there's no lump in my throat.

"For example, at Castle North"—Daniel reaches his arm out toward me—"do you dance?"

"Do we *dance*?"

Daniel takes my hand, still talking as he leads me away from the window. "Yes. Do you dance?"

I shake my head, looking at our hands. "No. We definitely don't dance at Castle North."

"How about here, now?" He has that twinkle in his eye.

"Oh." I blink, looking first at my feet, then around us. I'm surprised to find that we're in the very center of the room, what I guess could be called the dance floor. Daniel lifts my arms up so that my left hand is on his right shoulder and my right hand is holding his left hand. He's as close to me as Randy was in the kitchen the other night; as close as Eleanor and I were, trudging through the snow; as close as Nathan and I were, lying in his bed together.

Almost that close.

"I can't dance," I mutter.

"Everyone can dance," Daniel insists. He doesn't keep his voice down. He moves his feet slightly, almost imperceptibly.

I shake my head. "Look, I don't want to give you the wrong impression," I say. "I know my roommate seems plenty cozy with Henry already, but I'm—I'm not—"

"Moira," Daniel breaks in seriously, the twinkle in his eye vanishing. "It's just a dance." He sways slightly. "I love this song."

"Me, too," I say. "It's my best friend's favorite."

I say it like Nathan's still alive. Daniel doesn't know that he isn't. Daniel doesn't know what my best friend's name is or whether my best friend is a boy or a girl. It's nothing like being at home, or at school, where mentioning anything about Nathan elicited some kind of response.

"And by the way," Daniel adds, "just so you don't worry about this kind of thing again—I'm gay."

I feel myself blushing, but Daniel just pulls me closer.

"That's not why my parents sent me here," he adds quickly. "This place is bad, but it's not, like, *that* kind of bad. And my parents are idiots, but not, you know, monsters."

"Thank goodness for that," I say, but I'm thinking, *Do you really think this place is bad?* Compared to Castle North, Castle South seems kind of great.

The next song that comes on is a fast one, so Daniel and I break apart. Then Eleanor and Henry are dancing next to us. Another song comes on after that, and a few other boys join in. I feel myself smile.

"Hey!" someone calls out. "Dr. Prince says we've got to turn the music down—we're keeping her up."

Eleanor grabs me, and we crouch on the floor behind Daniel and Henry.

"What are you doing?" Daniel asks.

"Hiding," Eleanor explains. "In case your Dr. Prince comes down here and sees us."

Henry shakes his head. "You don't have to worry about that.

144

Dr. Prince thinks it's important to give us unsupervised time each night."

"Unsupervised?" I echo.

Daniel grins. "Yup. That's where we got the idea to lure you girls over here in the first place. We knew we wouldn't get caught. Don't you have unsupervised time at Castle North?"

"Not exactly," Eleanor answers. Technically, I suppose we're unsupervised at this hour, but we're also supposed to be in bed. Asleep.

Is it strange that Dr. Prince—*our* Dr. Prince—doesn't have someone who checks on us all night to make sure we're still in our beds? When I believed we were alone in the middle of nowhere, I didn't think much of it—where could we possibly go? But now that I know we're not all alone out here, I think maybe he should check on us more often.

Or maybe bedtime is his idea of unsupervised time.

It all must be part of the experiment.

"You better get back, though," Daniel adds. He's panting a little bit from dancing. "It's almost one in the morning. If you get caught now, it'd spoil all our fun."

# *twenty*

Back in our room, neither of us can sleep. We don't talk, but we both lie there with our eyes open, each of us knowing the other is awake.

Eleanor sighs over and over. She's probably thinking about Henry—tall, handsome Henry—and wondering whether he likes her back. (I'm assuming from her sighs that she likes him, even though she hasn't actually said so.) I'm thinking about magic. Of course, I know life isn't a fairy tale and magic isn't real—*very pragmatic.* But still, here we are, trapped in a cold, dreary castle, having snuck out to the warm castle on the other side of the woods. I'm pretty sure I read something like that in a fairy tale at least once. And in that warm castle, I was able to say something was my best friend's favorite without choking on the words. And my scarred roommate could roll up her sleeves. And both of us could dance and laugh.

It's got to be part of the Princes' experiment. *(There's no such thing as magic.)* All that stuff my mom found so convincing in the brochure about the fresh Maine air and the healthy food and the student bonding is a cover for the Princes' real plans. Maybe they're the ones who broke the lock because they wanted to see what would happen if Eleanor and I snuck out.

No, that's not right. Daniel said he and Henry broke the lock.

Besides, isn't the point of the Princes' experiment that the two schools are kept separate, so they can compare notes on whose tactics are most effective? They've probably done this experiment dozens of time, tweaking their methods slightly each semester to see what kinds of effects the changes bring.

But now, Eleanor and I are sneaking out at night.

Maybe this semester's experiment will have anomalies that the Princes can't explain.

And they'll never know why, because we'll never tell.

◇◇◇◇

In group the next morning, I smile every time Eleanor yawns, and she giggles when I yawn. Dr. Prince's "time to wake" obviously didn't account for our late night (and early morning) out.

Halfway through the session, Carol threatens to separate us.

"And send us where?" I ask, laughing. "Anyway, isn't this the point of therapy?"

"Isn't *what* the point of therapy?" Carol snaps impatiently.

"Well, we're laughing. Doesn't that mean we've made progress?"

The ends of Carol's mouth curl up like she's trying not to smile.

"Ryan," she says eventually, "do you have anything you'd like to share with the group?"

Ryan reaches shyly into the front pocket of her sweatshirt. She always wears shirts and sweaters with big pockets across the belly, like she's a kangaroo. She places my shampoo bottle on the table in front of her and pushes it away until her arms are straight and she can't push it any farther. She doesn't look at me when she says, "Sorry."

I look up at Carol, not sure what I'm supposed to say.

"Why did you take that shampoo, Ryan?" Carol asks.

Ryan shrugs. "I couldn't help it."

"You know we don't use those kinds of words here. Halsey can *help* having a drink. Beth can *help* using drugs. And you can *help* stealing things."

I glance at Halsey and Beth to see if they find Carol's choice of words as jumbled as I do. *Beth can help using drugs.* Well, yes. She'd be the person here most equipped to help any of us who had questions about opiates. But I don't think that's the meaning Carol has in mind.

Carol says, "Ryan, let's try again. Why did you steal Moira's shampoo?"

She shrugs. She looks like she's going to cry, and before I can stop myself, I say, "She didn't steal it. I lent it to her."

Ryan looks at me, whipping her head up so suddenly that the tears lingering in her eyes quickly fall to her chin.

I'm not sure why I said it. I wonder if this is how Mei felt when she drank the rest of Alice's Ensure. Ryan is off the hook, but now Carol is focused on me, along with everyone else in the room.

"You lent it to her?" Carol asks.

I shrug. "Sure." It's obvious Carol doesn't believe me. No one at the table believes me. I brace myself, ready for Carol to call me a liar. But she doesn't. Instead, she looks down at her notebook and scribbles something.

I wonder if she's writing about Ryan, or about me.

Suddenly, Eleanor says, "Hey, I use your shampoo all the time, too. It smells better than mine."

It's not that funny, but the whole table erupts into laughter. Carol keeps writing.

After lunch, Eleanor grabs me on the staircase leading up to our rooms. Even though Virginia said that private study means we can essentially do whatever we want, Alice told me that technically we're supposed to divide our time between our dorm rooms and the drawing room. Shelly's in charge of watching us and sometimes organizes a group activity like a board game or making feeling paintings. Alice said that sometimes Carol shows up, and when she's there, she takes notes on our interactions.

Now Eleanor says, "I'm nervous for my private with the Prince."

"Why?" I ask.

"What if I say the wrong thing?"

"You won't."

149

"What if he's suspicious because we're so happy?"

I shrug. "Don't act happy."

"But if I pretend to be upset, he might send me to the infirmary again." Eleanor looks desperate. A night in the infirmary means a night she can't go to Castle South.

"You'll do fine. Just let him do most of the talking."

"Right. Okay."

She scurries down the stairs. It's kind of annoying how you have to go down the stairs from our rooms and then up another narrower, winding set of stairs to Dr. Prince's office. I wonder if Castle South has all the same twists and turns.

I don't tell Eleanor that I'm nervous for my private therapy, too. Dr. Prince opens our session with a question.

"Do you like my castle?" He crosses his legs, sitting straight and tall in his chair across from me.

I shrug. "Not especially."

"No?"

"Well, no offense, but I find the whole idea of having a castle in America pretty tacky."

"Oh?"

"Yeah. We don't have royalty here, no princes and princesses or dukes and duchesses, so what do we need castles for? They're inherently fake. America is too young for a castle."

"Does my castle seem young to you?"

I think about the stained glass in Castle South, imported from Europe a century ago. "No."

"Fake?"

"Not fake," I say slowly. *Fake* isn't the right word.

"So you do like my castle?" Dr. Prince says, smiling. He looks pleased with me.

"I don't like *your* castle," I say. I don't mean to the put the emphasis on *your*, but it comes out that way before I can stop it. Quickly, I change the subject. "Why twelve girls?"

My question seems to startle him. "I'm sorry?"

"Why twelve? Why not more? The building is certainly large enough to accommodate more."

Dr. Prince smiles. "Well, the building may be, but I am not. I pride myself on giving each of you individual attention."

"Well, then, why twelve? Why not ten or eight? You could pay even more attention to a smaller group."

"I don't think anyone would benefit from too small a group."

I finger the ponytail holder around my wrist. I wonder if Carol's ever confiscated ponytail holders. "And why only girls?"

Dr. Prince smiles. "It can get complicated when you have girls and boys running around together."

I roll my eyes but stop myself from lecturing him about being so gender normative. Cass and Virginia are a couple. Daniel's gay. And what about gender-nonconforming kids? Do the Princes admit nonbinary students?

Maybe Dr. Prince isn't talking about romance when he says a coed environment can get complicated. When I was in ninth grade, my mom got on a kick about sending me to an all-girls private school. She'd read that girls performed better in a single-sex environment. Never mind that I already got straight A's at my coed school. I think she just wanted to get me away from Nathan but gave up when she realized that sending me to a different school would probably mean that I'd spend even more time at the Kaplans' outside of school. "It must be expensive," I say, "maintaining a place like this with the tuition from only twelve students." I pause. "Do you accept insurance?"

Dr. Prince shakes his head. "This is a school, not a medical facility, so we can't accept insurance. And I'm afraid many treatment centers aren't covered by insurance, either. It's a terrible shame—the cost keeps so many people from getting the care they need."

"But not the twelve of us."

"No," Dr. Prince says.

"So everyone here is rich?" It's not like I haven't noticed that some of the girls wear designer jeans, cashmere sweaters. But not all of them. Not me. My family isn't rich, exactly, but I went to a private school in Manhattan, and I know its tuition wasn't cheap. I'm guessing my parents aren't getting my tuition back for the days I'm missing, so they probably had to dig into their savings to send me here.

I wonder if Nathan's parents got a refund from our school for his senior year. He never got to attend a single day.

"I accommodate every student as best I can," Dr. Prince says.

"What, like with scholarships or something?"

"Something like that," Dr. Prince says, and I wonder how financial aid is awarded here. Some schools base it on merit—like, academic achievement—but how would you quantify that for a place like this?

I guess scholarships could be based on need rather than merit. The tuition could be adjusted based on each family's income.

But seriously, it must be expensive to maintain this place. Even if it's not as old as the real castles in Europe, it's still almost a hundred years old, which means rusty pipes and outdated wiring, plus the cost of electricity for such a massive footprint. I wonder if Dr. Prince makes a profit on us troubled girls. Maybe he loses money every year. Maybe he's independently wealthy, and he runs this place out of the goodness of his heart.

Or maybe he and the other Dr. Prince think that they'll publish the findings of their experiments someday and get rich.

I don't know how long I sit there quietly, but it must be a while, because suddenly Dr. Prince says, "Will you send in Grey, please?"

"What?" I ask dumbly.

"Our time's up. Please send in Grey."

"Oh. Okay. Right."

Dr. Prince doesn't seem all that bothered by the fact that I spent half our session silently thinking. In fact, right now he's bent over his pad, taking notes as though I just shared some kind of revelation, like he can read my mind.

No; if he could read my mind, he'd have fixed the lock on our window by now.

Besides, there's no such thing as mind readers.

Right?

# RYAN

Ryan wants to make one thing clear: she knows that stealing is wrong. Which is why she tries to take things of little value, things that won't be missed, things that are easy to replace.

She still remembers the first thing she took. She was at a mall with her mother, and she was four years old. It was December, and Ryan was wearing a bulky pink jacket. In one store, there was a plastic wand filled with silver streamers, tipped with glitter. Ryan thought of the magic she could do with that wand, the twirls and tosses she could perform. She held the wand up to her mother, who smiled and shook her head. The wand was junk, her mother explained, the sort of thing that would clutter the house and then end up in the trash. But Ryan knew the wand was already hers.

So she slipped it up her sleeve. She brought it home and hid it under her bed, next to her leftover Halloween candy. She didn't tell anyone it was there, and she never took it out. Never twirled and tossed it like she had imagined. Never performed any magic tricks. But just knowing it was there, that she slept above it every night, made her feel better, made her calmer. She believed it gave her good dreams.

*It wasn't stealing*, she thought. It was bringing home something that belonged to her.

When she was ten, she got caught slipping gum into her pockets at the pharmacy. Her mother, embarrassed, said it was a misunderstanding, paid for the gum, and pulled Ryan out of the store. Later, chewing the gum, Ryan felt anxious, twitchy— the same way she'd felt before she'd taken it. Usually after taking something, she felt calmer. *What's the difference*, she wondered, *between gum my mother pays for and gum I take?*

She went back to the pharmacy after school the next day, her fingers clenched into fists, her jaw set. She hadn't been able to relax, not for one minute, since her mother had paid for the gum.

She took her time, browsing the candy aisle. It had to be something bigger than gum. She eyed an entire bag of candy bars. She could taste the chocolate, the nougat (whatever that was). She imagined bringing the candy to school the next day and sharing it with her friends.

Only when the bag was tucked away under her sweatshirt, only when she could hear the rustling of the plastic as she moved, only when she could feel it sticking to her sweaty skin, did her fingers relax, her shoulder blades slide down her back, her breath grow steadier.

Stealing, Ryan knew, *should* make a person nervous.

She got caught sometimes, and her parents punished her. But they had no idea how often she took things. She stole the flowers she gave to her mother on her birthday and the tie she gave her father for Christmas. She kept her favorite items under her bed, the things she couldn't eat or share or give away: the popular girl's favorite hair tie, her gym teacher's whistle. Her ballet teacher's handkerchief and the principal's stapler. The wand lay exactly where she'd left it when she was four years old. She never moved anything once it was under the bed.

Until one day, when her mother announced that she was hiring a housekeeper to clean the house from top to bottom. Spring cleaning, she called it, even though it was October. Ryan left a note on her door for the housekeeper: SKIP THIS ROOM.

But when she got home from school, her parents were sitting, white-lipped, on her bed. The wand lay in her mother's lap. Ryan knows now that she was foolish to expect a collection to remain hidden. And she shouldn't have been surprised when her parents sent her to her school's guidance counselor, then to therapy, and finally, away to the Castle School.

# twenty-one

"It's freezing!" Eleanor blows gray clouds of air in my direction, stomping in some frozen snow.

This afternoon, for the first time since I've been here—I don't have a calendar, but I think it's been about a month—Dr. Prince let everyone who doesn't have private therapy come outside, which isn't exactly a treat when it's bitterly cold and there's nothing to do but wander around the driveway. The air isn't just cool but also clammy, like wrapping yourself in a towel that's still wet after a shower.

"It's gotta be February by now, right?" I blow on my hands. I feel like a first-grader who's been let out for recess.

Eleanor grins. "It's Valentine's Day next week. Hank told me. I think he wants to make a big deal about it."

"How big of a deal can he make?" I ask. "It's not like he can take you out on a date or give you a present."

"He could ask his parents to send him something," Eleanor counters defensively. "They sent him soda, remember?"

"Yeah, but how could he ask them to send him a present for a girl without giving away that we've been sneaking into his school every night?"

"He'll manage to make it special." Eleanor makes it sound easy. "Hank's good at things like that. I mean, it's bad enough that we can't, you know, talk and text during the day. I mean, *he* could, *he* has a working phone, but we're stuck in Siberia over here. So anyway, he'll make it special. You have to when you only have so much time together."

I want to ask how a few hours each night is enough time for her to know what Henry's good at. And I want to ask if Henry has told her why his parents sent him there. I've been dancing with Daniel every night, and other than telling me it wasn't because of his sexuality, he hasn't said what he's doing here. He hasn't said why *any* of the boys are there. I know that A.J. is good at picking locks and Henry's parents believe in care packages. I know that Daniel has a crush on a cute boy named Drew, though Daniel explained that Drew is too busy keeping up with his schoolwork to get distracted by romance.

If next week is Valentine's Day, then my math was right—I've been here a month. Back home in New York, my former classmates are surely complaining about the cold, just like us. But unlike us, they've probably also sent out their college applications, anticipating acceptances and rejections come spring.

About eight of us are out here now, gathered in the drive that

158

circles the castle like a moat. We keep close to the building, as though we think we'll be a little bit warmer that way.

Eleanor and I are up front, near the doors. Alice is power walking up and down the cobblestones. Ryan and Halsey found a flat, untouched patch of snow just off the driveway, and they're building a tiny snowman. I notice that the snowman's hat looks a lot like one I saw on Eleanor's side of the room a few days ago.

"Guess that's Ryan's way of giving it back to me." Eleanor laughs when she sees the hat on top of their fairly pathetic snowman. I don't think he's even a foot high.

I wonder what would happen if Eleanor and I snuck off into the woods right now, this afternoon, once Shelly turns her back on us. I want to see Castle South in the daytime, if only to assure myself it's there no matter the hour.

I know it's a ridiculous thought. Buildings don't disappear depending on the time of day. But when you only have access to a place for a few hours each night, it's hard not to wonder if it exists the rest of the time.

Eleanor moves so that she's standing close to me. "I want to talk to you about something."

I drop my voice. "Maybe we should start being more careful. About where and when we talk about—*you know*."

"Shelly's not paying attention to us," Eleanor points out reasonably. "She's too busy making out with her cigarette."

We both glance toward Shelly, who's leaning against the Castle door, smoking. She's not wearing gloves, as though she doesn't want anything coming between her and her cigarette.

She holds it gently, bringing it to her mouth quickly, like she just can't wait to feel it between her lips.

"Shelly shouldn't smoke in front of us," I say. "And anyway, what about the other girls? If they hear us talking about"—I pause—"*anything*, they might ask questions."

"Well, that's what I'm getting at," Eleanor says. "I *want* them to ask questions."

"What?" I forget to keep my voice down. "Are you crazy?"

Eleanor grins. "Of course. Aren't you? Aren't we all?"

"Eleanor, be serious."

"I *am* serious." My roommate stops smiling. "I don't think it's right to keep this to ourselves."

I drop my voice back to a whisper. "If they know about it, they'll want to come." Eleanor nods, like, *duh*. "But the more of us who go, the higher our chances are of getting caught. And let's not forget that Reva is a flight risk. You think it's a coincidence that the Prince let us out when the runaway has her private session?"

"Don't pretend you want to keep this to yourself because you're worried about Reva's well-being."

"I'm not pretending." Ryan and Halsey have taken their snowman apart in favor of using his parts for a snowball fight, Eleanor's hat left to freeze on the ground. "It's not safe. What if someone gets hurt in the woods?"

"Nothing's happened to us."

I turn and focus my gaze on anything but her face: the stone castle, the driveway, the wrought-iron gate.

"Moira, this is what girls do," Eleanor whispers to my back.

"What's that supposed to mean?"

"If we have something that might make our friends happy, we share it."

I shake my head, but I don't turn around.

Eleanor pauses, and when she speaks again, I hear a catch in her voice, like she's begging. "I don't even think about cutting when we're there. And I know you feel better, too. You're not constantly chugging water."

It's not like I didn't know Eleanor noticed. Our first night at Castle South, she said, *You're the one who's always thirsty.*

She continues, "Before I came here, I spent every day counting the minutes until I'd be alone so I could cut myself, then hating myself for cutting because I knew it was sick, and then cutting again because it was the only thing that made me feel better."

"I didn't know that," I say softly.

"Yeah, well." Eleanor stomps on the snow again.

I understand how she feels, sort of. I spend every day with the pain of missing Nathan buzzing under my skin. I spend every day with a painful lump in the back of my throat that's always trying to rise into my mouth and out through my lips so it can shout, *he's gone, he's gone, he's gone.*

He *is* gone.

He's *been* gone.

The only thing he'll ever *be* from now on is gone.

The lump is a constant reminder.

Except at Castle South.

"Come on, Moira," Eleanor pleads. "It's not fair to keep something this good to ourselves."

*Ourselves.*

*Our* castle.

Eleanor's and mine.

*Our/we/us.*

Eleanor and me and the ten other girls.

That's why I covered for Ryan about the shampoo that time, isn't it? Because I see myself as aligned with these girls against Carol?

Like how I snuck champagne to Nathan for his birthday when the grown-ups weren't looking.

I didn't bring any water out here with me. I thought it would be too cold. Stupid mistake.

In the time we've been having this conversation, the last private session must have ended. All twelve of us are out here, even Reva. (So much for my theory that Dr. Prince wouldn't let her outside.) My classmates are stomping the snow, packing snowballs, whispering in the nooks and crannies of the castle's stone walls.

"I'm going to take a walk." I have to speak carefully to get the words out.

"Moira, please."

"Please what?"

"Think about it."

"About what?"

"About the other girls."

162

I nod and back away from her. I'm not looking where I'm going, and I slip on a patch of ice on the ground. I fall backward, knocking my head hard against the stone wall of the castle behind me.

"Ow!" I shout.

A male voice speaks up. "What happened?"

Randy.

He's only a few paces away. He's wearing a sweatshirt with the hood up and a scarf tied tightly around it. His sweatpants and sneakers are caked with snow. Despite the cold, there's a layer of sweat on his face, which is ruddy and pink. He must have just gotten back from a run.

"How long have you been standing there?" There's some dull sunlight coming in from between the clouds, making me squint when I look up at his face. I picture him jogging through the woods, making a path through the snow just wide enough for his legs, like a deer.

"Long enough to see you whack your head against the Castle. Come on, I'll take you to the infirmary."

"The infirmary? I just knocked my head."

"You knocked it pretty hard," Randy says. "I'll get you some ice."

Randy takes me by the elbow. I let him lead me away, but I keep my eyes locked with Eleanor's as we walk toward the Castle's entrance. I know we're thinking the same thing:

How long was Randy standing that close, and how much did he hear?

163

# twenty-two

The infirmary is on the first floor, down the hall beyond the drawing room. It looks just like my high school nurse's office: a desk and two sets of bunk beds. But there's no nurse sitting at the desk, ready to send you back to class as long as you don't have a fever.

I sit on the edge of one of the beds and Randy holds out a ziplock bag full of ice. He steps toward me and gently places the bag against the back of my head. Some water drips onto my neck, and I shiver.

"Too cold?" Randy asks, pulling the bag away.

I shake my head. "Just startled me." With one hand, Randy softly presses the bag back onto the bump that's forming. With the other, he gestures to the blanket folded at the foot of the bed. I reach for it and wrap it around my shoulders like a cape.

"No nurse, huh?"

"Hmm?" Randy stands over me so that he blocks the light. He's so close I can smell him: the shaving cream he probably only just started using, the conditioner he maybe uses to tame his curls.

And something else, something warm and comforting. It takes me a second to identify it, but I realize it's *Randy*. He doesn't smell sweaty and hot like you'd think he would after a run. Or anyway, the scent of his sweat doesn't smell bad to me; it's not the sweat of sickness, the kind that comes after tossing and turning with a fever or nausea or pain all night. Randy smells *healthy*. He holds the ice pack so gently I can barely feel it, like he's scared to touch me.

"No nurse," I repeat. "Usually infirmaries have nurses."

Randy nods to a door on the opposite wall. "Shelly's rooms," he explains. "She keeps her door open whenever anyone stays here."

I tilt my face up toward Randy's. He moves the ice pack as my head shifts so that it's still resting over the right spot.

When I was five years old, my dad decided to take the training wheels off my bike. He took me to the park and did the whole holding-the-back-of-the-bike thing, but once he let go, I fell down after about thirty seconds. He didn't ask me to get back on the bike, just brought me home, where Mom put ice on my skinned knee. She wasn't nearly as gentle about it as Randy is being now, and she looked so disappointed that I apologized.

For the first time, I wonder if maybe she wasn't

disappointed in me. Maybe she was disappointed in my dad. Maybe he didn't always go along with what she said, not back then.

Randy says, "We don't need a nurse. We have my dad. He's a doctor."

"Yeah, but not, like, a *medical* doctor."

"Sure he is."

"He is?"

"He went to medical school," Randy says. "Almost became a neurosurgeon."

"Really?"

Randy nods.

"How'd he go from that to teaching a bunch of troubled girls?" I'm genuinely curious.

Randy shrugs. "It's a long story."

"Yeah, but, c'mon—who studies neurosurgery and ends up in the woods like this?" Something must have happened, right? Maybe Dr. Prince had too many patients die in his OR and he lost his medical license. Maybe he was experimenting on patients even back then.

"Seriously," Randy says, "it's not that interesting."

I try another tack. "What's the deal with Shelly, anyway? She's, like, the worst teacher ever."

Randy laughs. "Call her a leftover from the old days."

"The old days?"

"Shelly was a counselor back when—" He pauses, then says, "Well, they used to run this place a little differently."

166

So the Princes do tweak their experiment from one semester to the next, like I thought.

I should keep track, take notes on everything I notice about the experiment. Maybe when I get out of here, I can track down the Princes' former students and interview them. Someday, maybe years from now, I can write an exposé. When I'm grown up enough that people will believe me.

Then again, maybe no one will ever believe a girl who got sent to a place like this.

Randy continues, "My parents used to have more students, more teachers. We even had a nurse you'd approve of."

"Your parents?" I ask. Well, that answers one question—Dr. Maura Prince *is* Randy's mom.

Randy sighs. "Long story short, it was my parents' dream to have a school of their own. After Dad went to medical school, he got his master's in education. That's how he met my mom—she was the TA in one of his classes, but she was also getting a PhD in psychology, made him want to study it, too."

I want to ask why he doesn't live with her. Did he *choose* Castle North over Castle South? Did he have a choice? Does he alternate between castles, part of his parents' experiment?

My confusion must show on my face, because Randy says, "Don't look so surprised. Didn't you think I had a mother? I mean, everyone has a mother, one way or another. Didn't you ever wonder where she was?"

"I didn't think—" I don't know how to explain without telling him that we've been sneaking out to Castle South without also telling him that I think his parents are a couple of Dr. Frankensteins, experimenting on us all.

Suddenly, Randy's face hardens. "You didn't actually *think* about me at all. None of you girls do."

"What are you talking about?"

"You know, you're the only one who ever even talks to me."

"You told me we're not supposed to talk—"

"Don't you girls wonder what I'm doing here? Why I don't go to a regular school? Why I live with my dad in the middle of nowhere?"

"Of course we do," I say, though the truth is, I haven't heard any of the other girls mention it. And I'd simply assumed there wasn't a regular high school nearby for Randy to attend. "It's just—"

"But instead of talking to me, you talk *about* me behind my back." I can feel Randy's fingers trembling over the ice pack, but it doesn't frighten me. One of the few advantages of having had so many fights with my mom is that raised voices barely even register with me.

Randy puts the ice pack down and backs up two steps.

"Sorry." He stuffs his hands in his pockets. "I didn't mean to get so worked up."

"It's okay."

He shakes his head. "You should ice that bump yourself."

I pick up the ice pack and press it to my head. "Why don't you go to a regular school?" I ask finally. "Do you ever—I don't know, want to be around other kids? Other guys, I mean." Does Randy ever hang out with the boys at Castle South?

"Other guys are overrated." I can tell that in the pockets of his sweatshirt, Randy's hands are balled into fists. He looks trapped here in the nurse's office, a room he's about six inches too tall for.

"What made your dad decide to make this place so much smaller?"

Randy shrugs. "Things got... complicated."

"Oh," I say softly. *Complicated*, like someone found out they were experimenting on their students and there was a scandal? *Complicated*, like they had to make this place smaller so they could pay for that person's silence?

No, that makes no sense. If they needed money, they'd admit more students, not fewer.

Right?

Randy adds, "I don't know why Dad ever thought this was a good place for a school. We hardly get any sun up here. This castle's too damp to ever feel warm or, you know, cheerful."

*This* castle, I think. As opposed to the other one—is that what Randy's getting at? Is he trying to find out how much I know? Even if he didn't overhear Eleanor and me talking earlier, he might have seen our footprints in the snow when he was out running and put two and two together.

"I think that's enough ice," I say finally, holding out the ice pack for Randy to take.

"Well, good," he says. "I shouldn't be in here with you, anyway."

"Right, you're not supposed to be alone with any of us."

"Right."

"But I don't think you'd get in trouble for giving ice to a girl who hit her head. I mean, every rule can be broken under the right circumstances, right?"

"My dad's rules are in place for a reason." Randy looks at me meaningfully. "I know it seems lame, but the rules keep us safe."

*Us?*

*Ours/we/us.*

That night in the kitchen, I thought Randy saw me as just another one of his dad's troubled students. But he's including himself in the *us* he's referring to now.

"It may seem fun to be lax with rules, but it's actually really selfish."

"Selfish?"

"Parents trust my father with their kids. It would be irresponsible not to take their trust seriously."

"Or people are just sick and tired of their kids, so they send them away to punish them."

"You think it's a punishment to be sent away?"

"Maybe it depends on *where* you're being sent." We lapse into silence until I add, "You know, mythology has stories of people without mothers."

"Huh?"

"You said everyone has a mother in one way or another. But, like, the goddess Athena in Greek mythology—she was said to have simply sprung from her father's head."

"You always fill silences with trivia like that?" Randy asks, but he doesn't roll his eyes like Eleanor.

"It's interesting."

"It is," he agrees, then adds, "But Athena's a goddess, not a regular person. I'm not sure there are any stories about *regular* people who didn't have mothers. I mean, there are plenty of stories about people whose mothers abandoned them or died—"

"Romulus and Remus," I offer.

Randy nods. "Cinderella and Snow White." Nathan never added to my trivia, just let me rattle it off.

"What is it with fairy tales and dead moms?" I ask.

"Or sometimes dead*beat* moms," Randy adds. "Hansel and Gretel—their mom sent them off into the woods to die."

"I think that was their stepmom," I correct.

"Okay, then how about Sleeping Beauty? Her mom sent her to be raised by a bunch of fairies, right?"

"But Sleeping Beauty's mom did it to protect her daughter, right? To hide her from the spinning wheel or whatever."

"And how did that work out?"

I laugh. "Okay in the end. Sleeping Beauty lived happily ever after."

"Only after sleeping for a hundred years."

"Something like that."

Randy sighs. "I better go."

"Right," I agree. "The rules."

Randy's face is silhouetted in the dim light as he leaves the room and heads back to whatever it is that he does to pass the time around here. I linger in the nurse's office. Before I came to Castle, I spent so much time alone—not just in my room, but on the subway or walking through the city. That's the thing about New York: you can be stuck in a crowd but still be completely alone.

There are so many fewer people here that you'd think it would be easy to be alone, but it's not.

Is that part of Dr. Prince's method, too?

Is it part of this semester's experiment?

# twenty-three

At dinner, Virginia whispers something to Beth, who giggles in response. Beth is my age, but she's so tiny that she looks like she's even younger than Virginia, who's the youngest girl here. If we were in a regular school, Virginia would be a sophomore, not a senior like I am. Or like I'm supposed to be.

When we finish eating—Mei finishes off Alice's Ensure again—we pile our plates on the sideboard, and Shelly counts the silverware. She nods in our direction, signaling that we can go.

"What do you think of Randy?" I ask Eleanor as we trudge up the stairs to our room.

"Randy?"

"Dr. Prince's son."

Eleanor opens our door. "I don't think of him." She disappears into her closet, her voice muffled by all those long sleeves and sweaters. "What do you think I should wear tonight?"

"At all?" I ask.

"At all what?"

"You don't think of Randy at all?"

"At all." Eleanor comes out of her closet and plops down on the edge of my bed. "I have nothing to wear."

"What are you talking about? Your closet is stuffed."

Eleanor shakes her head. "Everything I own is two sizes too big. I buy my clothes that way on purpose—you know, so that the sleeves will be long enough."

"You can wear something of mine," I offer. Eleanor is a little bit smaller than I am, but my clothes will probably fit her better than her own anyhow. She looks relieved and heads for my closet with the ease of someone who's used to sharing. Maybe she has a sister back home. I don't actually know; we don't talk about our families much. She emerges with a black sleeveless dress. "This is pretty." If she notices how much black dominates my closet, she doesn't say so. For two months before Nathan died, I obsessed over what I would wear to his funeral. In his bedroom, while he slept, I browsed different websites, looking for the right dress, the right sweater, the right shoes.

I made my way through the little black dresses that were meant for nights out on the town, the smart black shift dresses that were meant for older women to wear to the office. I needed one outfit for cold weather and another for warm, because there was no telling when it would happen.

If Nathan woke up and asked what I was doing, I always lied. Checking email, I said. Or reading an article, or playing on

Instagram. I knew it was wrong to shop for a dress to wear to the funeral of a boy who was still alive in front of me. I'd squeeze my eyes shut, trying to get rid of the images of black dress after black dress floating across my phone's screen.

In the end, the dress I wanted to wear was on back order. It showed up at my apartment almost a month after Nathan died. I didn't even open the box before sending it back. Finding that dress was the only thing I'd bothered doing to prepare for his death, and I'd failed at it. Everyone else at the funeral looked right— people from our school who barely knew Nathan were better prepared than I was. I guess I shouldn't have been surprised that they just happened to have the right things to wear to a funeral; they always knew the right things to wear to school, too.

I hated what I wore that day, hated myself for wishing that Nathan had lived a little longer, long enough for the right dress to arrive.

"Too fancy?" Eleanor asks, holding the dress up under her neck.

I shrug. I rejected that dress as a funeral option because it was sleeveless, but it was final sale, so now I'm stuck with it. I don't remember packing it. Did I really think I'd need it here?

Eleanor turns back to the closet and selects a tank top instead. I look away as she takes off her sweater and slides the top over her head.

"What do you think?" Eleanor asks, and I face her.

There are goose bumps up and down her arms. It's too cold for a sleeveless shirt here, but it won't be at Castle South.

175

On the inside of Eleanor's right elbow is a series of dots, as though she poked herself over and over with a needle. On her left wrist, the angry red line that got her sent to the infirmary last month has faded into a pink scar. I wonder how long it will take until it turns white like the others.

Eleanor folds her arms across her chest. "Henry says he doesn't mind them, you know."

"You talk about them?"

"It's hard to avoid."

Eleanor and Henry have taken to disappearing for at least part of our time at Castle South. I guess they go to his room, like they did on our first night there. But I don't think they're going for anything as innocent as soda anymore.

"What does he say?" I ask.

"That he hopes I won't do it anymore."

"And what do you say?"

Eleanor doesn't look at me when she answers, "That when I'm with him, I don't want to." Her quiet voice makes me blush, like I've walked in on her and Henry making out. "Anyway, the shirt looks good, right?"

I nod. She sits on the carpet to lace up her boots. I sit facing her.

"You did that right before I got here, huh?" I ask, gesturing to her wrist.

"Yeah."

"How? Didn't they confiscate anything sharp enough for you to cut with?"

"I can be pretty creative when I need to be."

"What'd you use?"

"A book."

"A book?"

She nods, a sheepish sort of smile crossing her face. "Yeah. I took the sides of the pages and started by giving myself paper cuts."

I wince.

"Then I took the front cover—the corner of the cardboard part, it was a hardcover book—and used it to open the cuts up wider."

"Were you trying to kill yourself?"

"What?" The question seems to surprise her.

"Well, opening up your wrist like that. Seems like a suicide attempt."

Eleanor shakes her head. "Lemme try on your sweater," she says, reaching for the cardigan I'm wearing. "I think it'll look good over this top."

I slide off my sweater and hand it to her. "It looks like it hurt."

Eleanor gestures to the bottom of my arrow tattoo, peeking out from under my T-shirt sleeve. "Some people would say that looks like it hurt."

"It's not the same thing," I say.

"Isn't it?"

"Of course not."

"When they drew the tattoo on your arm with a needle, did it hurt?"

177

"Sure," I answer.

"And when it broke the surface of your skin, did it make you feel better, just for a second?"

I don't want to answer, but I find myself nodding. It hurt—I knew it hurt—but it was also a relief to have something that hurt other than missing Nathan.

"It's not the same thing," Eleanor agrees finally. "But you have to admit, it's not completely different, either."

I went to the tattoo parlor alone. I used a fake ID that had been intended for nights out with Nathan. The last—and only—time I'd used it was at a liquor store on Nathan's birthday, when I bought us that champagne.

When I got to the tattoo parlor, I realized that I'd left the printout of the arrow I'd chosen at home. I tried to find it on my phone, but I couldn't remember where I'd seen it and I didn't want to risk going home to get it—what if Mom figured out what I was up to and kept me from coming back?—so they brought me books and books of pictures, pages and pages covered in different arrows. It took me almost an hour to find the right one. I worried someone might kick me out, tell me I was taking too long, say they didn't have time to help a little girl get her first ink. But they left me alone while I ran my fingers over the pictures. When I finally found the perfect arrow, the lump in my throat grew bigger than ever. I couldn't even get the words out to tell them I'd found the right one; I just pointed, and they understood.

"We can't tell the other girls about Castle South," I say

suddenly. "I'm worried Randy knows we've been sneaking out. He might tell his dad."

"So then there's no reason not to tell the others," Eleanor says cheerfully. She practically bounces to her feet.

"What are you talking about?"

"You said the more of us who knew, the higher our chances of getting caught, right?"

"Yeah?"

"Well, if we're going to get caught anyway, we might as well tell them."

I can't argue with that. "May as well be in for a penny as in for a pound," I say softly.

"Huh?"

"It's an expression. It means if you've done a penny's worth of something wrong, you may as well do a dollar's worth."

"Did anyone ever tell you that sometimes you sound like an old lady?"

Nathan said so all the time. But he didn't mind it. He was an old soul, too.

"Well, however much money we're in for, it doesn't matter, anyway," Eleanor says.

"Why not?"

"'Cause I already told."

# twenty-four

"You told them?" I ask furiously.

"I told *Raina*," Eleanor corrects carefully. "It's not like she's going to spread the word, right?"

"So, what, you took it upon yourself to use Raina's"—I struggle to find the right word—"*problems* as a convenient cover, or something?"

"Don't be so melodramatic," Eleanor counters calmly, tucking her hair behind her ears. "We had to start somewhere."

"No, we didn't. We didn't have to start *anywhere*."

I'm so cold without my sweater on that I rub my hands together to keep warm. I can't remember the last time I fought with anyone but my mother.

Eleanor says, "Raina will be here after lights-out."

I shake my head. "What about Reva?" Reva is Raina's roommate.

"I told Raina to wait until Reva's asleep."

Actually, I can remember fighting with someone else—with Nathan. But there were no raised voices, no pulsing veins. Just the pleading in his voice.

"What if Reva wakes up? I mean, she's *literally* a flight risk."

"Not *literally*," Eleanor corrects. "She's not going to sprout wings."

I'd normally be the one to point out that sort of technicality. "This isn't funny. If she sees an opportunity to escape—"

"She didn't make a break for it when we were outside this afternoon," Eleanor points out. "Maybe her therapy with Dr. Prince is actually working."

This makes us both start laughing.

None of the fights I ever had with my mom ended in laughter.

Neither did my one and only fight with Nathan.

"Okay, fine," I say, not that Eleanor actually asked my permission. "Raina can come."

◇◇◇◇

Raina is a good dancer. And though she doesn't talk, I hear her humming along to the music. Even singing the lyrics, at one point. A.J. spins her around in time to the music, and then another boy with dark hair takes her hand. He's wearing plaid flannel pajama pants with a crewneck burgundy sweater.

"Remind me of his name," I ask Daniel, nodding toward Raina and her new partner. It's been a month, but I don't quite have all the boys' names memorized.

"Greg," Daniel answers. "Remember? Greg Dhali and Dave Packer are best friends."

I nod, locating Dave—tall, skinny, with close-cropped light hair—sitting at the table at the other end the room, looking intently at his laptop, seemingly oblivious to the music, the dancing, and his best friend's moves. Greg leans in and whispers something to Raina. She doesn't speak, but she nods in response.

"You gonna bring the other girls one at a time, too?" Daniel asks.

"What do you mean?"

"I mean, why haven't you brought the rest of your friends yet?"

Abruptly, I stop moving my feet. Daniel keeps dancing, and my stillness against his movement creates distance between us. My hands hang in front of me like a marionette's.

In the days after Nathan died, my phone buzzed with calls and texts that I never answered or returned. Mom noticed all the unanswered messages and said, "Why don't you write back to your friends?"

They weren't my friends. They were just girls I went to school with. They'd barely spoken to me before Nathan died.

*Nathan* was my friend, and Nathan was gone. I didn't have any friends left.

But fighting with Eleanor tonight and then laughing over something no one else would find funny—is *she* my friend now?

"Earth to Moira," Daniel prompts.

"Sorry." I shake my head and drop my hands. "I think I need to take a break from dancing." I wave my hand in front of my face like I'm hot, and I am—my hair is moist with sweat.

"No problem." Daniel leads me to one of the soft chairs near the fireplace. "So, are you gonna bring the other girls here?"

"If you wanted more girls here, why'd you guys break the lock on just one window?"

"Touché," Daniel concedes with a grin. Then he asks, "Don't you like the other girls?"

I shrug.

Daniel adds, "I mean, believe me, none of us came here to make *friends*. Some of the guys barely talked to the rest of us when they got here. They were too busy being pissed about being here in the first place. But most of us are friends now, more or less, because what else is there to do?"

"Okay, so if you and Henry were walking down the street back home—"

"We don't live in the same town," Daniel interrupts.

"Okay, but for the sake of the story, just pretend."

Daniel raises an eyebrow but says, "Fine."

"So, you and Henry are walking down the street, and you bump into someone you go to school with—normal school—and you introduce your *friend* Henry, and the guy asks how you met each other, you'll say, oh, we were at reform school together?"

"This place isn't a reform school."

I snort. "Maybe *your* castle isn't."

Daniel folds his arms across his chest. "So you don't want to make friends here because later you'd be embarrassed about where you made them?"

"I didn't say that."

Nathan is my best friend.

I never needed any friends besides him.

Okay, I know he's gone. People say the first stage of grief is denial—that when someone you love dies, you're struck by the urge to call, to text, and then you remember the person is gone and you can't call or text.

I never get that urge, because I never forget Nathan's gone.

But I don't think about his absence as much, not here in Castle South.

Eleanor wants to come back every night because of Henry.

I want to come back because it's so bright and so warm that sometimes it's hard to remember I ever lost anything. Here, there's never any quiet—no hidden spaces between words and sentences, between sighs and laughter—so I don't hear Nathan's voice commenting on my every move.

Or maybe I don't hear him because I'm losing him.

Isn't that what they say about Neverland in *Peter Pan*—stay too long, and you'll forget where you came from?

But Castle South isn't a magical land, it's a psychological experiment.

And I'll never forget Nathan.

I would never abandon him just because he abandoned me. It's not like he wanted to.

It's not like he had a choice.

He's still my best friend.

He'll always be my best friend.

# RAINA

Raina had always been quiet. Starting in kindergarten, there was usually a line or two on her report cards about how quiet she was. At first, it read like praise, because she never disrupted the classroom. But as she grew older, her teachers expressed concern—though they also said that she always did well on tests and that whenever they met with her one-on-one, she was more talkative.

They thought she was shy. *Raina* thought she was shy. She looked at other kids with wonder, the ones who spoke up in class, who didn't seem cowed by crowds.

Raina's parents never complained that their daughter was quiet. In fact, her mother appreciated peace and quiet in the house at the end of a long workday. She said that some things were too terrible to talk about. She said it when Raina's grandmother was diagnosed with cancer, when one of Raina's classmates died in a car accident, when Raina's father stopped picking

Raina and her sister up for their monthly visits. Raina always believed her mother: when terrible things happened, talking made them worse.

It's not that she was silent at home—sometimes, when it was just Raina, her mother, and her sister, she could be positively chatty about a TV show, a book, a meal. But the minute one of her mom's friends came over, Raina went quiet again. And her mother would explain that Raina was shy.

Raina was almost fifteen the day she saw a girl get attacked after school. Raina didn't know her well, but she knew the girl's name was Jennifer and that she went by Jenn with two *n*'s to differentiate herself from the half dozen other Jens they went to school with. Raina had always liked that about Jenn; she had decided that if her name were Jennifer, she would spell Jenn with two *n*'s, too. But she'd never said so to Jenn, since she barely knew her at all.

Raina was running late. She'd been halfway home when she realized that she forgot her French textbook, which she needed for that day's homework assignment. So she turned around.

It looked like Jenn knew at least one of the boys, because she got into the car willingly. One of them even opened the door for her; Raina heard Jenn say, "Thank you."

Raina heard sounds that were familiar and harmless: a door closing, a seat belt locking, a turn signal clicking over and over.

But then there were other sounds, sounds that Raina had to concentrate to identify: a slap, a whimper. A skull hitting a car window.

The boys couldn't see Raina from where she stood, leaning against the school, just outside the door that led to the parking lot. Even if they had seen her, maybe they wouldn't have worried: the quiet girl wouldn't tell.

When the car finally drove away, Raina walked home with her French textbook clasped to her chest. She said hello to her mother and went straight to her room and did her homework. She came down when her mother called her for dinner, and if she was quieter than usual at while they ate—it was just the two of them that night, her sister was at a friend's house—Raina's mother didn't seem to notice.

On the news that night, they said a local girl had been found unconscious in the parking lot of the school. Raina guessed that those boys had brought Jenn back there. Authorities were asking anyone who knew anything to contact the police. Raina's mother clucked at the television and said that it was such a terrible thing. No one, she said, wanted to hear about such a terrible thing.

Four days went by before Raina's teacher called her mother and said that Raina had gone from quiet to positively silent. Her mother asked Raina if her throat hurt; she took Raina to the pediatrician. Raina was able to open her mouth when the doctor told her to, but she couldn't say "Ah." Just the thought of making a sound made her shake.

The doctor suggested therapy, and Raina's mother scoffed, "She doesn't need therapy, there's something wrong with her throat." Raina's mother took her to an ear, nose, and throat specialist next, then to be fitted for hearing aids.

On the news several weeks later, they mentioned that the local girl had identified her attackers: the guilty parties would face charges. Raina knew she should come forward as a witness; she hated herself for staying silent, but she *couldn't* speak. She wondered how Jenn had been able to talk about it.

Six months went by before Raina's mother sent her to therapy. Raina was diagnosed with severe social anxiety disorder, of which her selective mutism was a symptom. They gave her medication and a speech coach, tried to reassure her about "safe spaces" like home and the doctor's office. They told her school was a safe space, but what Raina had witnessed proved otherwise. She started speaking again, but only to the doctor, only to her mother—and she never told them about what she saw.

A year later, Raina's therapist gave her the brochures for the Castle School.

# twenty-five

In group the next day, Carol begs Raina to speak. Years ago, I read a book about a girl with selective mutism, and it specifically said not to do that.

"Raina," Carol begs, "tell me something, anything. What's your favorite food? Do you want more cereal? You're safe here. No one will judge you."

Raina blinks at Carol and looks at her plate. Carol chews her lip in frustration. I swallow the last bite of my toast and peanut butter.

Much to my surprise, Raina opens her mouth, and for a second, every girl at the table holds her breath.

Raina's voice comes slowly, like it's stuck down inside her belly and needs time to find its way out. When she finally speaks, her voice sounds dry.

"I'd like to talk about secrets," Raina says.

Carol smiles so hard I think her teeth are going to crack. I can see her imagining the paper she'll write, arguing against the conventional wisdom regarding selective mutism. I can hear the sound of her fingernails clicking against the keyboard as she types it.

"What an interesting topic, Raina. Are there any specific secrets you want to talk about?"

"I have a secret."

Everybody freezes, like they think Raina's voice might be startled by sudden movements, like it's a shy animal that has emerged from its hole in the ground and might crawl back in if we frighten it.

Everybody, that is, but me. Before I can stop myself, I push my chair out and stand. The heavy chair scratches against the hardwood floor.

"Raina," I say, "maybe this isn't the right time to talk about this."

Everyone at the table looks at me like they hate me. What kind of a person, their eyes are saying, tries to silence a girl who has only just found her voice?

"Some secrets aren't..." I don't know how to finish, but I know that I have to stop Raina from telling everyone about Castle South.

Even if Randy knows already, he must not have told his father yet.

But if Raina tells now, they'll replace the lock on Eleanor's and my window right away.

The other girls will hate us for keeping it to ourselves for so long.

We'll never get to go to Castle South again.

I glance at Eleanor; isn't she as concerned as I am? If they keep us from going to Castle South, she won't get to see Henry. But Eleanor looks as disgusted with me as the other girls do.

I know I should sit down. My knees are shaking, trying to bend me back into my chair. I hold myself up by placing my palms on the table in front of me.

"Some secrets aren't for sharing with *everyone*," I say, and Raina blinks her dark eyes at me.

Carol says, "That's an interesting point, Moira, but this is Raina's secret, and we don't interrupt each other in group."

Suddenly, I hate Carol. She must know about the other castle, the other doctor, the other methodology. She must be in on the Princes' experiment, too.

My hair is still wet from the shower I took this morning. My lips are cracked from the cold air and the water I keep pouring into my mouth.

Carol says, "Please sit down and let Raina speak."

I shake my head, looking desperately at Eleanor. She pulls her sleeves down even farther over her wrists, until her hands are completely covered.

"No," I say.

"Then I'm going to have to ask you to leave," Carol says.

It takes me a moment to move. I lift my hands from the table and whisper, "Okay." Eleanor watches me go.

In our room, I sit on my bed, waiting for Dr. Prince and Carol to burst in, open the window, secure a new padlock on the bars, and call me a bad girl.

That's why we were sent here, right? This place is our punishment for being so bad.

At least, it's mine.

When I hear footsteps coming down the hall, I hold my breath. But it's not Carol, or Dr. Prince, or a team of muscular men in black T-shirts like the ones who brought me here. It's just Eleanor.

"Carol told me to come get you. It's time for class."

I lift my head from my pillow. "That's all?"

Eleanor nods.

"How can that be all? Didn't Raina tell about sneaking out?"

"Raina had more important things to talk about."

I swing my legs over the side of my bed so I'm sitting up. "What could possibly be a bigger secret than this?" I gesture to the window.

Eleanor moves toward me, holding a book close to her chest.

"Remember the first time we went there?" she says softly. "How we thought it might be an alternate universe?"

"Sure."

"What if it is? What if it's a place where Raina can talk, and that's the Raina we brought back?"

"You're not serious."

"Do you have a better explanation?" She pulls her sleeves down over her wrists again, the way she never does at Castle South.

I consider telling Eleanor what the Princes are really doing, but then I remember how easily she dismissed the idea that doctors experiment on patients.

Eleanor believes in magic. She doesn't know this is all part of the Princes' plan.

She doesn't know that if we feel better over there, it's due to conditions the Princes control.

Well, they can't control everything.

We're not helpless pawns in their experiment.

By going back and forth between the castles, we're *changing* their experiment.

I imagine the doctors Prince comparing notes at the end of the semester.

They'll be completely confused by their results, skewed by the nocturnal activities they don't know about.

Maybe no one will believe me if I try to expose the Princes, but at least I can mess with them.

My roommate sits carefully on the edge of my bed. "You know, Moira, no one thinks you were really sent here because of a tattoo."

I consider telling her about the late nights and endless arguments with my mother.

The arguments started before Nathan died. I'd stay at his apartment until midnight, one in the morning—he lived only two blocks away from us, but Mom freaked out at the idea of me walking home alone at that hour. I used to tell Nathan every detail of all these fights. He did an imitation of my mother that made me laugh so hard I thought I'd cry.

I consider explaining to Eleanor that Mom got every bit as angry about those two-block walks through our perfectly safe Upper East Side neighborhood as she did about my middle-of-the-night visits to the cemetery, but if I told her that, I'd have to tell her about Nathan. And she'd ask why I had to visit his grave so often, and I'd have to explain that I went there every night to apologize, and she'd ask why, and I'd have to tell her about the first time he was ever angry at me.

How anger was the last thing he ever felt for me.

How I never got a chance to apologize before he died.

And I never want to tell anyone that.

*Some secrets aren't for sharing.*

The lump in my throat is going to choke me.

With enormous effort, I swallow. "It's time for class. Shelly will notice if we're not there."

Before I step into the hallway, Eleanor whispers, "We're inviting the others tonight. All of them." She squeezes my hand, and I drop my shoulders. I didn't realize I'd been holding them up around my ears.

"Okay," I agree.

What better way to make this semester's results completely useless to the Princes?

# twenty-six

For class today, Shelly leads us to a large empty room across from the drawing room. She tells us to do jumping jacks, then to touch our toes, and then to reach into the air, swaying our arms from side to side like a tree in the wind.

"I'm dancing!" Virginia says, and she breaks whatever position we're supposed to be holding and begins spinning circles around the room, grabbing Beth along the way, then Halsey, then Reva, then Alice, then Raina, then Ryan, then Cass, then Mei, then Grey, then Eleanor, then me.

The ceilings are high in this room, so the windows are covered by the longest curtains I've ever seen. I wonder if the windows behind them are imported stained glass, like the windows in Castle South. The fireplace in the center of the wall is as tall as I am, though it's as clean and unused as the fireplaces in the kitchen and the room is cold and drafty. The floors are made of dark brown narrow wooden planks and would be shiny if they weren't buried under layers of dust that rises when we step on it. Still, our footsteps echo off the wood. This room is enormous.

It's exactly the same size and shape as the ballroom at Castle South.

◇◇◇◇

"You should be the one to tell them," Eleanor says after lights out.

I shake my head. "They're mad at me."

"No, they're not."

"Sure they are, after the way I silenced Raina this morning. Tried to silence, anyway."

"Well, soon they'll know why, and if they *are* mad at you, they'll get over it." Eleanor's impatient voice reminds me of my mother.

"*You* know why, and you're still mad at me."

"I'm not mad at you!"

"You're shouting at me."

Eleanor surprises me by laughing. "Well, even if I am mad at you, I'm almost over it."

I nod. "Okay. Go get the girls."

Everyone gathers in our room. They all have their coats on; Eleanor must have told them we were going someplace.

"Moira has something to tell you," Eleanor begins.

I open my mouth to speak, but I don't know where to start.

Sometimes I feel like a freak, legs too long and tongue too thick, around all these girls.

"Okay," I start. "So, the lock on Eleanor's and my window is broken, and we've been sneaking out at night—"

Virginia squeals, and Cass shushes her.

"And we discovered that we're not really in the middle of nowhere. I mean, we are, but we're not alone. We've been going to another place. A better place. I mean, not, like, 'a better place'"—I mime air quotes—"but, like, a more fun place—"

"Are you talking about the boys' castle?" Cass breaks in.

"You know about Castle South?" Eleanor says.

Cass shrugs in the darkness. "It's not a secret. I mean, didn't any of you research this place after your parents said you were coming here?"

"I didn't have that kind of time," I say, though it's not entirely true. The bodyguards who escorted me here didn't take my phone. I could've looked up the Castle School in the car, at the airport, on the plane. But I didn't bother. I was coming here regardless of what I found out about it, wasn't I?

"Well, anyway," Cass continues, "if you Google the Castle School, two websites come up—the boys' school and the girls' school. I didn't bother clicking on the site for the boys' one, since I wasn't going there."

"I did," Alice volunteers. "It honestly didn't look that different from the girls' site. You know—organic food, a chance to bond, that kind of thing. No specifics."

That makes sense. The Princes can't get too specific about

their methods if they change them from one semester to the next for their experiment.

Hearing the other girls talk about Castle South like this—like a place anyone could easily find online—feels strange. But I guess the Princes couldn't conduct their experiment without at least a semblance of legitimacy.

Finally, I say, "You guys knew there was a boys' school close by and you never said anything?"

"What would've been the point?" Alice says. "It's not like we could've gone there. It's all boys."

"Well, actually," I say, "we *can* go there. Not, like, to enroll, but—to hang out."

"Why?" Cass asks. "I mean, isn't it just as boring there as it is here?"

"No." My voice comes out so defensive it surprises me. "They don't have lights-out over there. We listen to music, dance, that kind of thing." It doesn't sound nearly as exciting as it is. "And Eleanor and I thought—" I pause. "We thought you could come, too. Only if you want to," I add quickly.

"If we want to?" Alice echoes. "Are you kidding?"

The room is dark, but I can still see that every single girl is grinning.

I am, too.

# twenty–seven

When we walk through the woods, I keep my eyes trained on Reva, worried that she might make a break for it. The girls chorus, "Ooh," when they see the lights from Castle South, and when we enter the ballroom—Daniel doesn't wait by the door to escort us in anymore—the boys cheer in welcome. Within seconds, Cass grabs Henry's phone and takes over as DJ. Virginia and Raina dance, though Raina is quiet again—whatever made her speak up in group today wasn't a cure.

Eleanor shrugs off her coat and sweater and makes a beeline for Henry. From across the room, I can't even see the scars on her arms; her pale skin looks smooth and radiant against Henry's darker complexion as he folds her into his arms. She looks at him and tucks her hair behind her ears instead of letting it fall across her cheeks.

I take off my coat and hang it over one of the heavy wooden

chairs at the table. It's so warm here that I lift my hair off the back of my neck and twist it around my fingers, wishing I'd brought a ponytail holder to pull it back with.

Daniel pulls me to dance in the center of the room. "We thought you'd never bring the others. Though I can't blame you for wanting to keep me to yourself," he adds with a wink.

"The more of us who know, the higher our chances of getting caught," I explain.

Daniel shrugs. "What're they gonna do?" he says. "Send you off to a castle in the woods until you learn your lesson?" He laughs, and I do, too, though of course, we both know there's so much more they could do. They could lock us back into our respective castles, for real this time. They could send us someplace else, someplace colder and stricter.

I shake my head, hoping it looks more like a dance move than an attempt to get rid of my nagging thoughts.

◇◇◇◇

"Typical," Cass says as we trudge north a while later.

"What's typical?" I ask, still keeping my gaze on Reva.

"That my parents would send me to Castle North when a place like that exists."

"Well, they didn't know how different it was," I answer reasonably. "And anyway, it's all boys. What choice did they have?"

"Oh, like there aren't a zillion 'special' boarding schools to

200

choose from. But no, my parents had to choose the place with bedtime and zero internet access."

She makes it sound like her parents shopped around before choosing to send her to Castle. I'm not under the impression that my parents did. The guidance counselor suggested the Castle School, so that's where they sent me. I wonder—would they have chosen this place if they'd known there were others out there?

"I mean," Cass continues, "it's like we're being *punished* for having problems while those boys are being... I don't know. *Not* punished."

I nod absently, then say, "Those boys were still sent away from home like we were, shipped off into the middle of nowhere." It must be part of the experiment. Like dog trainers who reward dogs for good behavior versus punishing them for bad behavior.

Cass leans against me as we walk. "Being sent away from home isn't always a punishment," she counters, and I can't argue. How many times did Nathan and I talk about leaving? Going away for college taking a gap year in Europe first. Nathan wanted to backpack across the continent, visiting as many museums as possible; I wanted to travel from one library to another. We figured that when the time came, we'd work out a compromise that allowed both of us to do what we wanted to do.

"They still have to do therapy and things," I say. Daniel told me that their days aren't structured all that differently than ours: group therapy in the morning, then class—but, like, *real* class with computers and textbooks and things—and individual therapy with their Dr. Prince in the afternoon.

But all the while, their castle is more cheerful, their fires are blazing, and their phones are in their hands.

"*This* is better than therapy," Cass says.

"What?" I ask. "Freezing our butts off in the woods in the middle of the night?"

"No." Cass laughs. "Sneaking out. Going someplace fun. How are we supposed to feel better when that place"—she gestures ahead of us, where Castle North is coming into view—"is so depressing? I mean, even our *teachers* seem bummed to be there. Have you ever seen the Prince smile? And what's with his creepy son skulking around in the corners?"

"He's not creepy—" I begin, but Cass keeps talking.

"And why does he live here instead of there?" Cass says. "I mean, his mom is at Castle South, right?"

I nod.

"Maybe she didn't want him with her," Cass suggests. "Maybe there's something wrong with him."

I shake my head. "If his mom didn't want him, there's something wrong with *her*, don't you think?"

"Like there's something wrong with our parents?" Cass retorts, and again, I can't argue. "There's got to be a reason he's stuck with us, right?"

"I don't know," I answer honestly.

Eleanor points the flashlight at the bars over the windows. One by one, my classmates start to climb.

"Makes you wonder," Cass says.

I nod. I thought Randy might be in on his parents' experiment or that he might have chosen our castle over the other. But maybe his parents didn't give him a choice.

*Other guys are overrated*, he said. *Things got complicated.*

"It definitely makes you wonder," I agree.

# twenty-eight

In group the next morning, when Carol asks who'd like to start, no one speaks. Maybe, like me, the other girls are nervous that if they open their mouths, the truth about where we were last night will come out.

Carol looks around the table, and we each avoid eye contact with her. My classmates at my regular school used to do that—no one wanted to get called on when they didn't know the answer. But I used to look right at the teacher. I always knew the answer. At least, until about halfway through sophomore year.

"Grey," Carol says finally, "how are you feeling today?"

Grey mumbles that she's feeling fine.

"Is there anything you'd like to share with the group?"

Grey shakes her head.

"I notice you didn't eat much breakfast today. Why is that?"

Grey doesn't answer. Cass told me that Grey actually asked

her parents to send her to the Castle School—she didn't get sent off the way I did. I imagine her body, her brain, her neurotransmitters or whatever they're called, working against her like an army countering her efforts to feel better.

Grey shrugs, and Carol moves on. "Mei," she says, "how are you feeling today?"

Mei's hair has begun to grow in a little bit, but she still doesn't have eyebrows. She runs a finger over her right one—or over the place it would be if she had one. It looks like she's not even aware that she's doing it.

"Mei?" Carol prompts. Mei looks Carol straight in the eye, even though it's pretty obvious that she wishes Carol would go back to begging Raina to speak.

I wonder what goes on in Raina's private sessions with Dr. Prince. Has she been talking to him all this time? In my next private session, I ask him.

"How does it work in here with Raina?"

"Why do you ask?"

"Well, I just wonder how talk therapy goes with a patient who doesn't usually talk."

Dr. Prince doesn't answer, not even to correct my use of the word *patient*.

"I mean, that is the technical term for what we're doing here, right? *Talk* therapy?"

"It is."

"Well, then, how does it work with a patient like Raina?" Maybe Dr. Prince somehow made her feel safe enough to talk in here from the day she arrived. It's hard to think of him that way—as a soothing presence—with his perfect posture, non-smiles, and contraction avoidance.

Oh, and the fact that he and his wife are experimenting on us.

He says, "I try to tailor my approach to each of my students."

"Yeah, but it's different with a patient who won't communicate."

"I consider you a student who won't communicate." Dr. Prince takes off his glasses and cleans them with a handkerchief from his front pocket.

I plant my feet firmly on the soft rug beneath my chair, as though I might need to stand at any moment. I remember how quiet Grey was in group this morning. "Who talks the least in here?" I ask. "Me, or Raina, or Grey?"

"It's interesting that you bring up Grey," Dr. Prince says, surprising me by (sort of) acknowledging the question.

"Why's that interesting?"

"Because your mother thinks you're suffering from depression." My surprise must show on my face, because Dr. Prince adds, "I assure you, that's what she said when we first spoke."

I shake my head. "She was probably just trying to sound concerned." My mother doesn't think I'm depressed. She thinks I'm a troublemaker. She thinks I'm out of control.

"Parents don't send their daughters here unless they are *truly* concerned."

"Parents send their daughters here to get them out of their hair."

"Is that why you think you were sent here?"

I don't answer. I look at my lap and then toward the window. I fold my legs up onto the chair and sit crisscross applesauce. (That's what my kindergarten teacher called it.) I take a drink from the glass of water I brought from downstairs. Maybe my hands wouldn't be so cold if I wasn't constantly holding a glass of cool water.

"Moira," he says slowly, gently; he doesn't even emphasize the *oy* sound. "Why do you think your parents sent you here?"

I look down again and let my hair fall across my face. "You talked to them. You know why I was sent here."

"I want to know what you think."

Through my sweater, I rub my arm right at the place where my tattoo is. I try to trace its ink.

"My mom was sick of my acting out."

"People who are depressed sometimes act out."

"So you think I'm depressed, too?"

"No—well, not in the same way that Grey is depressed."

"I thought you couldn't talk about other patients."

"You already know that Grey's been diagnosed with chronic depression, so I'm hardly breaking confidentiality by acknowledging it. Your behavior before you came here was a reaction to something that happened to you. There's such a thing as circumstantial depression."

"Nothing happened to *me*," I object, looking up. Everything that happened, happened to Nathan: the diagnosis, the treatment, the pain, the suffering.

"You lost your friend," Dr. Prince says. "You're mourning."

"Do you even know his name?" I ask, suddenly angry.

"You've never told me."

"Yeah, but I'm sure my mom did, right?"

"She did," Dr. Prince concedes, but he still doesn't say it.

I ask, "What's my presenting problem?"

"Your presenting problem?" Dr. Prince echoes.

"Yeah, Cass told me that a presenting problem is why a person starts therapy, right?" Dr. Prince nods. "So what's mine—that my best friend died?"

Dr. Prince shakes his head. "No," he says. "You told me your presenting problem in our first session—you got a tattoo."

Last night, Eleanor said no one believes I got sent here because of my tattoo, and now Dr. Prince is admitting that's exactly why I got sent here?

He continues, "Your tattoo isn't just about the fact that your friend died. It's also about your relationship with your mother, your need to punish yourself—"

"My mom punished me when she sent me here."

The universe punished me when it killed my best friend and left me all alone.

"Do you think you deserve to be punished?"

I take a drink from my water glass. I remember the way my black-clad escort crouched when he thought I might make a run for it.

I didn't run. In fact, I came here rather peacefully. Sure, I argued with my mother, but that was nothing compared to the way I yelled to defend my right to spend Thanksgiving with the Kaplans the year before last, or the way I shouted on the first day of school in September, when Mom practically had to drag me out the door.

I came here almost willingly.

I accepted my punishment.

I knew that I deserved it.

Dr. Prince asks, "It was cancer that killed your best friend, correct?"

I nod. Brain cancer. He had a brain tumor. He and I actually laughed when he first got diagnosed. I'm sure no one else would have found it funny, but it seemed so unreal that it struck us as hilarious. What fifteen-year-old boy halfway through his sophomore year got a *brain tumor*? Brain tumors were things you only saw in movies, on TV shows, in tragic novels. Brain tumors didn't happen in real life.

Except, of course, they do.

Radiation first, to try to shrink it. (But not enough.) I made jokes about Spider-Man and superpowers, trying to ignore how exhausted the treatment made Nathan, how many classes he (and I) missed.

Then surgery, to try to remove it. (But not entirely.) Nathan's bald head, so pale and so much smaller than I thought it would be. I joked that it made him look like an old man. I never told him the truth: it made him look like a baby.

Finally, chemo, to try to keep the cancer from growing and spreading. The poison that kept his hair from growing back beyond a little bit of peach fuzz, that made him too sick to go back to school, that made him so susceptible to infection. The hope that all that suffering would be worth it in the end.

I shift in my seat. I hate this wingback chair. I hate how hard it is to look anywhere but at Dr. Prince's face.

I know that Dr. Prince will say what anyone would say: *Cancer killed your best friend, not you.*

He'd dismiss me if I tried to explain.

He wouldn't understand that it was my fault Nathan died the way he did.

Dr. Prince puts his hands on his knees and leans forward, his perfect posture curling for just a second. "I'll tell you a secret," he says, and I ready myself for him to insist I'm not to blame. "Every single girl I take on has the same presenting problem."

"What, they all get tattoos?" I ask nastily.

Dr. Prince continues as if I haven't spoken. "Their parents send them away. Now, some people *need* to be sent away for treatment—for many people, inpatient treatment can be lifesaving—"

"So you admit that none of us needed to be sent away?" I interrupt, but Dr. Prince keeps talking.

"And I believe that the students I accept here benefit from being in this environment, but..." He pauses. "Sometimes, parents—even the best of parents, with the best of intentions, with the best resources at their fingertips—find themselves at a loss."

He sits up straight again.

"What do you think is so beneficial about this environment?" I ask. "Cutting us off from the rest of the world, from the internet and our schools and our parents and our friends back home—"

"I was under the impression that your only friend back home was dead."

I lean back in my chair as suddenly as if he'd slapped me.

"If you were back home, do you think you'd be speaking to your mother any more than you are here?"

"I don't want to speak to her."

"Why not?"

"She's the reason I wasn't there when Nathan died!" I shout angrily.

It's the first time I've said his name out loud in…I don't know how long.

Months.

Maybe since he died.

Yes, since he died.

I know exactly how long.

I break eye contact with Dr. Prince to take another sip from my water glass, but it's empty.

Dr. Prince stands and walks to his desk on the other side of the room, lifts a mug, and brings it back to me.

"Here," he says. "Tea. It's lukewarm now, but help yourself."

I take the mug and hold it for a second before drinking.

"Moira," Dr. Prince says, emphasizing my name in that way he always does, "if you were in your school back home right now, do you think you'd be making friends?"

I shake my head fiercely. "I don't want to make new friends."

"Why not?"

"*Nathan* will never make new friends." I'm surprised by the gravelly sound of my own voice. It's like a stranger is talking, someone whose voice is lower than mine.

Dr. Prince nods. "So, to rebuild your relationship with your mother, to make new friends, would be a betrayal of Nathan?"

I sniff. "What do you mean, *re*build my relationship with my mother? That implies there was a relationship there to begin with."

I expect Dr. Prince to argue, to remind me of my strawberry shortcake memories, but instead he says, "All right, then. But to attempt to have any kind of civil relationship with your mother—that would be betraying Nathan?"

I nod.

"But Moira—surely you know that just as Nathan can't make friends, he can't be hurt by your actions. You *can't* betray him."

"You don't know what you're talking about," I say fiercely. "You think I should move on like Nathan never even existed."

That's what Mom said when we fought, when she saw my tattoo. That I had to *let go, move on.*

"Not move on," Dr. Prince says, "but to accept that he's dead."

I put Dr. Prince's mug on the floor. "I know he's dead."

Dr. Prince shakes his head. "If that were true, you wouldn't be worried about betraying him now." I don't answer, and Dr. Prince explains, "To accept his death is not to say that his death was okay. Instead, it's to say that what is, is."

"So, that's your goal? I'll be cured when I accept that *it is what it is*?"

*Cured.* There are diseases for which there is no cure, no matter how much medicine the doctors give you.

Nathan had that kind of disease.

Maybe I deserve one, too.

Dr. Prince shakes his head. "I'm not trying to cure you."

"Then what's the point?"

Dr. Prince holds his hands in front of him and presses his fingertips together, making a little tent. It reminds me of the game someone taught me in kindergarten: *Here's the church, and here's the steeple. Open it up, and here are the people.*

"The point is that you're in pain." I'm not sure whether he means me specifically or all the girls here. "It's my job here—my *goal*, to use your word—to provide you with a place to recover."

*A place to recover.* That's almost exactly what Mom said when they sent me here—*You'll have space to recover.* Now I know where she got it from.

I stiffen in my chair, defensive now. "So, being in pain—you think that's enough reason for my parents to send their daughter off to a mental institution?"

"This isn't a mental institution."

"Well, what the hell is this place, then?" I stand up and grab one of the brochures from a stack on Dr. Prince's desk. I remember the way my mother held it up the day she sent me here, like the brochure meant something. "How is anyone supposed to get better in a place like this?"

I manage to stop myself from asking about Castle South, about the cheerful sconces and blazing fires.

In the hospital, Nathan was young enough that they put him in the pediatric ward. There were cartoon animals painted on the walls. He hated the fake cheer of it all. Maybe he'd have preferred a place like this. It's dark, it's cold, but it's not lying to you. It's not pretending to be Disneyland.

My heart is pounding. The glossy pages of the brochure feel hot in my hand.

Dr. Prince says, "I think our time is up."

"It is?" It feels like I've only been in this room for five minutes.

"Yes, Moira," he says, standing up and taking off his glasses. "It is. But good work today. Will you please tell Grey I'm ready for her?"

# twenty-nine

*Good work today? Good work today?* What is Dr. Prince talking about? I don't know what that was, but it wasn't *work*, and it certainly wasn't *good.*

And what were my parents thinking, sending me off to "recover" with a quack like Dr. Prince? In my room, I look at the brochure, wrinkled from my tight grip. On the cover is a picture of the Castle—not of any girls or teachers, just the building. I guess some parents would respond to that, the same way you think something is high quality because it's expensive. *This place must be good; it's so beautiful.*

The first page is a letter from Dr. Prince to parents of prospective students. Not to the students themselves; this brochure isn't for us. *We're* not necessarily involved in the discussions that lead to us being sent here.

> At the Castle School, we encourage our students to
> build a community through group therapy, class discus-
> sions, and team-building problem-solving exercises.

The brochure for the boys' school might say the exact same thing. This description is vague enough that it could apply to either place.

Cooking dinner is supposed to be one of those team-building exercises. I remember the first night we cooked after I arrived here—I wasn't even sure what we were cooking. Randy ate cereal rather than risk eating whatever we were making.

It was our night to cook again last night. Cass picked a recipe for chili from a cookbook she found in the drawing room. Alice chewed gum while she diced the onions because, she said, that way you don't cry. Cass made me slice carrots. Eleanor offered to open the can of beans, but everyone was worried that the edges of the can might be too tempting for her, so Ryan took over. Halsey browned the meat, and when Beth said she was a vegetarian, we all agreed to keep the meat on the side.

Shelly stood in the corner and didn't say a word. Were we doing exactly what we were supposed to do, working these things out ourselves? Deciding not to let Eleanor handle anything sharp and keeping the meat on the side?

Standing over the stove, surrounded by the other girls, I wasn't cold. When we ate, I actually tasted all the herbs and spices we'd so carefully measured and poured and mixed together. Even Randy took a bowlful of the chili we'd made. And for the first time since Nathan died, I had a second helping at a meal. Each bite didn't feel like a choking hazard.

I return to the brochure:

> By building a community of young women here at Castle, students become part of a fully functioning whole, distancing themselves from the dysfunctional patterns in which they'd found themselves trapped at home.

Interesting choice of words. *Found themselves trapped.* Like Dr. Prince is subtly telling the parents of prospective students that our problems aren't our fault—sometimes they really are the result of parents, or genetics, or outside circumstances.

> We give our students a safe space in which to interact with one another, keeping them engaged in their lives back home by holding classes while allowing them the freedom to structure the discussions themselves. We stand back, allowing our students to take the lead and feel empowered.

I think about Shelly's inability to hold court during class. The way we veer off topic when we're supposed to be talking about books or math or history. The way she kept quiet when we spilled tomato sauce last night—she didn't yell at us to clean up the mess, and eventually Cass told Virginia to grab some paper

217

towels. I assumed Shelly hung back and let us change the subject because she's incompetent. But maybe it's intentional.

I flip to the end of the brochure. On the last page are pictures of Dr. Prince, Shelly, and Carol, each with an accompanying bio.

Shelly Banks has been with the team at Castle since the very start. A graduate of Barnard College, she has a master's in education from Teachers College at Columbia University as well as a master's degree in child psychology from New York University.

I feel a pang when I read that Shelly went to Barnard. I'd wanted to go there, but I wasn't going to apply because Nathan didn't want to stay in New York for college. At the start of sophomore year, we agreed that we'd go to college in the same town, if not at the very same school. We agreed on a list of schools in Boston, another list of schools in and around Chicago, and a handful of schools in LA.

I shake my head. That was a thousand years ago, when I still thought about what might happen in the future. Since Nathan died, my fantasies have worked in reverse, and I only imagine the things we might have done while he was still alive.

Carolina Santos has a master's in psychology from Brazil's Universidade de São Paulo and is currently pursuing her PhD in developmental psychology with an emphasis on adolescent development from Princeton

University. She is joining us at Castle while she completes her doctoral thesis.

I read Dr. Prince's bio next—just like Randy said, he studied to be a neurologist, then got a master's in education and psychology. I turn back to Dr. Prince's letter on the first page and read the final paragraph.

> At Castle, we believe that something magical happens when young people are given a safe space in which to build a community and the freedom to share their problems without judgment. We keep their bodies healthy with a diet of local and organic food, fill their lungs with fresh Maine air, and monitor their pharmaceutical needs carefully. Although we pride ourselves on offering extensive talk therapy, much of the work gets done when our students are left on their own to build a bond based on shared experiences and common ground—a bond that will last a lifetime.

Vague language aside, it's easy to see why parents would be drawn to Dr. Prince's philosophy. Who doesn't want to hear that there's nothing wrong with their daughters that a little fresh air, good food, and girl bonding can't fix? *(But we do throw in plenty of therapy and the occasional antidepressant as needed.)*

The door to my room opens, and Shelly sticks her head inside. "Checks," she says. There are murmurs coming from across the

219

hall; Cass and Virginia are chattering in their room like an old married couple. Before Shelly can close the door, Eleanor walks in and starts going through my closet without asking permission. Is that a sign that we've bonded?

I fold the brochure in half and drop it in the trash can at the foot of my bed. It strikes me that *subjects* is the word for patients undergoing experimental treatment as well as for citizens living under royal rule. *The* Prince, indeed.

There are things missing from Dr. Prince's bio: the fact that he met his wife when he was in medical school and she inspired him to study psychology; the fact that together the Princes opened not one but *two* very different schools; the fact that they're raising their son on the premises, surrounded by their troubled students.

There's nothing in the brochure about the empty fireplaces, the shoddy heat, the dim lights. Nothing that indicates that nearby is a school full of warmth and brightness.

Who in their right mind would pick Castle North over Castle South if they had the choice?

# *thirty*

A couple of weeks later, instead of following the other girls upstairs after dinner, I sneak into the kitchen.

"Why do you live here?"

Randy is sitting on a bar stool pulled up to the butcher block kitchen island, curled over a bowl of soup, an open book on the counter in front of him. He's in his usual uniform of slim-fitting sweatpants and a windbreaker, plus a pair of well-worn sneakers. He's cracked the book's spine so that it lies open on its own, something Nathan and I always agreed was practically sacrilegious.

"What do you mean, why do I live here?" Randy echoes, looking up from his soup. "My dad lives here, so I live here."

I shake my head. "But you don't *have* to live here," I insist. "Couldn't your parents send you to a school for non-troubled kids somewhere? We're here because we don't have a choice. You do."

"You don't know anything about my choices." Randy straightens just a bit, not all the way like his father.

"I know more than you think."

"Oh?"

I take a deep breath, then ask, "Why didn't you ever mention Castle South?"

He doesn't ask how I know about Castle South. Like Cass said, it's easy enough to find out about. Instead, he says, "Why would I?"

"Because—because it would have been nice to know that we weren't stuck in the middle of nowhere, that there was someplace else, another option—"

"It's not an option," Randy interrupts, his tone reasonable. "It's all boys; this place is all girls. You couldn't go there."

I keep talking like that doesn't matter. "It's not an option for *us*." I walk around the counter so that I'm standing beside Randy. Even sitting, he's taller than I am. "But it is for *you*. Wouldn't you rather live in a cheerful castle with your mom instead of here in a freezing building full of troubled girls?"

Randy doesn't ask how I know it's cheerful there. "You're not troubled."

"Sure we are," I say. "Says so right on the van."

"We painted over that." Randy smiles, and I almost laugh.

"Seriously, though," I say more quietly, "why do you live here when you could live there?"

Randy pulls out the bar stool beside his.

I sit. "Where's your dad?"

"Working."

"You don't have dinner together?"

Randy shakes his head. "Family meals every night is more my

mom's style than his. You know, all those studies about how it's good for kids to eat as a family, that kind of thing."

I nod. "My mom used to say the same thing."

"How'd that work out in your house?"

At home, family dinners usually led to family fights. Before Nathan got sick, I'd have dinner at his place more often than not, forgetting to tell Mom ahead of time, so she'd cook a whole meal and wait for me. (I told her she could just assume I'd be at Nathan's every night after school, but that only made her angrier). Later, I'd eat dinner at the hospital. Some nights, I didn't come home until long after Mom and Dad were asleep, the leftovers cold in the refrigerator.

"It didn't go well," I admit.

"Yeah, well, not for us, either. I mean, I get the concept behind the whole family dinner thing, but I don't think it applies when your parents fight as much as mine. Listening to your parents scream at each other all through dinner might be more damaging to a kid than, you know, letting him eat on his own."

I have so many questions. What do his parents fight about? Their methodologies? But looking at Randy's pinched expression, I get the feeling he doesn't want to talk about it, and it would be really insensitive of me to ask, especially when he's never asked me why I'm here. So I say, "That sucks."

"Yeah."

"Is that why you don't live with your mom at Castle South? Because she forced you to have family dinners even when she and your dad were fighting?"

Randy looks at me, his light brown eyes locked with mine. There are darker flecks scattered around his irises, like his eyes are just as freckled as the rest of him. "You think *dinner* is why I live here, not there?"

I shake my head. "But I just can't imagine why you'd pick this place over that one."

"Oh, no?" Randy asks. "You can't *imagine* that anyone might not want to live with their mom?"

Now I slump in my seat. Randy pushes his bowl of soup in my direction and hands me a fresh spoon. I take a bite: broccoli cheddar. I can't remember the last time I ate something this rich, and the saltiness is sharp on my tongue. Still, it's so delicious that I find myself wanting another bite, then another. Finally, I put my spoon down and say, "You have a point."

"You and your mom don't get along?"

"What gave it away?"

Randy stretches his long arms overhead. "Well, most of you girls aren't sent here because you and your parents are getting along really, really well."

This time, I do laugh.

"Don't reduce me to a *type*," I insist, but I'm not really offended.

"I'm not. Believe me, you can't live here and not realize that everyone's problems are different. Like, even people who come here with the same problems are different."

"What do you mean?"

"Like, you know how Cass dropped out of high school?" I nod. "Well, last year, we had another high school dropout, and she was *nothing* like Cass. She wanted to drop out of life altogether, you know? Barely talked to the other girls. Cass is still curious, still reads, is still interested in everyone else."

"I didn't realize you'd been paying such close attention."

"There's not much else to do around here."

"Exactly," I agree, sitting up again. "So why live here when you could live—"

"In Castle South?"

I nod. "I bet your mom doesn't have rules that you're not allowed to interact with the kids there. You'd be able to do more than observe. You could make, like, actual friends."

"Did *you* come here to make friends?"

"It's different."

"Why?"

"Because this place isn't, like, my whole life. I'm here now, but I don't live here, not really."

"It's not going to be my whole life, either," Randy says. "I'm going to get out of here."

I push the bowl back toward Randy and stand. "I should get going. Rules, you know."

"Right."

Before I reach the door, Randy says, "Hey, Moira?"

I turn back around to face him.

"I know you don't like it here, but you should know—"

"Know what?"

"Castle South isn't any better."

# *thirty-one*

"I don't know how he knows, he just knows," I tell Eleanor as we walk through the woods later, the other girls scattered around us. "Like I said, he's observant." After our conversation in the kitchen, I'm positive Randy knows we've been visiting Castle South.

"Well, short of following us out of the castle every night, I don't see how he would know."

Randy didn't seem the least bit surprised when I let it slip that Castle South was cheerful and not freezing, that I knew his mom ran one school and his dad ran the other. He didn't ask how I could have known that. Somehow, he already knew I'd been there.

Eleanor adds, "And if he has been following us, then he's a creep for doing it."

"He's not a creep."

"Well, then, he's an idiot."

"Those are the choices—idiot or creep?"

"Only an idiot would live at Castle North when he could live at Castle South. Unless he likes following around a bunch of girls who barely know he's there, in which case—creep."

I shake my head, my hair falling across my face in the cold. "It's not like that."

"You don't know what it's like." Eleanor breaks away as the lights from Castle South come into view. I know I won't have a chance to continue this conversation with her anytime soon. She'll spend the rest of the night glued to Henry's side.

I can't blame her. If I could be with Nathan, I wouldn't be interested in talking to anyone else, either.

It's not the same thing. Nathan was my best friend. We knew each other for years. Henry is just some guy Eleanor's…I mean, I guess you can't call it *dating*, exactly, but whatever the Castle School equivalent is.

I'm about to step inside the castle gate when someone gently grabs my wrist from behind. "Hey," a low voice whispers, and I turn and see Randy. He doesn't have a winter coat on, just the same windbreaker he was wearing in the kitchen. He must be freezing.

"What are you doing?" I ask. "I thought you hated it here."

"I never said I hated it." Randy rubs his hands together to keep warm.

"Then come inside."

Randy hesitates.

"Come on," I say. "The guys are all super nice."

"Are they?" Randy asks.

"Of course," I answer, but even as I say it, I realize I don't really know. I've mostly spoken only to Daniel, and we don't actually *talk* that much—we dance, and we banter, but that's not really *talking*. "Come on," I say again, and Randy and I walk into the ballroom side by side.

Daniel makes a beeline for us, drawn to a new face. "Who's this?"

"Randy," I answer when Randy doesn't.

"I thought Castle North was all girls."

"He's not a student there."

"Then where did he come from?"

I glance at Randy. Does he want to answer any of these questions himself? But Randy keeps his mouth shut, his hands in his pockets, his eyes on the room. I guess I can't blame him for keeping quiet—the first time I saw this place, I was awed by the warmth and the brightness, too. I can only imagine what it looks like to someone who has lived in Castle North for months or years, not weeks.

Then again, maybe that's not why he's being quiet. For all I know, he comes here all the time.

"Dr. Prince—*our* Dr. Prince—is his dad," I explain.

"Wait!" Daniel says. "That means our Dr. Prince is his mom. *You're* Bertrand?"

Finally, Randy speaks. "She talks about me?"

Daniel continues as though Randy hasn't said anything. "I see it, I guess. The family resemblance."

Randy shrugs.

"Hey, guys!" Daniel shouts to no one in particular. "This is Bertrand Prince Junior!"

The boys scattered around the room—sitting in the cushy chairs by the fire, playing on their laptops, picking which songs to play next—look up and stare at Randy. The girls look as if they've never seen him before. I realize most of them probably don't know *Randy* is short for *Bertrand*.

"What's it like to have the coolest mom on planet Earth, Junior?" Daniel asks, clapping Randy on the back.

"I'm not sure I'd call her that," Randy says carefully.

"Are you kidding?" Daniel counters. "Your mom is so much nicer than my parents. I mean, for starters, they sent me off to a reform school in the woods, right?"

I'm surprised to hear Daniel call it a reform school. He corrected me when I called it that. He never hints at why he—or any of the boys—were sent here. I remember the way Cass introduced the girls my first morning at Castle North. I never had to wonder what anyone did to be sent away.

"My mom raised me in a school in the woods," Randy answers smoothly.

"Yeah, but you don't, like, *have* to be here," Daniel says, just like I did a few hours ago. Then he narrows his eyes and adds, "Do you?" Daniel's wearing a slim T-shirt and jeans that fit him perfectly. Even though Randy is taller than he is, Daniel somehow looks older, or at least more authoritative, than Randy.

"What's that supposed to mean?" Randy asks.

"I mean, maybe you were your parents' very first case. You know, patient zero and all that."

Randy shakes his head but doesn't say anything.

"I mean, maybe you're the reason your parents started running their schools in the first place. Their *inspiration*."

"Daniel, why would you say that?" I ask, hoping to change the subject. "Let's just dance or something." For the first time ever at Castle South, there's no music playing. Someone must have turned it off.

Daniel won't be distracted. "Come to think of it, when your mom mentions you, it's not like she's telling us stories about the most popular kid in school."

"Randy doesn't go to school," I interject. "I mean, he's homeschooled."

"In fact"—Daniel speaks as though he's remembering something long forgotten—"she always brings you up when we're talking about bullying. Why do you think that is?"

Randy doesn't answer. His face is white, but maybe that's just the light.

"Hey, A.J.!" Daniel calls out. "Do you remember what Dr. Prince said about Junior in class the other day?"

Sitting at the table across the room, A.J. shrugs. He's leaning in close to Raina and seems uninterested in anything else.

"Actually," Daniel continues, "I can't remember if she said it was you. She might have just said *a boy she used to know*. But you can always tell when a mother is talking about her son, can't you? Then again, why would she refer to her son as someone she *used* to know?

Don't you two get along? I suppose not—otherwise, why would you live at Castle North with a bunch of girls instead of here?"

"Stop it, Daniel," I say fiercely. Even though it's not that different from what I asked Randy a few hours ago, Daniel's question feels very different.

"What?" Daniel says, all innocence. "I'm just trying to get to know my new friend here."

Finally, Randy speaks. "I'm not your friend," he says through gritted teeth.

"According to your mom, you're not anyone's friend, Junior."

"Shut up," Randy says.

"I mean, my mom may have sent me off to this place, but she still calls me every day. When was the last time you and your mom *talked*?"

"I haven't talked to my mom in weeks," I break in, desperate to interrupt whatever this is. "Not since she sent me away. And honestly, for months before that, we barely spoke."

Randy looks down at me, startled. I guess it's the most he's ever heard me say about myself.

I said it loudly enough that almost everyone in the room heard me. From Henry's lap by the fireplace, Eleanor blinks in surprise.

"So I'm just saying," I continue, though I can feel myself blushing, "it's not that unusual for moms and their kids to go weeks without talking."

"Yes, it is, Moira," Randy says quietly. "My mom and I didn't stop talking because things were going great between us."

231

Randy's so tall that even when he's slouching, I need to angle my neck to look into his light brown eyes.

"Most of the girls call their parents," he adds. "My dad lets anyone call anytime."

For the first time ever at Castle South, the lump in my throat is growing instead of shrinking. But why? I'm not thinking about Nathan.

"Oh my goodness," Daniel breaks in, sounding excited. "I just figured something out."

Randy turns to Daniel wearily. "What did you figure out?"

"You have a little bitty crush on our girl Moira, don't you?"

"Don't be ridiculous," I snap.

"You're right," Daniel agrees. "It's not little, is it, Junior? It's an enormous puppy-dog crush, isn't it?"

"Stop it, Daniel," I say. "What's with you tonight?"

"Just having a little fun," Daniel says, but Randy uncurls from his slouch and takes a step toward Daniel, who only comes up to his shoulder.

"You want to take this outside?" Randy asks, but his tough-guy voice just makes Daniel laugh.

"*Take this outside?*" Daniel echoes. "Are we in an old movie?"

"Seems to me that you've been trying to pick a fight with me since the moment I walked in."

Something about the word *fight*—or maybe how close Randy and Daniel are standing—finally captures the attention of everyone in the room. Greg and Dave stand and walk toward us, ready to spring to Daniel's defense. Henry places his hands on Eleanor's hips like he's ready to push her off if the need arises.

I guess it shouldn't be surprising how quickly the boys choose sides. After all, Randy is the stranger here tonight, even though this place belongs to him more than it does to any of them.

"I'm going to get Dr. Prince," I say, feeling frantic. "Randy, where's your mom's office?" I don't care that we'll all be in trouble if she sees us here.

"Don't bother," Randy growls. He steps back from Daniel and turns on his heel. He jogs across the room and out the door.

I follow.

# *thirty-two*

I thought I knew the woods between Castle South and Castle North well, but I don't know this terrain half as well as Randy does. When he followed us tonight, he didn't bring a flashlight. He could probably run between Castle North and Castle South with his eyes closed and one hand tied behind his back.

Not me. I left my flashlight in Castle South, and now I'm lost.

Okay, not *lost*. I can hear the music coming from Castle South—they must have started it up again after we left—so I could turn around and go back.

But for the first time, I don't want to be there.

"Randy!" I call into the darkness. He might be long gone by now. Unlike me, he's a runner. Even before Nathan was diagnosed and I started spending every spare minute in the hospital with him, I never joined any teams at school. I hated gym class, and I never worked out if I could help it. I got winded the first few times I climbed down from our window in Castle North and woke up with sore muscles.

"Randy!" I shout again.

I jump when a hand lands lightly on my shoulder.

"I'm here," he says, out of breath. He jogs in place.

"I'm sorry," I say quickly.

"Not your fault."

"You wouldn't have come here if it weren't for me."

There are reflective patches on Randy's clothes, I guess to protect him in the dark.

He shrugs. "I'll walk you back."

He bounces on his toes like he's still running, even though we're moving at a normal place.

We walk quietly for a few minutes, and then Randy says, "I told you Castle South wasn't any better."

"How did you know? It's not like you'd met Daniel before, right?"

"I haven't met any of those guys before."

"So you couldn't have known what it would be like over there."

"I know my mom."

I shake my head. "Your mom can't control what her students do and say."

"Exactly," Randy says.

"That's not how I meant it," I insist. "I meant—she's he's not to blame for how they act."

"But she's to blame for the way she runs the place." Randy keeps bouncing up and down. "For the types of kids she takes."

"So you think they're bad, all the boys over there?" Randy doesn't answer. "Then what do you think about *us*—about the girls your dad takes? Our parents sent us away, too. We're not so different from those boys. What, you think that just because we're girls, we can't be mean?"

Before I met Nathan, I watched in the lunchroom as girls were invited and then disinvited to sit at one table or another. I try to remember—did I start going to the library at lunchtime because I wanted to or because of the girls who wouldn't let me sit at their tables?

And then, when Nathan got sick, those same girls came up to me with their sticky voices to tell me how sorry they were. When Nathan died, those girls cried, even though they barely knew him. Maybe they were crying simply because *someone* died. Or maybe they were crying for themselves, because they realized they weren't invincible after all. If one of us could get a terrible disease, any of us could.

I hated them for crying. I hated when they offered me their sympathy.

I know girls can be mean.

I was mean to those girls.

As we approach Castle North, Randy slows down and stops bouncing. "I just meant…my dad would never let something like that happen."

"Even your dad can't dictate what people say when he's not in the room."

In ninth grade, back when I still paid attention in class, our bio teacher told us that pharmaceutical companies always have a control group when they test new drugs—a group who thinks they're getting an experimental new treatment when really they're getting a placebo, a nothing pill that's intentionally ineffective.

And sometimes those patients report that their symptoms are improving. It's called the placebo effect. When people don't know the drug they're getting is worthless, they sometimes still think it's effective just because a doctor gave it to them. Their brains can make their bodies react like they're getting the real thing.

That's the problem with experimenting on human subjects, isn't it? You can't *really* have a control group with people involved.

Randy kicks at the ground. "I'm not—I don't—I know my dad can't control everything." He doesn't look at me. He starts bouncing up and down again.

Daniel said that Randy has a crush on me. What made him so sure? He barely spent ten minutes with Randy. And anyway, Daniel has a crush on Drew. What's wrong with having a crush on someone?

Slowly, I say, "You don't have to be—I mean, it's okay if you're embarrassed." I stuff my hands in my pockets, wishing for the millionth time that I'd remembered to pack gloves. I'm so cold that I can barely feel my cheeks. I don't know how Randy is managing without a coat.

Randy laughs. "I'm not embarrassed. Not because of anything that guy said, anyway."

"Okay," I say. "Good."

Randy leads the way to the bars beneath my window. "You okay from here?" he asks. "I really gotta get going."

"Yeah, of course," I say. "Your dad will notice you're gone."

Randy shakes his head. "I'm not going inside yet. I'm gonna run for a while."

"Now? At this hour? In the dark? In the cold?"

"It's always cold this time of year," Randy answers, ignoring the rest of my questions. "Anyway, I gotta get rid of all this energy before I explode or something. Do you know that feeling? Like if you don't let it rip, you'll burst?"

The only part of me that ever feels like it's going to burst is the lump in my throat. Maybe someday it'll get so big that instead of choking me, it'll tear my throat open.

"Are you going to tell your dad?" I ask softly. "About us sneaking out?"

Randy hesitates. "I should," he says finally. "It's not safe, you trudging through the woods in the middle of the night."

"You're about to run through the woods in the middle of the night," I point out. "And you're alone. At least the girls and I have each other."

"It's different," Randy says. "My dad's responsible for what happens to you."

"Isn't he responsible for what happens to you, too? You're his kid."

Randy starts bouncing again. "You need any help getting back inside?" I shake my head. "Okay, then. Good night, Moira."

"Good night," I answer, but he's already gone.

# REVA

Reva doesn't actually remember the first time she ran away. She was only two years old. It's not her story but her mother's, told to great effect at different family gatherings over the years. Sometimes, Reva's mother made it a comedy, and Reva's relatives laughed when they heard how her mother found her in the makeup aisle, her face covered in lipstick. Sometimes, Reva's mother made it a drama, and their relatives scolded Reva for giving her poor mother so much trouble. As though she were still responsible for something she did as a two-year-old, something she can't even remember.

And anyway, it's not like she actually *ran*. She merely wandered off when her mother dropped her hand in the Target, then toddled up and down the aisles until she found something that interested her.

At least, that's what she guesses happened. Because when she runs now, it's because she wants to find someplace more interesting than wherever she's running from.

It started with recess in fifth grade. (This is the first time she remembers herself.) One Wednesday, it occurred to Reva that when her teachers announced that recess was over, she didn't really have to go inside. She could stay *outside*, which had always been infinitely more interesting to her than *inside*. She didn't go anywhere; she stayed in the schoolyard. Almost an hour went by before her teachers noticed that she was missing; they didn't take attendance after recess the same way they did each morning. (That policy soon changed.)

By sixth grade, Reva had learned that she had to leave the schoolyard. If she stayed, the teachers found her and insisted she come inside. And so one day she started walking. She didn't actually *run*, though they'd call it *running away*. She simply waited until no one was looking and then away she went.

Unfortunately, the thing about being a flight risk was that soon everyone was watching, so Reva had to run to get to the interesting places. If she moved too slowly, they caught her and made her come back inside, back to her desk, back to her bedroom—always back, back, back. Reva wasn't interested in going back. Reva was interested in *forward*.

When Reva's mother put a lock on her bedroom door, Reva climbed out the window. When Reva's mother put a lock on her window, Reva ran out the back door. When her teachers called her a truant, Reva countered that she was an *explorer*. When her mother called her a runaway—she'd long since stopped playing up the Target story for laughs; now it was always tearful—Reva countered that she wouldn't have to run if her mother didn't insist on giving chase.

By the end of sophomore year, Reva's mother had stopped letting her walk to school alone; instead, she dropped Reva off and picked her up each day. Reva's teachers kept close watch on her in their classrooms. She wasn't allowed to go to the bathroom by herself—she always had to bring a companion, who was supposed to report it immediately if Reva so much as looked at the door funny.

Reva's life had never been so dull. She wasn't bothered when the brochures for the Castle School showed up in their mailbox.

At least it looked interesting.

# *thirty-three*

Carol has stopped opening group with "Who'd like to start today?" She didn't announce the change; one day she simply started asking questions instead. Maybe after her success with Raina, she wanted to try the direct approach with the rest of us. Or maybe our giggling and whispering drove her to it.

Today, Carol asks Halsey about her first drink.

Halsey looks up at the chandelier that's perfectly centered above the long, skinny table. "Wine," she says. "At my birthday party."

"How old were you?"

"Six."

Carol can't hide her surprise. "Why do you think you wanted to drink when you were so young?" she asks.

Halsey shrugs. "I didn't *want* it. My dad gave it to me."

Across the table from me, Virginia leans into Cassandra, whispers something in her ear. Cass shakes her head, then puts her arm around Virginia and rubs her shoulder vigorously, like she's trying to keep her girlfriend warm.

"Did it make you feel close to your dad, sharing his wine?" Halsey shrugs again. "Can anyone else think of a time when they did something they shouldn't have in order to feel closer to someone else?"

Like cutting class to spend more time with Nathan when he was too sick to come to school?

Or sneaking out to visit his grave?

Carol continues, "People talk a lot about peer pressure—doing something to fit in with the other kids. But of course, not all the other kids are doing the same thing, are they? Doing things to feel closer to someone can also distance us from *other* people." Carol pauses to let this sink in.

"When you drank with your father, Halsey, did you feel separate from the other kids at your party? More grown up?"

The chairs in the dining room are so heavy that it takes effort to push them back from the table. They're uncomfortable, too; the slats on the back dig into the space between my shoulder blades. My mouth is sticky with peanut butter. I've had the same thing for breakfast for days now: toast with peanut butter.

"My dad didn't mean anything by it." Halsey's wearing a light gray scarf that brings out the blue of her eyes, and she fingers its tassels absently. "He wasn't trying to get his six-year-old daughter hooked on alcohol."

"Of course not," Carol agrees. "But I'm willing to bet you were the only six-year-old at the party with a drink in her hand."

"I didn't have a drink in my hand. He just let me have a sip of his."

After group, Shelly leads us into the gym-ballroom and tells us to mime our feelings.

She says, "If you're feeling sad, you can curl into a ball and rock from side to side. If you're feeling happy, hold your arms over your head like you've won something."

Then, "If you're feeling anxious, pace the length of the room."

I raise my hand and ask to go to the bathroom.

◇◇◇◇

I don't actually know where the bathroom is on the first floor. I've always gone upstairs, to the bathroom near our bedrooms.

But it doesn't matter, because I don't really have to go to the bathroom. I want to find Randy.

Is he feeling okay after everything that happened last night?

Has he decided whether to tell his dad about us sneaking out?

If Randy already told, surely we'd know by now. Surely Dr. Prince would have burst into group/breakfast and meted out some kind of punishment.

Right?

I know where the dining room is, and the classroom/drawing room, the kitchen, and the gym/ballroom. I know the way to the other set of stairs—the skinny winding ones that lead to Dr. Prince's turret. I know where the infirmary is.

But somewhere, there's a hallway that leads to Randy and

his father's rooms. I try to imagine it. Is Dr. Prince's bedroom the most ornate room in the entire castle? Is there wood paneling and wainscoting—a word I didn't even know before I came here—and a vaulted ceiling and crown moldings?

I'm still frozen outside the dining room, trying to figure out where to go, when Alice and Reva find me.

"Hey," Alice says. "Thought you were heading to the bathroom."

I nod. I haven't told any of the girls—not even Eleanor—about my conversation in the woods with Randy. They saw me run after him, but when they came back to Castle North later, I pretended to be asleep. I'm sure they all knew I was faking—who could sleep while eleven girls climbed in her window?—but they were polite enough to accept that my feigned sleep meant I didn't want to talk.

"I'm not sure where it is."

"There's one next to the computer room," Reva says. "We'll show you."

"Computer room?" I echo.

"Yeah."

"I didn't know there was one."

Alice laughs. "Neither did I. Reva and I only got internet privileges last week."

"Internet privileges?"

"Yeah," Reva says. "We get to use the computer for thirty minutes a day. Dr. Prince stays in there with us, but he doesn't look at what we're doing."

Alice adds, "I could email someone for you, if you want. All of my friends back at home thought I'd dropped off the face of the earth until last week."

I follow them down a new hallway. The floors and walls are made of stone; it's so damp that it smells like mildew. I keep my eyes peeled for Randy. Maybe he'll be in the computer room, too.

"How'd you swing that?" I ask.

"Swing what?"

"Internet privileges."

"Oh." Alice stops walking. "I gained some weight." She clasps her hands, twisting her arms around herself. She's wearing one of those long-sleeved workout shirts with holes for your thumbs like fingerless gloves. Her shirt is bright pink and would be cheerful were it not for the awful lighting here. "I can feel it," she says, pressing her arms against her torso, "but they don't let me see."

"What do you mean, they don't let you see?"

"They make me stand on the scale backward. Some places even have scales that don't show your weight at all. They're hooked up to computers that show your doctor the number. But that's only at places that specialize in eating disorders."

I wonder how many places Alice has been sent to. Her cheeks are a little less sallow than they were when I first got here.

"How about you?" I ask Reva. "How come you got internet privileges?"

Reva grins. "I guess because I haven't made a break for it."

"Why not?" I ask. "I mean, the first night we went to"—I drop my voice—"Castle South, I was so sure you would run."

Alice interjects, "But that *was* running away, wasn't it? Going to Castle South?"

"Maybe." Reva cocks her head, considering. "But the truth is, I haven't wanted to leave since I've been here, you know? *This* was never the place I was running from, if that makes sense."

Alice drops her arms to her sides. "Maybe Dr. Prince's therapy actually works."

I open my mouth to laugh, but Alice and Reva look so serious that I don't make a sound. I realize that although Cass technically told me everyone's reason for being here on my very first day, I don't *really* know all that much about how any of the other girls came to be at the Castle School—how and when and why they developed the problems Cass listed so easily. I don't know what they talk about with Dr. Prince or what he might say to make them feel better, or worse, or to feel anything at all. I don't know if Alice is really getting better, if she only gained weight because they forced her, or if she'll relapse the minute she leaves here. I don't know whether Reva will run away all over again as soon as she gets home.

Does Dr. Prince keep tabs on what happens to us after we leave here, to add to his data? Will he keep track of us for years to come—if and where we go to college, whether or not we end up as productive members of society, whether we get married or hold down good jobs or have kids—to assess the success of his experiment?

Alice and Reva start walking again, and I follow. Alice asks, "So, do you want me to tell someone where you are?"

"Tell someone?" I echo.

"Your friends? Your boyfriend?"

I picture Alice sending email after email to the friends who'd been wondering where she was. I shake my head.

Our shoes click against the stone beneath our feet, and the sound echoes off the walls, making our footfalls sound so much heavier than they actually are. I wonder if that bothers Alice. We turn a corner, and there's Dr. Prince, standing outside a heavy wood door, a large key ring in his hands. He's wearing a dark green sweater under a tweed blazer (he must have an endless supply), brown corduroy pants, and brown loafers. Maybe he doesn't wear all those layers to look like a college professor; maybe he's just trying to keep warm in his drafty castle.

"Alice, Reva, I see you've brought a friend." He sounds so calm that I think Randy can't have told him about what happened last night.

Alice shakes her head. "Just showing our friend to the bathroom," she says. A shiver runs down my spine.

"There it is," she adds, gesturing to a door directly across from where Dr. Prince is standing.

"Thanks," I say.

Dr. Prince unlocks and opens the computer room door for Alice and Reva, and I peek inside. On the opposite wall is a row of narrow windows, the kind with metal diamond shapes across them. Through them I can see snow, gray and frozen, on the wide trunk of an enormous bare tree directly outside. It hasn't actually snowed in a couple weeks, but it hasn't been warm enough for any of the snow that's already there to melt, either.

Dr. Prince hovers in the hallway, his long fingers wrapped around the black metal doorknob. I'm tempted to ask him where I can find Randy, but according to Dr. Prince's rules, I'm not supposed to talk to Randy.

I stifle a sigh and wonder what Dr. Prince would do if he knew how much Randy and I have spoken this semester.

I smile just a little, thinking that talking to Randy is another way I'm messing with the Princes' experiment.

# *thirty-four*

By midday, I still haven't found Randy, and it's time for my private therapy with Dr. Prince.

"Good afternoon, Moira," Dr. Prince says in his achingly slow voice. I'm still not used to the way he emphasizes the *oy* sound in my name. Maybe he's trying to distinguish it from his wife's name.

"Good afternoon, Your Highness," I say, my voice high and treacly.

Dr. Prince laughs. "Do you think you're the first student to make that particular joke?"

"I guess not," I say. I sit up straighter, trying to mimic Dr. Prince's posture.

"Then why make it?" he asks.

"Just because a joke isn't original doesn't mean it's not worth making. People do perfectly useful unoriginal things all the time."

"Do they?"

I nod, trying to make my neck long like his. Holding my spine this straight feels like pulling a rubber band taut. Maybe that's why Randy always slouches. Or maybe it's his way of silently rebelling against his father.

I say, "It's not as though my parents are the first parents to send their daughter away when they don't know what to do with her."

"So you admit that your parents sending you here was worthwhile."

"I didn't say that."

Dr. Prince leans back in his chair. I relax my spine. "Perhaps you didn't intend to say it."

I sit up tall once more. I replay our conversation. If I believe that something unoriginal can still be worthwhile, does that mean I think my parents sending me here, like so many parents before them, was worthwhile?

"Why all girls?" I ask finally.

"I'm sorry?" Dr. Prince says.

"Why is this place only for girls?" I ask. "What about kids who are gender-nonconforming? Or non-cisgender girls? Can they come to school here?"

"Of course," Dr. Prince agrees. "I would never discriminate in that way."

"The other day, you said that coed environments can get complicated, but—I mean, you do know that people don't need to be around members of the opposite sex to be distracted by romance, right?"

"Of course," Dr. Prince repeats.

"And even if you somehow ended up with a group of students who weren't attracted to each other for one reason or another, so there was no chance of romance—their relationships could still get complicated."

That definitely wasn't *romantic* tension between Daniel and Randy last night. But it was still tension.

"Quite right," Dr. Prince says. "Your mother tells me that your relationship with Nathan was not romantic, and yet it sounds as though it was quite intense."

I shake my head. "That's not what I was talking about." Anyway, Mom did occasionally suspect that my friendship with Nathan wasn't entirely platonic.

"Then what were you talking about, my dear?"

"I was talking about—" I stop.

Dr. Prince fills the silence by saying, "Carol tells me that in your group session this morning, she spoke about the ways finding closeness with one person can distance us from others."

"That was about Halsey and her drinking."

"It didn't resonate with you in the slightest?"

I blink. "There's nothing wrong with being close with another person."

"Not at all."

"There's nothing wrong with having a best friend."

"Indeed. But Nathan was not merely your best friend, Moira. It seems he was also your only friend."

I shrug. "Maybe once you find someone you can be that close to, you don't *need* anyone else."

"I know it may feel that way, but it also leaves you quite susceptible to loneliness."

"I was never lonely when I had him."

"Yes, but—you couldn't have Nathan forever, could you?"

"What's that supposed to mean?" I stand and start pacing the room, just like Shelly told us to do in gym class this morning. "That I should've—that when my best friend got sick, I should've found a new best friend so I wouldn't have had to be alone when he died?"

What kind of monster is Dr. Prince?

Oh, right—the kind who experiments on troubled kids with his wife.

"Of course not," Dr. Prince answers smoothly. "But perhaps— perhaps it might have helped if you hadn't rejected friendships with everyone else."

"No one else wanted to be my friend."

"How do you know that? Did you ever give anyone else a chance, once you had Nathan?"

I look at Dr. Prince darkly. There's only one table in the dining room at his school. He doesn't know how much easier it is to eat fast and run to the library than to try to get a spot at one of the acceptable tables in the cafeteria, how terrifying it is to find yourself sitting alone halfway though seventh grade because everyone else at the loser table made the jump to a better one.

He continues, "As I understand it, you barely went to school over the last year. Perhaps you would have found a friend there, someone who could have comforted you—not just after Nathan's death, but during his illness, when you were suffering."

I stop pacing. I feel hot. I take off my sweater and tie it around my waist so I'm just in my T-shirt. "*I* wasn't suffering. He was."

"Perhaps you weren't suffering in quite the same way that Nathan was, but I have no doubt you suffered."

"Is that what my mother told you? That she pestered me to go to school—to leave my friend alone at the hospital or at home—so I could make new friends?"

"Certainly, that was part of why she wanted you to go to school. And I know she was also worried about you falling behind."

Finally I sit. "See? All she cared about was my grades. How it would look bad if I got held back a year."

"You misunderstand me, my dear. Your mother wanted you to care about *something*—another friend, your schoolwork, *something*—so that when Nathan was gone, you wouldn't feel quite so alone, quite so abandoned."

"He didn't *abandon* me. He died."

"I'm afraid it amounts to much the same thing in the end. You're alone. You rejected your teachers, your mother, your classmates, all in favor of Nathan, whom I know you loved deeply. But by loving him exclusively, you made your loss enormous."

I narrow my eyes. "It would have been enormous either way."

Dr. Prince nods. "Of course it would. But it might have been somewhat easier to bear if you'd allowed yourself a life outside of your relationship with him. Because, my dear, that's what you're left with now. You have a life to live, even if Nathan does not."

Eleanor is waiting for me outside Dr. Prince's office when my session ends. She grabs my arm so tightly I can feel my pulse beneath her fingers.

"Well?" she says.

"What?" I feel the itchy wool of her gray sweater against my bare arm.

"Did Randy go running to Daddy and tattle?"

I twist my arm from her grasp and put my own sweater back on. We walk down the twisted stairs and into the front hall.

"What makes you think Dr. Prince would've waited until my private to say something if Randy had told?"

Eleanor shrugs. "I don't know what you two talk about."

"Well, he didn't say anything about it, so I'm guessing Randy kept his mouth shut."

"Is he going to tell?"

"I don't know."

"You have to stop him!" Eleanor whispers, but it comes out like a hiss. "The Prince could put a new lock on our window! He might call our parents and make them come get us. We'd never get to go to Castle South again."

"I know," I say, but much to my surprise, I don't sound nearly as worried about it as Eleanor does.

I look through one of the large windows in the hall. March comes in like a lion and goes out like a lamb, right? Right now, it's hard to imagine it'll be sunny and bright—lamb weather—in just a few weeks. (Daniel keeps me apprised of the date and time each night.) The sky is as gray as ever, the castle shrouded in fog like a film over the air.

But spring is coming, whether it looks like it or not. "It'll be April before we know it," I say. "Eventually, the semester will end and we'll go home, and then we won't be able to go to Castle South anyway."

"Exactly," Eleanor says. "Hank and I need all the time we can get to figure everything out."

"What's there to figure out?" I ask. "In a few months, we all go back to where we came from, right?"

Eleanor shakes her head. "A few months is nothing. It'll go by like that." She snaps her fingers. "And I don't want to just go back to where I came from. I mean, do you want to go home to the same problems that got you sent here in the first place?"

I shrug. "What choice do any of us have?" When I get home, my mother isn't going to magically love me more, because I won't magically have become the daughter she wants.

Dr. Prince isn't a sorcerer, he's a psychiatrist.

Eleanor shakes her head again and walks away.

# *thirty-five*

That night, Dr. Prince joins us for dinner.

"Ladies," he says, sitting down at the head of the table, where Carol sits during group. He flips his tweed jacket out behind him as though it were a tux with tails he doesn't want to wrinkle. He sits up so straight that his back doesn't even touch the chair.

Cass rolls her eyes at me from across the table, and I try not to giggle. Each of us has already filled her plate with food from the sideboard; tonight, it's chicken marsala (for those of us who eat meat), spaghetti in marinara sauce, and steamed broccoli with garlic. Virginia covers her pasta with a mountain of Parmesan cheese. I hate to admit it, but the food here is delicious.

"I thought it was about time I joined you for dinner," Dr. Prince says, though the plate in front of him is empty.

"What made you pick tonight?" Eleanor asks. I wonder if Dr. Prince notices that she looks at me when she speaks. I know she's worrying that Randy told his father about Castle South and that Dr. Prince is here to keep us from going ever again.

"Well," Dr. Prince says, "our time together isn't endless. The semester is moving along. But I think your parents will be very pleased with your progress."

Even though Dr. Prince hasn't mentioned Castle South, Eleanor still looks frantic. Quickly, I say, "My parents won't be pleased."

Dr. Prince turns to face me. "Why do you say that?"

I adjust in my seat, the wood hard beneath my thighs. "I still have my tattoo. You said that was my presenting problem, didn't you? Well, it hasn't been solved."

Dr. Prince nods. "I don't like to think of a problem as having been solved or not. I prefer to consider whether an issue has been addressed or unaddressed."

I shake my head. This afternoon, he said I was wrong to invest myself so completely in Nathan. Is that the issue he thinks needs *addressing*?

Suddenly, Castle South is the last thing on my mind.

The day Nathan died, my mother walked me to school to make sure I didn't sneak off and go to the hospital. She lectured me along the way. This was the start of my senior year, she said, and I shouldn't let my whole life get off track because of one friend. I heard every word, but I wasn't paying attention. In my head, I imagined the sound of Nathan's heart monitor. The beat of his pulse, one beep after another. I wondered how many beeps he had left.

How could she keep me away from him?

Beth spins some spaghetti around her fork. "My presenting problem was that I did drugs. Isn't that a problem that needed to be solved? Isn't sobriety the solution?"

Dr. Prince tilts his head to one side, reminding me of a German shepherd. "Excellent point, Beth. And of course your sobriety is essential to your recovery. But addiction isn't only about the substances we abuse; it's also about the reasons we abuse them. And some of us are genetically predisposed to addiction, which may increase the likelihood that we'll struggle with substance abuse."

Grey speaks up. "Like me with depression. There are environmental factors, but there's also the possibility that mental illness could be literally written into my DNA."

"Well, not *literally*," Dr. Prince corrects gently. He's the kind of person who cares about the precise meanings of words. Like me. "But I catch your meaning."

"You're making it sound hopeless," I interject. I feel hot, just like I did in his office today, even though the dining room isn't nearly as warm. In fact, it's so cold that I don't think I've had a properly warm meal since I've been here, not counting the soup I shared with Randy in the kitchen the other night. "Like we can't solve our problems no matter what we do. Like it's genetic destiny or something."

"Not at all," Dr. Prince says. "Our genes may play a part with some types of mental illness. But as Grey said, there are environmental factors as well." He pauses. "Whatever else may be true, certainly each of us is born with a particular temperament. And while there are no *solutions* for our problems, there is treatment."

The day my parents sent me here, I thought my mother wanted Dr. Prince to shrink me down to nothing so she could start all over again with a better baby, one who'd grow into the little girl she'd dreamed of having. The kind of girl who'd be interested in the knight-in-shining-armor part of fairy tales instead of the who-built-the-castles part. The kind of girl who'd be surrounded by a gaggle of girlfriends instead of one guy friend.

"So a problematic temperament requires treatment?" I say. "Isn't that just trying to change someone's personality?" For all I know, Dr. Prince and his wife are hoping their experiment will achieve exactly that.

Dr. Prince smiles again, and this time, the smile reaches his eyes. "You raise an interesting point, Moira. Occasionally, I get calls from parents who simply don't get along with their daughters. So many parents expect their children to be miniature versions of themselves, and when that's not the case, occasionally they convince themselves it's because something is *wrong* with their children." He pauses. "In those cases, the problem is with the parents, not the children."

I lean forward in my chair. "How can you tell the difference?"

"It can be difficult," Dr. Prince admits. "Some parents mistake *difficult* children for troubled children. And when they call me, I have only their description of the situation to go by, of course."

"So how do you determine who needs to be here and who doesn't?"

"Well, it's not a perfect science, but I've found that the parents whose daughters don't need my help talk a lot more about themselves than they do about their children."

I narrow my eyes. "Have you ever been wrong?"

"Of course I have," Dr. Prince answers, like it's simple, inevitable. "Believe me, I've been afraid many times that I've refused admission to girls who might have benefited from my help."

"Then why not let all of them in?"

"I didn't want to risk sending a message to those children that there was something wrong with *them* instead of with their parents. Moreover, our resources here are limited. We're equipped to manage only twelve students at a time, and this is a school, not a treatment center. Some young women—and men, of course—need a more controlled environment."

Eleanor breaks in. "This environment in plenty controlled." I know she's thinking about the boys at Castle South. But at least she no longer seems worried that Randy told his father our secret.

"Not compared to an inpatient facility," Dr. Prince explains. I remember what Cass told me my first morning here: that Eleanor's former roommate, Astrid, ended up in inpatient treatment. I glance at Alice; Cass said she'd been kicked out of places that specialized in eating disorders and she only got to stay here if she kept up her deal with Dr. Prince.

"Okay," I say, "but don't you think that at some point, you probably admitted girls who maybe didn't need to be here?"

Dr. Prince looks at me carefully, with that gaze that makes me think he can read my mind. Then he smiles again. "I know

I'm not right one hundred percent of the time. But I believe that every girl who has come here benefited in one way or another." Dr. Prince breaks his gaze away from me and looks around the table. "I do hope you girls feel that way about being here. If not now, then someday."

Well, that's convenient—he can tell himself that even the girls who hate being here might change their minds *someday*.

That *someday*, I'll believe my mother sent me here out of genuine concern instead of desperate disappointment.

Will Dr. Prince follow up with me years from now to see if that particular someday ever arrives? How long will this experiment of a school go on before he and his wife come to any conclusions?

Dr. Prince claps his hands together. "Now, enough talk. Your meals are getting cold." He stands and fills his plate with food from the sideboard, and the room is filled with the sound of forks and knives and chewing.

But I don't feel like eating anymore. In fact, the lump in my throat is so large at the moment that I don't think I could eat if I tried.

# BETH

Beth was an *athlete*. When she was a little girl, her mother signed her up for dance, gymnastics, swimming, ice-skating, and soccer. She had so much energy, but not in a frantic, all-over-the-place sort of way, like her little brother. No, Beth's energy was focused, like a laser. It simply needed somewhere to point.

Her first injury happened in second grade: a sprained wrist from gymnastics.

In fourth grade: a broken leg from skiing.

In eighth grade: her first concussion, during a soccer match.

Beth hated taking time off to recover. All she wanted was to get back out there, back to her life.

Her freshman year in high school, she made the varsity track team, the only ninth-grader to do so. The hurdles were her best event. She broke the school record, the county record, the state record. It was the perfect outlet for all her energy.

Until she fractured her pelvis the summer before her senior year.

Being bedridden was unbearable. When she'd had a sprained wrist, she could still work out her legs; when she'd broken her leg, she could use her arms. But this—this was something else. Suddenly, she was someone with a serious injury, someone whose broken bones needed time to heal.

She was determined to get better as quickly as possible.

She wasn't scared of the pills. She thought they were a means to an end, nothing more. She couldn't do the physical therapy without the relief the pills provided, and she couldn't get better without physical therapy. There was a college scholarship on the line. She knew she'd be that special patient who defied the odds, no matter what the doctors said about the limitations of her recovery and the importance of setting realistic goals. Beth was certain she'd be better in time for her senior year, the one who did best at physical therapy, the success story, the winner.

That was all she knew how to be.

And she simply couldn't bear the stillness.

But then, with the painkillers in her system, stillness stopped bothering her. The pills made the pain vanish, but instead of bouncing out of bed and back onto the track, Beth stayed in bed all summer, in between PT appointments. At first, her parents were proud of her for taking her recovery so seriously, giving her body time to heal. They didn't realize that she usually took her next dose a fewer hours earlier than directed. What did "use as directed" even mean, Beth wondered.

It was months before her parents realized what was truly going on.

They took the medication away, a gesture so futile she almost laughed. Didn't they know how easy it was to get a fix these days? Kids at school traded pills like candy.

And when you ran low on cash, there were less-expensive alternatives.

And so, in November of her senior year—time she had intended to spend meeting with coaches and filling out applications—Beth found herself in the back of a stranger's car, watching him turn powder to liquid, his precision like a doctor's. Then came the pinch that preceded a pleasure like nothing she'd ever known. It felt like the fantasies she'd had as a child of how lying on a cloud would feel.

But later, Beth saw how dirty the needle was. She looked at her arm; where there had once been muscle, now she was so thin. She couldn't remember the last time she'd been hungry. She couldn't believe what she'd done. She told her parents that night, even as she was jonesing for more.

When the brochures for Castle arrived, Beth was relieved. When her parents spoke to Dr. Prince on the phone, Beth watched their expressions change. It reminded her of the way her body relaxed when the pills kicked in.

She thought that if just his voice could do that to her parents, he had to be good.

# thirty-six

"I don't think I'm going to go tonight."

"What?" Eleanor spins around. She's holding one of my (black) T-shirts against herself, trying to decide which one to borrow.

"I'm beat," I say. "I think I'm going to stay in, go to bed early."

"Seriously?" My roommate sits down hard on her bed. "Why would you stay here when you could be there?" A phrase so similar to what I said to Randy about twenty-four hours ago.

"I'm really exhausted. It's been a long day."

I'm not lying. The idea of climbing out the window and traipsing through the woods makes my eyes feel heavy.

"I'd rather stay here," I add. I used to say that to my mother when she called to ask me to come home from Nathan's hospital room, from his apartment after school, or on Thanksgiving, or on New Year's Eve. *I'd rather stay here.* I wonder how many times I said those words to her.

And not just when the alternative was going home to be with her and my dad. I also said it when Mom saw that there was a dance at school or when I got invited to some girl's bat mitzvah or sweet sixteen (always because she had invited our whole grade, not because she actually liked me): *I'd rather stay here.*

When Nathan died, I didn't think I'd ever have a reason to say those words again, because there was nowhere I'd rather be than with Nathan, and he was gone. And I certainly never would have guessed that the place I'd *rather* be would be a cold castle in the woods. But here I am, lying on my narrow bed, and I don't want to move.

Eleanor narrows her eyes and tucks her wavy hair behind her ears. We both do that, I've noticed—tuck our hair back when we're thinking. "You're sure Randy didn't tell his dad?"

"What do you mean?"

"Well, if Randy did tell his dad and you know, tonight would be a good night be safe in bed while the rest of us get caught."

"You think I'm setting you up?"

"I'm just saying. You've never wanted to stay behind before."

"Well, I do now." I'm lying on top of the covers, but I roll over so that I'm facing the wall, then close my eyes. I feel Eleanor's weight on the bed when she sits.

"Don't—" She pauses. "I know Daniel was a jerk, but he didn't mean anything by it."

I shake my head, but I don't turn around. "Like I said, I'm really tired."

Eleanor waits a minute or two, like she's hoping I'll say

something more, but then I hear her stand and go back to evaluating T-shirts. I change into my pj's—soft gray leggings, a tank top, and a sweatshirt over that—and stay in bed while Eleanor and the others climb out our window and into the night.

I can't sleep. I'm the kind of tired where it feels like you're *too* tired to sleep, where all the things that are making you tired keep you awake. I felt this way for weeks after Nathan died. That's when I started sneaking out to visit his grave in the middle of the night. Thinking about him kept me awake even as missing him made me tired, so visiting his grave was literally the only thing I could do to address my insomnia.

They call this time of night the *wee small hours*—the hours after midnight but before the sun rises. The expression apparently originated in Scotland in the 1800s. *Wee sma'hours* (I imagine a Scottish brogue saying it) because the numbers of those hours—one, two, three—are so low.

The word *wee* has been used to mean *small* since the 1600s in southern England.

I looked all of this up on one of those visits to Nathan's grave. Looking up trivia was an excellent distraction from the fact that I was wandering through New York City alone in the middle of the night. Just as it had been a pleasant distraction in his hospital room. Just as it had been a pleasant distraction in middle school, before Nathan sat with me at lunch.

The months I've spent here at Castle North—cut off from the internet, with no proper library—is the longest I've ever gone without looking up facts and figures. I think about Dr.

Prince's brochure promising parents that without the distractions of modern-day life, his students form a special bond. It was Beth who explained to me what wainscoting was instead of Dictionary.com.

Come to think of it, not counting the first couple of nights, I've slept better here than I had in months before. Sure, I've been staying up late at Castle South, but after we get back, I fall into bed and sleep long and deep. When I dream, it's not about Nathan, but about music and dancing.

Maybe Dr. Prince would say it's a sign that his methods are working. He basically said in our session earlier that missing Nathan so much was my fault because I didn't allow myself to have experiences that didn't involve him when he was alive. And now that he's dead, I'm here, having new experiences whether I want to or not.

I imagine Dr. Prince and his wife poring over their notes on us, scribbling away about my "progress," never guessing that this semester's results are skewed by our visits to the other castle.

I roll over and punch my pillow, trying to make it more comfortable.

For months after Nathan died, I heard his voice in my head, commenting on everything I said and did. I didn't even have to try. It was just there—*he* was just there—all the time.

It occurs to me that right now is the first time I've really been alone in weeks—months, even. I try to call up Nathan's voice, to imagine his laughter, making fun of me for staying behind while the other girls are off having fun. But there's only silence.

269

I get out of bed.

I decide to go down the kitchen. Alone. In the wee small hours. Surely Nathan's voice will pop up when I stub my toe against a wall in the darkness, when I trip on my way down the stone stairs. He'll laugh at me for being a klutz, just like he always did, but in a way that didn't make me feel like an idiot.

Eleanor has my flashlight, so I make my way downstairs by feel, walking slowly, one hand against the wall. It's dark but not pitch black—there are lights at the end of each hallway and at the top and bottom of the stairs. When I get to the first floor, I panic for a second. How do I get to the kitchen from here? But then I hear something. Not music, like that first night—now I hear laughter. I follow the sound.

In the kitchen, the lights are on. (There's a switch by the door; they aren't on a timer like the lights upstairs.) It's so bright that it takes a minute for my eyes to adjust. Virginia and Raina are sitting cross-legged on the stained and scratched butcher block island in the middle of the room, passing a giant jar of peanut butter back and forth.

Virginia sees me first. Raina's laughter falls silent.

"Hey, V," I say. "Mind if I join you?"

"'Course not." She taps her fingers absently against the countertop. "We never eat much on Dr. Prince nights. Cass and I started sneaking down here last semester."

"Aren't you worried Dr. Prince will catch you?"

Virginia grins. "You've been sneaking out to Castle South every night, and you're worried about getting caught in the kitchen?"

"Fair point," I say, climbing up on the countertop next to her. It's so large that all twelve of us could probably sit cross-legged up here. Opposite us is the enormous six-burner stove with a double oven and rows of open shelving above it holding half-empty spice jars. To the left of the oven is an open door that leads to an enormous pantry; inside, I know, are neatly arranged rows of organic soups and nuts, bread and peanut butter, dried pasta and jars of sauce. To our right is an enormous farmhouse sink with a window above it. The window is shut, but I can feel the slightest breeze coming in from its edges. I pull my sleeves over my wrists, Eleanor-style. Maybe all the times I saw her do this, she wasn't trying to cover her scars. Maybe she was just trying to keep warm.

"Why'd you guys stay behind tonight?" I ask.

Virginia passes me a spoon. "Didn't feel like going." She gestures to Raina, then adds, "Don't take it personally—she's not talking to everyone yet." I nod. "Anyway, Raina says that some of the guys there—well, they can kind of be jerks, you know?"

I nod again.

"I mean, just 'cause Raina doesn't talk much doesn't mean she can't hear. She said…" Virginia pauses and glances at Raina like she's asking for permission, and something in Raina's face must grant it, because Virginia continues. "She said that she heard Dave and Greg rating us in terms of attractiveness. Like, making a list or something."

"Gross," I say.

"Yeah. So she doesn't feel like going over there anymore."

"How about you?"

Virginia bites her lower lip. Her short, light brown hair is pulled into a messy ponytail at the nape of her neck, but a few stray hairs stick to her cheeks. Her eyes get very bright. "Cass and I had a fight," she whispers. "'Cause I told her what Raina said and that I wanted to stay here, but she said she was going anyway, with or without me."

"Oh, V, I'm sorry." The nickname comes out easily, thoughtlessly.

Virginia sniffs. "We've *never* fought before. I wanted her to stay with me, you know? I mean, why would she want to hang out with those guys after what Raina said? But she still went, and so now—anyway. Now I'm here, and Cass is there."

I nod, taking a spoonful of peanut butter. "I think Eleanor's pissed at me for staying behind," I offer. "I know that's not the same thing."

"No," Virginia agrees. "It's not."

Raina hops off the counter and disappears into the pantry. Seconds later, she emerges with a chocolate bar.

"I didn't know there was any junk food in there," I exclaim.

"It's not junk food," Virginia says, taking it from Raina and reading the label. "See? Organic, free-trade, semisweet baking chocolate."

She breaks it into three pieces, and each of us dips some chocolate into the peanut butter. For a few minutes, we're quiet, chewing thoughtfully.

It occurs to me that the boys don't actually have that much

more freedom at Castle South than we do here at Castle North. Sure, Dr. Prince gave us a bedtime, but it's not like it's actually kept any of us in bed over the past few weeks. Even tonight, having stayed behind, here the three of us are in the kitchen, sharing a midnight (or whatever time it is) snack.

Virginia asks, "Why did you stay here? I thought you loved that place more than anyone."

"Not more than Eleanor," I say, but Virginia waits for more of an explanation. "I don't know," I answer finally. "I guess I thought I was tired, but then I couldn't sleep. And after what happened with Randy last night…" I pause. I told Eleanor that wasn't why I stayed behind.

"Yeah," Virginia agrees. "That was pretty terrible." Raina nods in agreement. "I know this sounds cheesy," Virginia continues, "but that's not what our parents sent us here for, you know?"

"What do you mean?" I ask.

"I mean, I came here because I *wanted* help with my problems. Going to Castle South every night—it was fun at first, but I don't think it was actually, you know, *helping*. And I don't know why those guys are there, but hanging out with us every night probably isn't helping them with their problems, either, right?"

"I don't know," I answer honestly. "I thought maybe it *was* helping. Eleanor seems happier. Raina, you're talking more than you were before."

"Yeah," Virginia agrees. "And you're not chugging water as much." She pauses, and I know she's thinking about asking me why I drank so much water, but she must decide against it,

273

because she continues, "That place definitely wasn't helping *me*. It was just another distraction, you know?" I nod, thinking of all the trivia I haven't gotten to look up since I got here. "And Cass and I never fought about anything until now."

I almost fall off the counter when a fourth—male—voice enters the conversation. It's so deep that for a split second, I think it's Dr. Prince, catching us out of bed.

"Hey, Moira," the voice says. "Can we talk for a minute?"

"Sure, Randy." I start to slide off the counter, but Virginia stops me.

"We'll go upstairs," she says. "You guys can stay here and talk. Just put the peanut butter away so the Prince doesn't know, okay?"

"Of course," I say. "Thanks, V."

"Sure," she answers. "Good night."

"'Night."

# thirty-seven

"Peanut butter?" I offer. Randy shakes his head and leans against the counter. I slide off the butcher block to stand beside him. Even with socks on, I can feel the cold stone beneath my feet.

"Why don't you guys ever build actual fires in the fireplaces?" I ask, gesturing to the enormous hearth behind us.

"How do you know we never do?"

"Look how clean they are." I point. "If there'd ever been an actual fire in that grate, there'd be ash or charred wood or something."

Randy nods. "Actually, when we moved in, all the fireplaces were black with soot. But Dad was pretty meticulous about cleaning them before they opened the schools. He thought it'd be too dangerous to light fires around the students."

"Doesn't stop your mom in Castle South."

Randy runs a hand through his curly hair. "Yeah, well, they don't agree on much anymore." Before I can ask what he means by that, Randy continues, "I just wanted to say—" He stops abruptly. His Adam's apple bobs up and down as he swallows. I wait for him to say that he's going to tell his father about us sneaking out, that he feels obligated to tell the truth, that he'd get in trouble if his Dad found out he was keeping something like this from him, that it's the right thing to do.

But instead he says, "I wanted to apologize for last night."

"Apologize?" I echo.

"For the way things escalated. I should never have let that guy get to me."

"Are you kidding? Daniel was being a jerk."

"Yeah, but I didn't have to be a jerk back."

"You weren't."

Randy shakes his head, the edges of his curls aglow from the overhead lighting. "You don't understand. I wanted—" He sighs heavily and presses a finger to the bridge of his nose. "I wanted to beat the crap out of him. That's why I left like that. I had to get out of there. If I hadn't, I don't know what I would've done." He tucks his hands into the pockets of his jeans. "My freshman year, I got into a fight with a kid at school."

"I thought you were homeschooled."

"Not back then. Anyway, my mother—I mean, you'd have thought I killed the guy, the way she reacted. She said I'd drive her and Dad out of business—this was before the divorce—"

"Your parents are divorced?" I interrupt.

Randy blinks in surprise. "You haven't noticed that they don't live together?"

"No, it's just—I thought—"

I don't know what to say.

*I thought they lived apart because they were testing different psychological methods and comparing notes as part of an elaborate experiment they were doing on their students.*

My breath catches in my throat.

A few months before Nathan died, his mother came across a promising new treatment the doctors at a university in Maryland were using on tumors like Nathan's. In June, the four of us—Nathan's parents, Nathan, and I—drove the five hours to Baltimore, spurred on as much by hope as by gasoline. Nathan and I sat in the back seat. He slept half the time, but somewhere in Pennsylvania he started quizzing me on vocabulary words the same way he did before he got sick.

It was only after we arrived that Nathan and I discovered his parents hadn't actually made an appointment. In fact, his mother had been begging them to put Nathan in their study for weeks, and they'd said no over and over again. Apparently, Nathan's mom thought that showing up in person might change their minds if they saw what a special kid Nathan was, how deeply he was loved.

Finally, after Nathan's mother had pleaded and cried, the doctor in charge let us into his office. It was nothing like Dr. Prince's office—no built-in wooden bookshelves or old-fashioned windows. This man's desk was covered with patient files, two enormous computer screens, and a slim wireless keyboard. The chairs were made of metal, and the room was cold. Patiently, kindly, the doctor—I don't remember his name—explained that Nathan wasn't a candidate for the study: his tumor had been found more than a year earlier and had already been treated, and they only accepted patients with new diagnoses. Moreover, the doctor said Nathan was "too far gone." Admitting him to their trial would corrupt their results.

Doctors never say that a patient is going to die. They say things like *prepare for the worst, hope for the best, we'll make him as comfortable as possible,* and, apparently, *too far gone.* They count on patients and their families to decipher the real meaning behind these phrases.

Nathan's mother asked if they could keep Nathan's results out of the study. No one would have to know. But the doctor still said no.

I hated that doctor then, for turning Nathan away because his death might mess up their statistics.

On the drive home, Nathan started talking about his end-of-life plan. He said he wanted to die at home. I flinched when he said the word, and I think his parents did, too. Nathan was the first one of us to actually say it. His mother cried in the front seat; his father drove with tears streaming down his face. But Nathan didn't cry, so neither did I.

"Don't let me die in the hospital," he said, squeezing my hand.

"I promise," I said.

After that, I hated every doctor. Not just the one who'd turned Nathan away in Maryland, but also the doctors who wouldn't let me into the ICU and the ones who slipped in and out of Nathan's room while I sat in the hallway. The doctors who wouldn't let him go home one last time.

So of course I hated Dr. Prince from the moment I met him. He *had* to be a bad guy—the villain, only doing what he did for money or for fame. He and his wife *had* to be experimenting on me. Nathan would have appreciated the irony—his mother did everything she could to get him experimental treatment, and my mother got it for me without even trying.

But as I look at Randy now, I finally understand that the Princes aren't experimenting on us. I'm not corrupting their results by sneaking out to Castle South. Like the couple who first built these two castles, they each got one in the divorce, except this time, the wife got the nicer castle. And now she allows fires to blaze around her students while her husband keeps his hearths spotless.

"Anyway," Randy continues, "my mom was worried that if it got out that they couldn't control their own son, no one would send their kids here for help ever again."

"Did she really think she could control you?"

Randy smiles wryly. "Dad said the same thing. But she pulled me out of school and made me attend classes with the boys at Castle South—therapy, group, the whole thing."

"You had therapy with your parents?"

"With my mom."

"Isn't that kind of—"

"Unethical? Frowned upon? Worth losing your license over?"

Just a few minutes ago, I thought the Princes were all of those things. "I was going to say pointless. I mean, how can you work out your issues with the person who probably gave you at least half of them?"

Randy grins. "Yeah, well, I didn't work out my issues. I got into another fight. Here—there, I mean, at Castle South. With one of their students."

"Oh," I say softly.

"My dad was actually kind of great about it. He said my mom had been wrong when she tried to keep everything a secret. He had me start seeing a therapist in town, doing anger management, that kind of thing. He's the one who suggested I start running."

He pauses. "But my mom—she was furious. After the fight, a bunch of students dropped out, and their numbers never quite rebounded. They had to let half the staff go. She blamed me, and I blamed her, and my dad got caught in the middle. You know how parents always tell their kids it's not their fault when they get divorced?" I nod. "I'm not sure that applies in my case."

"I'm sorry."

"Yeah, well. Anyway, they'd always kept the castles separate— one for boys and one for girls—but they split the campus into two different schools after the divorce. You know, the way it is now."

I nod.

"You don't have to be scared," Randy adds quickly.

"Why would I be scared?"

"To be alone with me. I have my anger issues under control. Even last night, I got out of there before things escalated, didn't I?"

"You did," I assure him. "Is that why you're not supposed to be alone with any of us?"

"Nah, that's just my dad being all puritan." Randy laughs. "You know, worrying that his gorgeous son might distract his students. The ones who are interested in that sort of thing, anyway."

I don't laugh, because the thing is, Randy *is* handsome. The freckles dotting his face are like a connect-the-dots picture calling out to be traced. A rush of butterflies flutter across my stomach.

"Dad never seems to notice that most of the girls here barely acknowledge that I exist. Some of them don't even know I'm his son—they think I'm, like, a very young groundskeeper or something. You were literally the first girl this year who actually talked to me on the way home from the airport."

"I thought I was doing something wrong."

"Well, you *were* breaking my dad's rules." He grins at me. "No one else even tried to get in the front seat."

"Can I ask you something?" I say, and Randy nods. "After everything that happened, do you hate Castle South?"

Randy shrugs. "You mean, do I hate my mom?" I don't answer, and Randy continues, "I'm angry at her, but I don't hate her, you know?"

I nod, but I don't really know. I've been so angry at my mother for so long that it feels like hate.

"Eleanor thought Castle South was magic at first," I whisper. Is that really any stranger than believing the Princes were experimenting on us? The first time we went there, it felt like there was something *unnatural* at work. The kind of thing that couldn't be explained by facts or figures or trivia. The kind of thing for which there's no logical explanation.

Like when your best friend dies, and even though you know *why*—cancer—you still can't make any kind of sense of it. And you hope that his voice in your head is more than just a memory. Maybe it's his way of staying with you forever.

"Eleanor felt so much better after we started going there. Raina started talking the morning after she first went, after who knows how many months of silence. And, and—"

Randy finishes my sentence for me. "And when you were there, you didn't feel like crying all the time?"

I must look shocked, because Randy adds, "When you've seen as many students come and go as I have, you learn to read the signs. You lost someone you loved, right?" I nod. "Your dad? Your grandma?"

I should be angry that Randy has reduced me to a type, but instead, it's somehow comforting that he recognized what happened to me. I thought no one here—well, other than the grown-ups, who'd been filled in by my parents—knew, but it turns out Randy could see it, maybe from the moment he met me. And Eleanor never believed I was sent here because I got a tattoo. She said no one believed that.

Even though they didn't know exactly what happened, they knew *something*.

"Boyfriend?" Randy guesses next.

"Best friend," I whisper. I try to say his name, to say the word *cancer*, but the lump won't let me. I almost stomp my foot in frustration, surprised by how much I want to speak. Randy is the first person I've actually *told* about Nathan's death. Everyone else—my mom, Dr. Prince, the kids at school—found out some other way.

"I'm sorry," Randy says.

I nod.

"Castle South isn't magic." Randy's voice is gentle. "If you're feeling better, *you're* the reason why, not my mom's bright and shiny castle."

"What about your dad?"

Randy smiles. "My dad—well, he has different philosophies about different kinds of problems, but I know he believes in giving people room to grieve. After the divorce, when I started home-schooling here and I couldn't even talk to my mom… I know it's not the same as what you went through," he adds quickly.

"It's okay," I say. "Go on."

"Well, my dad just kind of gave me space. And sure, he'd therapize every once in a while—he can't help himself." Randy smiles. "And he has his rules, his bedtimes and organic food"—he gestures to the enormous jar of all-natural, sugar-free peanut butter on the counter behind us—"but he also understood that I needed time."

Randy's standing so close that I can feel his breath when he speaks. I'm suddenly very aware that he's wearing jeans and a sweatshirt while I'm in my pajamas. I look down—he's wearing sneakers, and I only have socks on.

"My dad says the worst things I ever did—getting into those fights—don't have to be the things that define me. Like, he says I'm not an angry kid, I'm just a kid who struggled with anger and learned to manage it and move forward." He pauses. "My dad says we're more than the worst things that happen to us."

For months, I've been thinking of myself only as a girl whose best friend died. And before that, I was a girl whose best friend was sick. And before that, I was Nathan's best friend.

"Daniel was right about one thing," Randy says softly.

"Oh?"

"Well, he was right and he was wrong. He said I had a crush on you."

"You don't?" I try to feign offense, to play it off as a joke, but my voice comes out sounding nervous. I'm suddenly warm. I feel myself blushing.

Randy shakes his head. "That makes it sound juvenile." He pauses, then adds, "I *like* you, Moira."

"I like you, too," I say, feeling breathless.

Randy leans closer. I've never kissed anyone but Nathan, and that was more like the two of us testing to make sure we'd rather be friends. Halfway through our kiss, we started laughing because it felt too weird.

That kiss felt nothing like *this*. That kiss didn't make my heart pound, my knees wobble. I've read about that in books, but I thought surely a kiss couldn't *really* make your knees feel weak, right? But here I am, leaning on the kitchen island behind me like I'd fall down without it.

If I had my phone or internet access, I might look up the physiological explanation for what I'm feeling. But I don't, so instead I let Randy wrap his arms around me.

But then there's another feeling: the lump in my throat swelling so big that I think if I don't pull away, I'll suffocate. I press my hands against Randy's chest and shove.

"I'm sorry," I say, feeling frantic. "I can't."

"I know it's against the rules," Randy says. "And I don't want you to think I do this all the time, that every semester I hook up with one of my dad's students or anything. I swear I've never done this before."

"It's not that," I say.

Randy steps back and studies my face. "You look the way you did when you first got here."

"How's that?"

"Like you're about to start crying. Have you ever really cried, Moira, since your friend died?"

# thirty-eight

I run straight past our bedroom to the bathroom at the end of the hall. I duck into a stall and slam the door shut, curling over the toilet. I expect peanut butter and chocolate and bile. Instead, I dry heave a couple of times, and then there's nothing. I sit on the linoleum floor, my back against the stall door.

When I was with Randy, it felt like I was cheating on Nathan.

But why? Nathan was never my boyfriend. He was my best friend.

*Have you ever really cried, Moira, since your friend died?*

When Randy said my name, I thought I would choke. He didn't emphasize the *oy* the way his father does. He didn't sound impatient or tired, like my mother. He didn't sound familiar, almost giddy, like when Nathan used to say it, twisting it into nicknames: *Moys, Moyce, Mouse, Mini-Mouse, Minnie Mouse, Mighty Mouse.*

No one's ever said my name the way Randy did: softly, sweetly, warmly.

I haven't cried.

What if I cry until I'm drowning, like *Alice in Wonderland*?

Do I even deserve to cry, after everything that happened?

I get up off the floor. The linoleum reminds me of the floor in the hospital, in Nathan's room, in the chemo suite, and in the hallways where we walked—slowly, so slowly—so he'd get some exercise.

I stop at the sink and brush my teeth. Fill up a glass of water, drink it down, fill it again, and bring it back to my room.

I get into bed, but I don't sleep. The window is open, and I'm cold beneath my blanket. Any minute now—or maybe not, maybe it'll be hours—Eleanor and the rest of the girls will climb inside. I grip my glass of water like a stuffed animal, careful to hold it upright so it won't spill.

I don't know how much time goes by before the girls arrive. They're trying to be quiet—whispering, swallowing their giggles. Eleanor comes in last. She must see that my eyes are open, because she says a breathless, "Hey," as she changes her clothes and climbs into bed.

"Hey," I answer. She's smiling widely enough that I can see her teeth in the dark. "What are you so happy about?"

"Henry told me he loves me," she says.

"Oh," I answer, not sure what else to say. I didn't know love could happen like that, when you only see each other for a few hours each night. Some days, I spent every minute with Nathan. "Well, that's nice."

"He lives in California. Did you know that?"

"No." I don't know where Daniel's from, either. I only know that Eleanor's from Massachusetts because she said her parents drove her here. "So you'll do the long-distance thing after we all go home, huh?"

Eleanor shakes her head.

"You're going to break up?"

"Of course not. Didn't you hear me tell you he loves me?"

"Then what are you going to do?"

"Have you always been this dense?" Eleanor asks. "Is it really possible that I've shared a room with you all this time and never noticed how clueless you are?"

I sit up and swing my legs over the side of the bed, shivering as the cold air hits my bare feet. "What's gotten into you?"

"I haven't told the others," Eleanor says carefully. "Now I'm wondering if I should tell you."

"Tell me what?"

"You have to promise you won't tell." Eleanor slides out of bed, crosses the room, and stands over me. "I wish I had a knife."

"What are you talking about?"

"Don't go running for Dr. Prince, I didn't mean it like that."

"How did you mean it?"

"I'd cut your hand and you'd cut mine, and we'd seal the promise with blood."

"Sounds sanitary," I say, and Eleanor laughs. She takes my hand and grasps it. I wonder if the scar on her palm is a relic of a promise she made with some other girl.

"One of these nights, I'm not going to come back."

"You're going to stay at Castle South?"

"Hank and I—we're getting out of here. Before the semester ends. He has money saved. We're going to run away together."

I take a sip from my water glass. It's almost empty.

"What about your parents? Henry's parents?"

"What about them?" Eleanor scoffs. "They're the ones who sent us here."

"Yeah, because they were worried about you."

"Oh? Is that why your parents sent you here?"

I don't answer. Eleanor crosses back to her side of the room. She's scratches her neck absently, right where her collar meets her skin.

"You promise you won't tell?"

The last person I made a promise to was Nathan.

*Moys, Moyce, Mouse. You promised.*

"I promise," I say now.

Eleanor rolls over in her bed and sighs contentedly. I hear her breathing shift as she falls asleep. I wonder if she's dreaming of Henry, of the life they'll have together. I wonder if in her dreams, her skin is clear and smooth.

I finish my glass of water, tiptoe to the bathroom to refill it. Even though I brushed my teeth, I can still taste Randy's kiss in my mouth, sweet and salty, fresh and surprising.

But I can also taste the promises I made: to Eleanor, and to Nathan.

They taste sour.

# HALSEY

Halsey remembers the first time she tasted alcohol: a sip of her father's wine on her sixth birthday. She liked the purple-red color and expected it to taste like grape juice. Instead, it was bitter, though it coated her mouth the same way grape juice did, leaving a film on her tongue that she could feel for a long time afterward. Her father seemed proud that Halsey didn't mind the taste the way other little girls would have.

Her mother had never been much of a drinker. She never would have opened a bottle of wine at her daughter's sixth birthday party. While the other fathers drank beer, Halsey's father held his wineglass in one hand and a platter of hot dogs and hamburgers for Halsey's friends in the other. Halsey heard her parents arguing later, when her mother was cleaning up and found bottle after empty bottle of red wine.

*It was a party,* her father said. *I was opening the wine for everyone.*

But Halsey's mother knew the truth, and Halsey did, too. Her father drank all the wine himself. He didn't offer any to the other parents; wine was more expensive than beer. It was all for him, except for the sip he gave to his daughter, the girl who didn't wrinkle her nose when the tinny flavor hit her tongue.

After that, Halsey tasted her father's wine every chance she could. She wanted to like it every bit as much as he did. She wanted to be able to tell her mother that her father wasn't going through all of those bottles himself. It wasn't all his fault.

She was eleven when her father went to rehab for the first time. With him gone, all the bottles in the wine rack, all the extra bottles in his trunk, and the crate of bottles in the garage stayed closed and gathered dust. Eventually, Halsey's mother threw them away. Halsey missed the taste of the wine from her father's glass each night. She knew that her sips had grown into gulps, from gulps to a mouthful from every glass her father poured, until she was having at least a full glass every night, little by little, shared with her father. With him at rehab, dinner alone with her mother was much less satisfying. Halsey left the table every night with an empty space in her belly, as though she hadn't eaten enough.

Once she got to high school, it was easy to get drunk. She rarely got the red wine she favored—more often it was shots of some mysterious pink liquid at a party, swigs taken from someone's flask in between classes, keg stands on Saturday nights. She never lost a single drinking game. The boys all clapped her on the back. The pride in their eyes reminded her of the way her father had looked at her on her sixth birthday after that first sip.

But her father was sober now. It took more than one trip to rehab, plus the "meetings" he went to several nights a week. Her mother said that Halsey's drinking was her father's fault; he led by example, and he handed down the genes for addiction. Halsey shook her head, remembering the little girl who'd sipped her father's wine to get him out from the shadow of her mother's blame.

Halsey was only fifteen when she first tried (and failed) to quit drinking. Only a few months after that, her father threw the brochure from Castle down in front of her on the kitchen table. It landed with a smack, and Halsey felt a stinging in her cheek, as though her father had slapped her.

# *thirty-nine*

When I wake up the next morning, Eleanor is gone, and for a second, I think she and Henry must've run away already. But then I hear her voice coming from the hallway.

"Out of bed, sleepyhead," she says, flicking on the light. "Time for breakfast."

I get dressed, trying to ignore the feeling in the pit of my stomach, the rush of panic receding. She hasn't run away.

Not yet.

Crap. Should I tell Dr. Prince about her plan so he can stop her, so his ex-wife can stop Henry, so her parents can come and get her and take her home before she does anything dangerous?

More dangerous than the things she's already done, that is.

Will Henry know what to do if Eleanor starts cutting again?

But what kind of person would I be if I keep her from the boy she loves? If her parents find out what she has planned, they might send her someplace else, someplace with even stricter rules and tighter security, a place from which she'll never escape. She might never see Henry again.

Randy said his father's rules exist for a reason.

And Dr. Prince said the parents who send their daughters here are trying to help them.

But I promised.

Maybe I should ask Randy what he thinks. He's seen so many girls come and go, maybe he'd know what's right.

But I can't ask Randy. Surely he's angry at me after the way I ran off last night.

I pour myself a glass of water at breakfast, refill it twice. If the other girls notice that I'm back to chugging water, they keep it to themselves.

In group, we're mostly quiet. Virginia and Cass aren't sitting next to each other like usual, and Virginia's eyes are red. She's wearing the pajamas she had on in the kitchen last night. After group, I pull her aside.

"Hey," I say. "Are you and Cass still fighting?"

Virginia shakes her head.

"Well, that's good," I try. "So you made up after she got back last night?" I'm careful to whisper. I don't want Carol to overhear and ask *back from where*?

Virginia's eyes overflow with tears. "She dumped me. Said we were too different."

"Too different?" I echo.

"Yeah, you know, because I'm some kind of"—she sniffles

and gulps—"goody two-shoes, staying behind like that. She said I'm judging those boys when we're no better than they are." Virginia shakes her head fiercely. "But I never said I was judging them! I just don't like them and I'm allowed to have an opinion, you know?" She taps her hands frantically against her thighs.

"Of course you are." I hold out my water, thinking it might help with her crying, but she misinterprets the gesture—she must think I'm reaching for a hug, because she collapses against my chest. Instinctively, I put my arms around her and squeeze. I rock her back and forth and murmur that it'll be okay.

And then there's that feeling again—the lump in my throat, the nausea. Just like when Randy kissed me last night.

But how can I feel that way *now*? This isn't kissing another boy; this is comforting a friend.

A *friend*.

Virginia is my friend.

Randy is my friend.

Eleanor is my friend.

Cass, Raina, Beth…all of these girls. They're my friends.

But *Nathan* is my only friend. The only friend I need.

Nathan *was* my only friend.

This time, I don't run away. "It's going to be okay," I say again, patting Virginia's back. I'm not sure which of us I'm saying it to.

# forty

Every night for the new few weeks—I count the days—I hold my breath when Eleanor climbs out the window. Raina, Virginia, and I continue to stay behind. Sometimes we're not the only ones. One night, Halsey and Beth stay; another night, Reva sneaks down to the kitchen with us; another night, Mei braids everyone else's hair in the bathroom, explaining that when her hair was long, she loved braiding it.

Eleanor is the only girl who doesn't miss a single night at Castle South. Even Cass stays behind once or twice. Each time Eleanor leaves, I worry that *this* will be the night she doesn't come back. I try to ask her about her plan—where she and Henry will go, when they will leave, how much money Henry has saved—but Eleanor won't tell me anything specific. She says the less I know, the better, like she's imagining that Dr. Prince will interrogate me when he discovers she's missing and she's trying to inoculate me with a little plausible deniability.

Every morning, I consider telling Dr. Prince about her plan, but every afternoon—or actually every other afternoon, during our private sessions—I keep quiet. I promised not to tell, and I'm never breaking a promise to a friend again.

But keeping Eleanor's secret doesn't feel like the right thing to do any more than breaking it does.

*I don't know what to do.*

What would a true friend do? Who am I to decide the safest course of action? What do I know?

I screwed everything up the last time I was faced with this kind of choice.

Didn't I?

And so *I don't know what to do.*

Today (Eleanor tells me it's a Wednesday, courtesy of Henry's calendar in Castle South), I sit next to Cass in the drawing room. Shelly has given out worksheets again, but Cass and I are the only ones actually working on them.

"How's Virginia?" Cass asks suddenly, without looking up from her work.

"Huh?" I say dumbly.

"I know she talks to you," Cass says. "Like, you guys hang out."

"Oh," I say. "Yeah."

"So how's she doing?"

"Can't you tell?" I ask. They're still roommates, after all.

Cass sniffs. "She's not talking to me."

"Well," I explain, "she's heartbroken."

Cass nods, and now she does look up. "Me, too."

I sit up. "Then why not get back together? I know she wants to." She tells me so almost every night.

Cass doodles on her worksheet. "I know I seem like the bad guy, breaking sweet, innocent Virginia's heart."

"I don't think you're the bad guy," I protest, and Cass sighs. She slides off the couch onto the floor and pulls me down beside her.

"I don't like people telling me what do," Cass says. "Dr. Prince says I have issues with authority."

"I know."

"You do?"

"You mentioned it my first morning here."

Cass smiles wryly. "Guess it was my way of warning you. You know, *don't tell me what to do and we won't have any problems*—that kind of thing." Cass keeps doodling, holding the worksheet against her thighs. "I tried to warn Virginia."

I shake my head. "But there's a difference between someone disagreeing with you and someone telling you what to do."

"Is there?" Cass asks. I have to admit, I don't know. All those fights with my mom about where I should eat dinner, whether homework was important, how late I should stay out—was she telling me what to do or trying to express her point of view?

"I know I have to work on it," Cass says. "The Prince says if I ever want to have a healthy relationship with anyone—not just a romantic relationship, but with my parents, my friends, my brother, anyone—and if I want to finish high school—which I might, by the way, if it's up to me how I do it—then I have to learn the difference between someone trying to teach me and someone trying to control me."

"Isn't that *his* way of trying to control you?" I ask. "You know, him trying to make you trust your teachers?"

Cass laughs so loudly that Shelly looks up, but she doesn't shush us. I guess that would interrupt our bonding, which would go against everything it says in the brochure.

"You sound like me," Cass says. "A while back, I accused Dr. Prince of exactly the same thing."

"What'd he say?"

"He said shrinks who practice mind control only exist in the movies. Then he corrected himself and admitted that there are unethical therapists and teachers and physicians out there, even though it undermined the point he was making about how I should trust people. But the thing is, that made me trust *him* more, you know? That he wasn't pulling some 'all authority figures are good' BS, like my mom telling me to listen to my teachers even when I disagreed with them."

I nod, thinking about how certain I was that Dr. Prince was experimenting on us.

Cass continues, "Anyway, I felt myself getting so angry at Virginia, and I didn't want to fight with her the way I fought with my brother, with my parents, with my teachers. She doesn't deserve that, you know? So I thought, better to break up with her than fight with her."

"But you still love her," I protest. "Why wouldn't you want to be with the person you love?"

Cass's eyes are very bright. She pulls one of her twists from the bun on top of her head and wraps it around her fingers. "She deserves someone who won't get mad at her just for expressing her opinion." She sighs heavily. "You know, when we got together last semester, I promised I'd never hurt her."

"Breaking up with her *did* hurt her."

Cass nods. "I know. But I think I would've hurt her worse if we'd stayed together."

"So you were trying to keep your promise?"

"Yeah. Even if that meant breaking it, too. It was the only way I could protect her, you know?"

I shake my head. I didn't know it was possible to break a promise and keep it at the same time.

# CASSANDRA

No one was going to tell Cassandra Owens what to do.

Actually, that wasn't exactly true. Plenty of people told her what to do. Parents, teachers, guidance counselors, even her supposed friends.

But no one could make Cass *do* what they said.

Cass couldn't stand it when people tried to tell her what was right and what was wrong, like she couldn't form her own opinions about such things, or like her opinions were incorrect. She was perfectly capable of coming to the right conclusions on her own.

So screw anyone who tried to tell her what to do.

And screw anyone who tried to teach her right from wrong.

Wasn't that all school really was, when you thought about it? An indoctrination into *other* people's opinions about right and wrong, about the way the world should work? Just look at the way they taught history. It was so ridiculously biased, twisted and turned into the version of history *they* wanted it to be, the version in which the victors were right and the vanquished had it coming.

Screw that, too.

Cass's parents didn't understand. They said that she could get straight A's if only she applied herself. She had a high IQ, they insisted—she'd been tested in kindergarten. As though the results of a test she took when she was five years old had any bearing a decade later.

Her parents didn't understand. Cass wasn't worried about being *smart*. She knew she was smart. But she also knew there were different kinds of smart, and she was the kind teachers didn't give you grades for.

And she didn't think that was fair.

Anyway, who did her father think he was, trying to tell her what to do after all of his screw-ups? Not just the drinking, but the cheating, the fights, the benders that lasted for days, weeks, months. She was supposed to listen to *him*? No way.

Sure, she could stay in school day after day after day—but she could also go out in the world, make her own way. So she dropped out, got a job, made her own money.

Her parents acted like leaving school was a sickness. Like refusing to conform required treatment—a fix, a cure. They dragged her home, sent her back to school, but she simply cut classes all over again. They hired therapists to help her work on her "issues" who told her school was only temporary and eventually she'd make her own way. But didn't they see that she was already doing it? Already living life on her own terms?

Her parents tried sending her to private school, a special school for kids who learned differently. They didn't understand that it wasn't that she *couldn't* learn the old-fashioned way. She just wasn't *interested* in learning anyone's way but her own. She offered to move out—she was working, she could afford it—but they insisted that she stay. But then they said that living under their roof meant abiding by their rules, which meant school, which meant she couldn't stay.

When the brochures for Castle arrived, Cass didn't take much notice at first. Another special school. Another ultimatum. But eventually she read the brochures cover to cover. She even found mentions of the school on social media, posted by former students. She wasn't going anywhere she didn't know every last thing about.

She didn't think it actually sounded that bad. Or anyway, it sounded *different*, and different was good. Students weren't expected to sit in class all day long. Sure, she wasn't going to listen to this Dr. Prince any more than she'd ever listened to anyone else. But at least he'd provide her with a new set of rules to disregard.

So when her parents said they were sending here there, she surprised them by agreeing to go.

# forty-one

"I have to tell you something," I begin.

"All right," Dr. Prince says. We're in our private session, facing each other in the usual tall wingback chairs.

"God, didn't they teach you to provide your patients—"

"Students," Dr. Prince interrupts.

"Whatever. To provide your students with comfortable chairs?" I stand and start pacing. "Like, in medical school, didn't they tell you that if you want people to be comfortable enough to confide in you, it would help if they were actually, you know, *comfortable*?"

Dr. Prince smiles, a real smile that reaches his eyes. "I must have missed that day's class."

"It's not funny."

"No," he agrees. "It's not. In fact, most therapists put a lot of thought into how they arrange their therapeutic environments.

Some prefer couches to chairs. Some make sure the people they're working with are facing the window or the door, so they don't feel trapped."

"And you?"

Dr. Prince says. "I prefer looking at my students face-to-face. That's why I chose these chairs. It certainly wasn't my intention to make you uncomfortable."

"It's too late to do anything about it now," I say. "I've already had to sit like this for months."

Dr. Prince nods. "I wish you'd mentioned it sooner."

"Like you couldn't tell I was uncomfortable? Didn't they teach you that in school, too?"

"I could see you were uncomfortable," Dr. Prince admits, "but, my dear, I think you would have been uncomfortable regardless of how I arranged the seating. And, in any event, I believe this particular seating arrangement has value. It forces us to look at each other."

"You big into forcing your patients—students—to do things?"

Dr. Prince uncrosses and recrosses his legs. His posture stays stick straight. "Moira, what was it you wanted to tell me?"

"Huh?" I ask, though I know exactly what he's talking about.

"You said you wanted to tell me something."

I stop pacing, but I don't sit. I press my hands together, interlacing my fingers tightly. I said I *had* to tell him something. I don't want to tell him. I've never actually *wanted* to tell him anything at all.

Maybe I don't *have* to, either.

Maybe I should ask the other girls' opinions. Maybe they'd know what I should do.

But maybe they'd think Eleanor should go. Cass might encourage her, and Reva could give her tips on being a runaway. Maybe Virginia would be too scared to say anything because she's hoping Cass will change her mind about the breakup. Raina wouldn't say anything at all.

*Crap.*

"Moira?" Dr. Prince prompts.

"Umm," I begin. I start pacing again. What was I thinking, opening with *I have to tell you something*? I set Dr. Prince's expectations too high. It's warm in here. It's always so cold everywhere else but so warm in here. Sweat springs up on the back of my neck.

"I kissed Randy," I say, surprising myself so much that I stand still.

I didn't think it was possible for Dr. Prince to sit any straighter, but somehow, he does. "Oh?"

"Yeah, like, a week ago. In the middle of the night, after lights-out. Just for a second. But I stopped it before it went anywhere."

"Why?"

*Why* is the last thing I expected. Isn't he upset that his son and I were kissing when we were supposed to be in bed?

Or when *I* was supposed to be in bed. I don't know if Randy has a bedtime, too.

"I felt—I mean, it felt wrong."

"Why?" he asks again.

"Because Nathan will never kiss anyone ever again." This

time, I'm so startled by my own words that I sit down. Directly across from Dr. Prince.

"And you felt disloyal, kissing someone else when he couldn't?" I nod, and Dr. Prince asks, "Have you felt that way any other times, or only while you were kissing my son?"

"When Virginia told me she and Cass broke up." I pause. "I hugged her, and it felt like—it felt like I was cheating on Nathan. Which is ridiculous, I know. I mean, Nathan and I weren't a couple, not like that. How could I cheat on him?"

I bite my lip again, then take a long drink from my water glass. I hold it up.

"I'm back on the sauce," I say, a weak joke. If I had internet access, I'd look up the origin of that phrase. Dr. Prince smiles, but it's that smile that doesn't reach his eyes.

"Moira?" Dr. Prince asks gently. "Is that really what you wanted to tell me?"

I shake my head and curl up into the chair. "No," I admit. Dr. Prince doesn't say anything. He simply waits. I don't want to look at him, so I close my eyes when I say, "We've been—well, I've been—" There's no need to get all the girls in trouble. But no, I have to mention that Eleanor's been doing it, too. "We've been sneaking out. At night."

"You mean you left your room after lights-out to see Randy?"

I shake my head. "No. I mean, yes, that's true, but that's not what I mean."

Dr. Prince doesn't ask what I'm talking about. Again, he waits.

"We've been going to Castle South," I say softly. "Eleanor and I."

"Castle South?" For the first time, Dr. Prince sounds unsettled. Other than the shift in his posture, he managed to keep his composure even when I told him about kissing Randy. "How?"

"The lock on our window is broken." No need to tell him how it got that way. "We climbed out—"

"You climbed down from the second-floor window?"

I nod, opening my eyes. I actually feel bad when I see the worried look on his face. "It's not dangerous," I add quickly. "The bars are like a ladder."

"It is very dangerous," Dr. Prince counters firmly. "How long has this been going on?"

"Since my third night here."

Dr. Prince uncrosses his legs and leans forward, his posture finally curling slightly. "Why tell me now, Moira? After all this time?"

"Because..." I pause. Take a deep breath. "Because Eleanor—she's gotten really close with one of the students there. A guy named Henry Gordon."

"And?" Dr. Prince prompts.

"And she's thinking of... well, she mentioned she might... she's worried that after they go home, they won't be able to see each other for a while. She and Henry. You know, because he lives in California, and she's in Massachusetts."

"I see," Dr. Prince says. "And you're concerned that Eleanor might do something rash in order to be with this boy?"

I nod and take another drink of water.

"Thank you for telling me this, Moira," he says. Then he adds, "Our time is up."

# forty-two

We don't discover it until after lights-out, when Eleanor opens the window.

Dr. Prince must have done it while we were at dinner.

Maybe *he* didn't do it. Maybe the custodian did it. Or maybe Shelly or Carol. I guess *who* doesn't matter.

What matters is this: there's a shiny new lock on the bars outside our window.

Eleanor is fully dressed, ready to go. Her wavy hair is pulled back into a neat ponytail, and I see a tiny scar at the nape of her neck. I wonder if she got it from hurting herself or whether it's the result of some kind of accident. Maybe she fell and hit the back of her head as a little kid.

"What the hell?" she says, rattling the bars. Her fingers grip the cold metal tightly. If I'd been there when Nathan died, I would have held his hand just like that. I would have begged them to let me keep hanging on.

Eleanor twists to face me without taking her hands from the bars. "How did he find out?"

"Eleanor—"

"Did you tell him?"

"I didn't mean to—"

"You didn't mean to? What, it just slipped out by accident?"

"Not exactly," I admit. My voice sounds very small. I curl up into a ball on my bed. It's cold in here even when the window's closed; now I feel the breeze from outside. Unlike Eleanor, I'm in my pajamas: blue-and-white-striped leggings and a T-shirt under a hoodie with my old school's name on it. Our door is closed, and I wonder if the other girls who are going tonight—who were planning to go tonight—are standing in the hallway outside, listening to us, waiting for the fight to end before coming inside.

"You had no right!" Eleanor sounds panicked. She rattles the bars again. "You had no right to stop me. You don't understand. I *need* Henry."

She sounds like an addict, desperate because someone's keeping her from getting her next fix. I wonder whether being with Henry gives Eleanor the same endorphin rush that cutting gives her.

I've never cut myself, not like Eleanor, but when I got my tattoo, when the needle opened my skin, I didn't mind the pain. I wondered if my blood might not clot.

Some cancers can keep your blood from clotting properly.

310

"What about your parents?" I try. "They would have been so worried—"

Eleanor slams the window shut and turns to face me. "They'll have my perfect sister. They won't miss me."

I sit up a little bit straighter. "I didn't know you had a sister."

"What do you want to know? *She* never had a love affair with razor blades, so my parents can't help preferring her." Eleanor folds her arms across her chest and turns to face me. "Your turn."

"What do you mean?"

"You think it's weird that you didn't know I had a sister? Well, I've been living with you as long as you've been living with me, and I don't know *anything* about your life back home. Oh, right, except for the fact that your parents don't approve of your tattoo."

I stand. "I know you're angry—"

"Angry?" Eleanor echoes. "*Angry* doesn't cover it. What made you think you knew what was best? What made you so sure it was better for me to go back home than to run away with someone who loves me?"

"I'm sure your parents love you," I begin, but Eleanor cuts me off again.

"Oh? Because all parents love their kids? Like you're so sure your parents love you?"

"With my parents, it's complicated. They didn't want—"

"Didn't want a daughter who got a tattoo?"

"You don't understand. My mother—"

"Was disappointed in you from the moment you were born?

311

Was sad because you weren't the daughter she hoped you'd be? Yelled at you for acting out?"

I nod.

"Yeah, you're right, I don't understand," Eleanor says sarcastically. "And I definitely don't understand why you're trying to keep me from the one person who ever made me feel like I was enough just the way I am."

"But maybe there shouldn't be only one person who makes you feel that way. I mean, maybe *you* need to feel that way all on your own, even without Henry."

"Is that how you feel, all on your own?"

I shake my head. The only time I ever felt that way was with Nathan.

"I was scared that you'd get hurt out there, by yourself."

"Moira," Eleanor counters, "I've been hurt my whole life— at home, with my family around me. Maybe being out there by myself would've felt better!"

"Maybe it wouldn't."

There's a knock on our door. Whoever it is doesn't wait for an answer before opening it.

It's not any of the other girls. It's Dr. Prince.

"What the hell?" Eleanor shouts. "We might have been changing our clothes, and you just barge in like you own the place?"

"I do own the place." Dr. Prince's voice is as calm and even as always. He doesn't sound angry or offended. He doesn't even sound particularly concerned. "And given your raised voices,

I thought it was safe to assume you were not in the midst of changing your clothes."

He turns to face me. "Moira," he says, "could you please wait in the hallway for a few minutes? I need to speak privately with Eleanor."

I nod and step into the hall, where the other ten girls are waiting—not just the ones who are dressed like they thought they'd be heading to Castle South with Eleanor like usual, but also a few girls in their pajamas like I am, ready for bed. They all must have heard us fighting.

I turn away from them to look back into our room. "I'm sorry," I begin, but Dr. Prince has already closed the door. Eleanor can't hear me.

I slide down onto the floor, my back against the door. There's the sound of murmuring voices on the other side of it, but I can't make out what they're saying.

And then, raised voices.

And then, another sound: glass breaking.

I spin around and open the door. Dr. Prince is holding Eleanor by her arms, so drenched in blood that for a second, I think Eleanor attacked him. It takes me a second to realize where the blood is coming from, the way your eyes need to adjust to the dark.

Eleanor must have punched her fist through the window. Her entire right arm is a bloody mess: the backs of her knuckles, her palm, all the way up to her elbow.

"Eleanor!" I shout, rushing toward her. I press my hands over her cuts as Dr. Prince pulls the sheets from her bed to wrap around her arm like a tourniquet.

"She moved so quickly," he says breathlessly. The change in his voice makes my heart beat faster.

I always looked away when they took Nathan's blood. It made me feel lightheaded. But now I press on Eleanor's arm with all my might, wishing they'd covered this in ninth-grade biology. The blood doesn't drip or leak—it gushes between my fingers.

"Let me take her," Dr. Prince says, twisting the sheet around her arm and pulling it tight. I hold her closer. "Moira," he says, "I need to drive her to the hospital. This is more than we're equipped to handle here."

Carefully, Dr. Prince slides his hands beneath mine, and in one move, he lifts my roommate like a baby and carries her out into the hallway, where the other girls are waiting, watching. I follow him down the stairs to the enormous wooden doors and out into the night. He puts Eleanor into the back of the school van and turns back briefly.

"Go inside," he says. "I'll call from the hospital."

*How?* I think. My cell phone is dead, and there's no service here, anyhow. Then I remember: he's not leaving us here alone. He can call Shelly, or Carol, or Randy.

Dr. Prince climbs into the van and speeds away.

He's taking her to the hospital.

Because of me.

If I hadn't told him that she was planning to run, none of this would have happened.

This is my fault.

Her blood is literally on my hands.

# forty-three

I don't know how long I stand there before I feel the weight of a blanket on my shoulders and hear Randy's voice saying, "Come on, you'll freeze out here." It's not nearly as cold outside as it was a few weeks ago, but my clothes are wet—that's how much blood there was—and I'm shivering.

The other girls are standing in the entrance hall, but I let Randy lead me away from the stairs, past the dining room, and into a narrow hall where the walls are plain white Sheetrock instead of stone or wood.

"Where are we going?" I ask.

"To our rooms. Mine and Dad's."

Randy turns a sharp corner and opens a door into what looks like a living room in a small New York City apartment.

"Am I allowed in here?" I ask.

Randy smiles faintly. "I think *allowed* went out the window the night you showed up."

"I'm sorry," I say as Randy directs me to a soft, worn gray couch in the center of the room.

"Why are you sorry?" he asks.

The words won't come. The lump in my throat is as big as it's ever been. Randy offers me a glass of water, but I can't swallow anything.

"Moira," Randy says gently. His weight beside me on the couch is warm, comforting. "Maybe you need to cry."

I shake my head, but as I do, tears overflow onto my cheeks.

My face is collapsing. My whole body is collapsing. I curl into myself, the blanket falling from my shoulders. I'm crying so hard that I'm shaking. I go to wipe my face, but then I see that my hands are still stained with Eleanor's blood. Instead of offering me a tissue, Randy picks up the blanket and wipes my face, my nose, my chin, my neck—the tears, the snot, the blood. He doesn't seem disgusted. He doesn't look away. He takes my hands and doesn't let go.

My breaths come shallow and quick, like a machine gun: *rat-a-tat-tat, rat-a-tat-tat.* I'm going to hyperventilate, I think. I'm going to pass out. Maybe that would be better. Maybe passing out is the only way I'll be able to stop crying.

"You have nothing to be sorry for," Randy says, and I shake my head breathlessly, still unable to talk.

"My best friend died," I manage raggedly. "It's my fault."

Randy squeezes my hand. Maybe he thinks there was a car

accident and I was driving. If I tell him it was cancer, he'll say that of course I'm not to blame.

"He didn't want to die in the hospital." The words hurt.

We had a plan. Nathan's end-of-life plan. Hospice care in his apartment.

He was going to die at home.

We promised.

I promised.

But last August, we were in his room, and he stood up, lost his balance, and fell to the ground. He hit the floor hard. There was nothing to soften his landing; his mother had taken the rug out of his room months before. His immune system was so weak that the littlest germ could set off an infection, and it was easier to keep his room clean without carpet covering the hardwood floors.

I moved to get his mom, but Nathan grabbed my wrist, stopping me.

"Don't," he said. His grip was so much stronger than I thought it could be.

"I'm just going for help," I explained. "I can't get you into the bed by myself." I wasn't actually sure whether that was true. He'd lost so much weight that maybe I could've.

"Don't," he repeated. "They'll send me back to the hospital."

"They won't send you back to the hospital for losing your balance."

He shook his head. "The doctor said that if I got any worse—"

"You didn't tell me that." That was the part I was upset about. Not that Nathan—my best, only friend in the world—was so sick that the doctor had said he'd have to stay in the hospital, probably for the rest of his life, but that he'd kept it a secret from me.

"Don't tell my mom, Moira," he said. "You know what'll happen."

I said, "What if there's something the doctors can do?" Maybe there was some new treatment, some medicine that would help him.

Nathan looked at me like I was a fool. Had I learned nothing from our trip to Maryland? He understood that the next time he went to the hospital, it wouldn't be to get better.

"Moys, Moyce, Mouse. You promised."

I didn't know what to do. I'd never felt like that before. In every argument with my mother, I knew my side. I knew she was wrong and I was right. Every time I shared a piece of trivia with Nathan, I had complete faith in my facts and figures, my stats and stories.

But this—it was terrifying, not knowing what to do, not being able to look up an answer online or in the dictionary, or the library, or anywhere at all.

Nathan's mom knocked on his bedroom door. "Cover for me," Nathan whispered desperately. He was still on the floor.

Now, I explain, "*I'm* the reason he went back to the hospital." I shake my head. "He might still be alive if he hadn't."

If he'd been able to stay home—if I'd been with him—maybe he would have gotten stronger instead of being pumped full of drugs and painkillers and god knows what else. He'd still be sick, I know that—but maybe he wouldn't have died.

Not yet.

Randy thinks he likes me, but he doesn't realize what a terrible person I am. *I'm* the reason Nathan died the way he did, just like *I'm* the reason Eleanor's on the way to the hospital now. I deserve to be locked up in the woods. I don't deserve friends, and I definitely don't deserve for someone to *like* me—let alone *love* me—ever again.

Randy shakes his head firmly. "If he was sick, his parents would have sent him to the hospital, no matter what you did."

Nathan was admitted to the ICU. The doctors wouldn't let me see him, but that didn't stop me from going to the hospital. Every day, I walked the ten blocks from my apartment and sat in the waiting room. It was hot and humid, the summer before our senior year, when everyone else was on vacation or participating in internships or classes that would look good on their college applications.

Nathan's parents kept me up to date on his condition.

Eventually, the doctors moved Nathan to a regular room—the kind of room where visitors were allowed—but Nathan didn't want to see me.

I sat in the hallway outside his room every day. I caught glimpses of my best friend when the doctors and nurses opened the curtains around his bed.

He was so angry at me for what I'd done, he wouldn't even make eye contact with me.

His parents said he just needed some time, he'd come around. They said we'd be thick as thieves in no time. I looked up the expression *thick as thieves*. The idiom originated in the 1800s, when thieves often worked together in gangs and were extremely close, telling each other everything and completely replying on each other. In that context, *thick* meant very close or closely packed, like hair or grass.

Gently, Randy says, "Eleanor is better off at the hospital, too. If she'd run away with Henry—"

"How do you know about that?" I ask, startled when my voice comes out almost normal.

"Doesn't take a genius to figure out that's what she had planned. Anyway, if she'd gone off with Henry, who knows what might have happened?"

"You mean maybe she'd have cut herself so badly that she'd need to be rushed to the hospital?" I ask nastily.

"I do mean that," Randy says, ignoring my tone. "Or something worse. Think about it—think about what she did tonight, here, in a safe place, with a doctor in the room. You did the right thing, telling my dad, stopping her."

I shake my head. I've never done the right thing. I never did the things my mom wanted or expected, never acted like the other girls at school.

I did the wrong thing with Nathan.

And then he died, and I thought I'd never feel right about anything ever again.

But Randy just said I did the right thing tonight.

He said Nathan's parents would have sent him to the hospital whether I'd kept quiet or not.

I manage to take a deep breath and swallow. "Do you think my mom made the right choice, sending me here?"

"I don't know," Randy answers slowly. "But I do know this: she *believed* it was right. She didn't send you here to punish you for what happened to your best friend."

"Nathan," I croak. I've said his name so few times since he died, and it sounds strange, like a word in a different language. I say it again, trying to get used to the shape of it in my mouth. "His name was Nathan."

"Nathan," Randy repeats solemnly. "Your mom sent you here because she was worried about you. That's the only reason people ever send their kids here, to either of the schools. And that's why you sent your friend to the hospital, too. You were trying to help him, not hurt him. You did it because you loved him. Just like what you did for Eleanor tonight. Just like what your mom did for you. Even my mom—she thought she was helping me. It was misguided, but it was still love."

I never think of my mom as someone who loves me. Someone who's disappointed in me, sure. Someone who's frustrated with me, embarrassed by me, impatient with me. I thought those were the reasons she sent me here.

I definitely didn't think it was because of *love*.

I thought Nathan was the only person who loved me.

The only person I would ever love.

But now I realize that I love Eleanor. And I love Virginia, and Cass, and Raina. I love these new friends, friends I never thought I'd make or want and certainly didn't believe I deserved.

"Sometimes people come into our lives and make us feel better about ourselves," Randy continues. "It sounds like Nathan was that person for you." I nod. "But maybe it shouldn't be another person who makes us feel good about ourselves. Or bad about ourselves, either, you know?"

I said almost that exact same thing to Eleanor earlier.

Nathan and I never got to be *thick as thieves* again.

He died angry at me.

He died without me.

But not only because my mom made me go to school that day. Even if I'd gone to the hospital, I might have been sitting outside his room.

I wipe my face with the blanket.

"I want to call my mom." The force in my voice surprises me.

"Okay," Randy says. He reaches into his pocket and pulls out a fully functioning cell phone. "Here you go."

# forty-four

"Hello?"

I thought she might not pick up a call from a strange number. But maybe she recognized the Maine area code of Randy's cell phone and guessed it had something to do with me.

"Hello?" she says again, louder this time, her voice an octave higher.

"Hi," I say softly, and I'm crying again. I didn't think there were any tears left in me, but somehow they're still coming. It's different from how it was before. Now I'm able to breathe, and it doesn't feel like I'm drowning. I lean back on the Princes' soft couch, curl the worn, warm blanket around myself.

"What happened?" Mom asks. And then, "Do you need us to come get you?"

When Nathan's mother called me to tell me he died, I was in between classes at school. My classmates were milling around me, opening and slamming locker doors, rushing from one place to the next, thinking about this semester's syllabus, or whether they were going to take the SAT again, or which teacher they'd be able to ask for an extension on a paper or extra credit on a test.

Nathan's mom waited half an hour to call me. It had taken that long, she said, for her to be able to say the words. She was sorry to tell me like this, she said, over the phone, while I was at school, but she thought I'd want to know.

All I could think was that for half an hour, I'd been just like the kids around me: opening and slamming my locker door, rushing from one classroom to the next, looking over syllabi, arranging my books in my bag. I'd had no idea what had happened, that the world had changed forever.

I didn't tell a teacher or the guidance counselor or the school nurse. I simply walked out of school and hailed a cab and asked the driver to take me to the hospital.

By the time I got to Nathan's room, they'd taken his body away. His mother hugged me, and she cried, and she patted my back. His father stood silently in the corner; he looked shocked, as though he'd never actually *believed* his son was dying until after the fact. The three of us stayed in that empty room until it got dark, until the nurses told us we had to leave. Then I went back to their apartment, to Nathan's room—the room it was my fault he hadn't died in—and listened while Nathan's parents called their rabbi and the funeral home, bickered over whether to send out a mass email or call their extended family and friends.

By the time I got home that night, Nathan had been dead for

more than twelve hours. In all that time, it had never occurred to me to call my mother. It had never occurred to me that if I had called, she might have offered to come get me—from school, from the hospital, from the Kaplans' apartment.

Weeks later, when the letter from the Kaplans came, Mom called them strangers. Now I think that maybe it wasn't entirely her fault that she hardly knew Nathan's family. I had never invited her to be a part of my life with him.

"Honey," Mom says now. "Just say the word, and we'll start driving."

I shake my head, and somehow Mom must understand because she says, "Okay, then I'm just going to keep talking until you're ready to say something, all right?"

I thought she sent me here because I was too much trouble. I thought she sent me here because I was a disappointment.

"I'm sorry," she says. "I never should have sent you away."

I thought she sent me here because she needed a break from my silences and shouting.

"I just…" Mom pauses. "I didn't know what else to do."

I even thought she might have signed away her rights, given Dr. Prince secret permission to experiment on me.

"You were so sad—so terribly, desperately sad—and I was scared."

I never thought she sent me here because she was scared.

I never thought she sent me here because she *cared*.

Her voice when she picked up the phone, when she said hello a second time—it sounded high-pitched, louder.

It wasn't anger in her voice.

It was fear.

Maybe that's what it always was.

"I was worried," Mom continues. "I thought…you might hurt yourself. The way you snuck off to Nathan's grave at all hours—who knows what might have happened to you?"

I nod. I started losing weight, getting paler, months before Nathan died. I looked almost as sick as he did. Nathan said so once.

Mom keeps talking. "It was almost as if you were trying to get lost, to get hurt, and I… I was scared you'd do something that couldn't be undone. Be hurt so badly that you'd never recover. I guess that's why the tattoo set me off. Because there was no taking it back. Because it was permanent."

"I was sad," I say finally. And for the first time, I know that losing Nathan wasn't the only reason why. I was sad before Nathan died, even before he got sick. Sad because before he came along, I didn't have any friends. I didn't fit in. Not at school, and not at home.

I was sad because my mother didn't like me.

"I'm sorry," I say.

"For being sad?" Mom asks. "Honey, you don't have to apologize for that. Like I said, I was just so worried—"

"Not that." I shake my head and wipe my eyes. When I swallow, the lump is barely there at all. "I'm sorry for all the time I spent at Nathan's apartment instead of at home with you and Dad. I'm sorry"—my voice catches—"that I couldn't be the daughter you wanted me to be. I'm sorry I was such a disappointment."

"Oh, honey," Mom says, and now it sounds like she's crying. "You weren't—you *aren't* a disappointment. You never could be. Do you have any idea how much I love you, how proud I am of you?"

I shake my head. "I know I used to get good grades. After Nathan got sick, everything slipped."

"I'm not proud of you because of your grades," Mom says, then pauses. "Of course, I *was* proud of your good grades," she corrects. "You worked so hard for them. But I wasn't angry when your grades started slipping. It was absurd that the school expected you to do the same work as before under the circumstances."

I blink. "It was?"

"Of course." I imagine her nodding. "I told them they were being unreasonable, but they threatened to expel you, to hold you back a year—that's why I said you couldn't miss the first day of your senior year. I didn't want you to get held back on top of everything else." Mom takes a deep breath. "And I'm sorry for that, too. I was wrong to let the school scare me like that. I shouldn't have listened to them."

I've been so angry at her.

She was the reason I wasn't there when Nathan died.

But she was trying to do the right thing.

And she was trying to do the right thing when she sent me here, just like Randy said.

Just like I was trying to do the right thing when I broke my promise to Nathan.

And when I broke my promise to Eleanor.

Cass said that sometimes you have to break the promises you make to protect the people you love.

Mom says, "I should have let you take as much time as you needed instead of worrying that you'd fall behind. Dr. Prince said that people—consciously or unconsciously—believe grief will take a set amount of time, like they expect that after a month or two, things will go back to normal. But for the person who's grieving, there is no 'back to normal.'" She takes a deep breath. "Dr. Prince helped me understand that on some level, I was expecting your grief to *end*, waiting for it to be over. I didn't know I was doing it, but I was."

Softly, she asks, "Do you want to know the real reason I'm proud of you?"

I nod, and even though she can't see me, she must sense it, because she continues, "I'm proud because you knew how important being with your best friend was. Because you loved him so fiercely and fully. That kind of love, honey—to be able to love like that—it's a gift."

"But you always wanted me to have more friends. You hated how much time I spent at the Kaplans.'"

Mom sighs. "You're right. I was worried that with only one friend, you'd get lonely. And I was jealous—I wanted you home with me. Because the way you loved Nathan—with that fierceness, that fullness—that's the way I love you."

"I thought we didn't have anything in common," I explain. "I thought we had different ideas about everything—what was important, what was right, what was wrong."

"Well, we are very different people. And I know that's created a lot of strain between us." She takes a deep breath. "When you were little, strangers used to stop us on the street to tell me how similar we looked. They said you were my miniature, my clone, my doppelgänger. I guess it went to my head. I thought you'd grow up not just to look like me, but to *be* like me.

"Dr. Prince told me that at some point or another, every parent has to accept that their children aren't simply smaller, younger versions of them, aren't chances to relive their childhoods or their adolescences. That children are ours to guide but not to mold. He said that if we get too caught up in trying to mold them, we forget to guide them, and then we risk losing them."

I think about how Dr. Prince carried Eleanor to the van tonight: how gently he held her, how expertly he tied the sheet around her arm. I can't believe I ever thought the Princes were monsters. They're two doctors with very different approaches, trying their best to help the kids in their care.

Including me.

Mom cried at Nathan's funeral even though she barely knew him. I sat there dry-eyed, thinking that this was another thing we didn't have in common. I thought I would never be like my mother, would never collapse in—as Dr. Prince put it—a fit of grief. But tonight, I cried so hard I couldn't breathe. All this time refusing to say Nathan's name, even getting the tattoo—I thought I was being so reasonable, so careful. But maybe it was all one prolonged fit of grief.

"You haven't lost me," I say finally.

"I did for a while. But maybe I never should have thought of you as mine to lose instead of as your own person. But I'd like—I'd like for us to work together to find each other."

"Me too."

A phone rings. Not Randy's cell phone, but a landline phone. Randy opens the door to his bedroom—he went in there to give me some privacy while my mom and I talked—and picks up the phone from a small table on the corner.

"Hello?" he says. Then, "Okay. Okay, good." Pause. Then, "Yeah, everything's fine here. Yeah, she's fine." And last, "No, Mom hasn't called. Okay. Okay. See you then."

Randy hangs up the phone and looks at me. "Eleanor's stable," he says. "My dad's staying with her until her parents get there. Why don't you tell the other girls?"

I nod. "Mom, I've got to go. But I'll call you tomorrow, okay?"

"Okay."

# forty-five

In the morning, everyone is quiet on the way down to breakfast. Instead of Carol, Dr. Prince is there. He offers to answer any questions we have about Eleanor's condition, but beyond telling us that she's stable and that her parents are with her in the hospital, there's not much to say.

The sudden sound of high heels clicking on the stone floor in the hall outside the dining room startles us all, even Dr. Prince. Around here, there are a lot of slippers shuffling, maybe the squeak of sneakers' rubber soles and the occasional heavy *clomp* of winter boots. I can't remember ever having heard high heels. And then there's a woman standing in the doorway.

"Bert," she says. I guess Dr. Prince goes by Bert. "We need to talk."

I don't wonder for a second whether or not this is Dr. Maura Prince. She has Randy's exact coloring: the same freckles and curly red hair. But unlike Randy, she's short—hence the heels, I guess. Randy must have gotten his height from his father. I wonder if that's how he got into the habit of slouching, so he could look his mom in the eye.

Does she know that Randy was at Castle South a couple of weeks ago? Maybe her students told her they met him. I wonder if she's seen him or spoken to him since.

"Maura." Dr. Prince doesn't get up from the table. "As you can see, I'm working with my students at the moment. I'll call you later."

Unlike Dr. Prince—*our* Dr. Prince—Dr. Maura Prince's voice doesn't stay calm. "When would be a convenient time to discuss the fact that your negligence is going to cost us our schools?"

Now Dr. Prince does stand. So do I, and so do Cass and Raina. The girls who stay seated look poised to move, like we're all ready to spring to Dr. Prince's defense.

"Let's discuss this in the other room," Dr. Prince says calmly. He tells us he'll be right back, but I follow them anyway. My footsteps are barely audible over the sound of Maura Prince's, so maybe they don't notice, or maybe Dr. Prince knows he can't stop me.

"I can't believe you let this happen," Maura Prince says hotly as they walk down the hall toward the rooms where Dr. Prince and Randy live.

"As I understand it, it was several of your students who broke the lock."

"And you simply didn't *notice* that your girls were sneaking out every night?"

Dr. Prince opens the door and leads her though.

"Mom." I hear the surprise in Randy's voice. "What are you doing here?"

"Trying to clean up your father's mess."

"Dad's mess?" There's a hint of a challenge in Randy's voice.

"That girl's parents are threatening to sue," Maura Prince explains. She doesn't say hello or ask Randy how he's doing. "They could close our schools."

"I know," Dr. Prince says. He sounds tired, and I remember that he must have been up all night. I imagine him sinking onto the soft couch where I cried.

"Is that all you have to say?" Maura Prince speaks quickly. "We have to work together here. Hire attorneys, experts, former students to testify in our defense."

"We don't *have* to do any of that." The calmer Dr. Prince sounds, the more upset his ex-wife gets.

"They could close the schools, Bert," Maura Prince says again. "All the work we've done to create this place, to help these kids—"

"I know," Dr. Prince repeats.

"Don't you give a damn about the potential loss of our life's work? Then again," she continues, "you barely flinched when I told you I wanted a divorce."

Randy must decide that he's had enough, because he comes out into the hallway. He doesn't look surprised to see me standing here. He's wearing faded flannel pajama pants and a gray T-shirt. He hasn't even showered yet. He leans against the wall beside me.

"They always like this?" I whisper.

"This is actually one of their tamer fights." He smiles, and I smile back.

Inside the room, Dr. Prince says, "Maybe we *should* close, Maura, if we've been running our schools in a way that allowed this to happen."

"The girl hurt herself under *your* roof, Bert, not mine. She snuck out under *your* supervision."

"Yes, but where did she go? Neither you nor anyone on your staff noticed that twelve girls were spending each night on your property, in your common room."

"I can hardly blame the girls for preferring my approach to yours."

"An approach so permissive and unsupervised—"

"No more so than yours—"

"*We* put our students in danger, Maura," Dr. Prince says finally. His voice shakes the tiniest bit.

"No more danger than they were in back home," Maura Prince counters. "Isn't one of your girls a runaway? Is it any wonder she snuck out? Our students are troublemakers, Bert. That's why their parents send them here."

I consider telling Maura Prince that Reva never showed any interest in making a break for it.

"If you believe that, Maura, then it's all the more reason for us to keep a close eye on them. And you know that's not how I feel about my students."

Maura Prince sighs heavily. "So you're telling me that you're not going to fight this lawsuit? You're going to let this girl's parents win because you feel guilty about what happened to her?"

"Not because I feel guilty," Dr. Prince answers. "But if a judge rules that our schools aren't safe environments, I'll accept it."

"Well, I won't," his ex-wife says. I can hear her steps as she turns to leave. She steps into the hallway and stops in front of Randy and me.

"I suppose you agree with your father," she says.

Randy shrugs. "I'm not an expert like he is."

"I'm an expert, too."

Randy nods. "This is Moira," he says, gesturing to me. "She's a student here."

"Nice to meet you, Moira," Maura Prince says, but she keeps her eyes on her son. "If your father closes his school but I keep mine open, you could come live with me, you know. If you wanted to." There's hope in her voice. I think about my conversation with my mother last night.

"I know," Randy says. "But I'm going to college next year, so I won't be here much, anyhow."

"Of course, right." Maura Prince looks down at her dark leather shoes. "Well, I better get going. I have to find us an attorney."

"Right."

"I'll call you, let you know how it goes."

"Okay."

Their exchange isn't angry, exactly. It's more awkward, like a conversation between two people who used to know each other well but haven't spoken in years.

Randy's mother nods again and starts walking away. Once I can't hear her footsteps anymore, I say, "I didn't know you were going to college next year."

Randy smiles. "What, you think homeschooled kids can't take the SAT?"

"No, it's just—I didn't actually know what year you were in school."

"Yeah, my dad even wants to do some kind of graduation thing to celebrate. Even though it's just me."

"That's nice."

"I guess."

"Won't it be kind of strange, though? Being away at school after—" I pause.

"After I got kicked out of my last school and took classes all by myself for the last two years?"

"Well, yeah."

"Strange doesn't begin to cover it." Randy stretches his arms overhead. I can see a thin stripe of his skin between his T-shirt and pants. I wonder how he's not cold in just a T-shirt, then realize I'm not cold, either. Maybe I've gotten used to the temperature. Or maybe it's warmer than I realized. "But my dad and I agreed that I had to at least try."

I nod. "I guess I better go. The other girls will want to know what I overheard. And it seems like your dad is waiting for you in there." I start walking down the hall.

"Hey!" Randy calls out. "Aren't you a little bit curious about where I'm going to college?"

"Oh, yeah." I turn around. "Where?"

"Columbia." Randy grins.

"In Manhattan?"

"That's the one."

"That's where I live."

"I know."

"It'll be a kind of culture shock, you know—the big city after living out here." It occurs to me that *I* might be shocked by the noises, sounds, and smells when I got home. In the city, I never even would've noticed the music that lured us to Castle South in the first place.

Randy shrugs. "I'm looking forward to living someplace so big and so crowded that a freak like me won't stand out."

I regard Randy. The night we met, I thought his curly red hair looked almost like a clown's wig, that his freckles—some dark, some light—looked like tattoos. He was so tall and so thin that I thought he looked overgrown. Eleanor called him a creep for the way he kept to the corners here and for following us through the woods.

"You're not a freak," I say.

"Neither are you," he answers.

# forty-six

"It's not our usual day," I say when I'm alone in Dr. Prince's office that afternoon. "Or time," I add needlessly.

Dr. Prince shrugs; I think it's the first time I've ever seen him do so. He seems slumped, like the events of the last twenty-four hours have taken a toll on him. I wonder if they've done studies on posture and mood. I bet Dr. Prince would know.

"Your ex-wife is…" I pause, trying to think of a polite way to put it. Maybe he won't care if I'm polite. Finally, I say, "Different than I expected."

"Different?" Dr. Prince echoes. He's dressed in his usual tweed blazer, a sweater-vest, and brown slacks, but somehow the outfit looks less put-together than it usually does.

I nod. "I thought she'd be, like, hippie-dippy, the way she lets the boys wander around at all hours. But she seemed pretty intense."

"Would you describe your own mother as intense?"

I lean my head against the back of my chair. "You're really going to try to do therapy today?"

Dr. Prince smiles.

I ask, "When did you drop the 'for troubled girls' part of the school's name?"

"When Maura and I split the schools."

"Why?"

"She always thought the qualifier was necessary for clarity. I worried it might be stigmatizing, so once the school—*this* school, I should say—was mine alone, I changed the name."

I nod. We both know I'm only half interested. My focus is somewhere else, with *someone* else.

"What did the doctors say?" I ask finally, a familiar question. "I know you said she's stable and that her parents are with her, but how much blood did she lose? Will there be any permanent damage?"

"Moira, you know I can't discuss the details of Eleanor's condition with you."

"Yeah, but what if she, I don't know, damaged the muscles in her arm or something, and her hand will be paralyzed? It was her right arm, and she's a righty, so that would change her whole life."

Dr. Prince doesn't say anything.

"It's strange, you know, to worry about someone else," I say.

"Someone other than Nathan, you mean?"

I nod.

"Do you feel the way you described the other day, like you're cheating on him?"

"Kind of."

"When do you think you first felt that way?"

"I told you, when I kissed Randy. And then when I comforted Virginia about her breakup with Cass."

"Not before then?"

I shrug and look out the window.

"After Nathan died, why did you continue to cut class? You might have been able to catch up, graduate on time, even submit a college application or two."

"What was the point of worrying about grades and detentions once I had experienced bigger things—life-and-death things?"

Dr. Prince nods. "It's understandable that Nathan's illness shifted your priorities. But let me ask—if he had recovered, would you have gone back to class together? Would you still have hoped to attend college together?"

"Maybe. Probably."

"Even though you would have gone through such an enormous—as you say, life-and-death—thing together, you still would've cared about your future?"

I nod.

"So I ask you again: Why did you continue to cut class after Nathan died?"

I look from the window to my hands folded in my lap, my fingers twisted tightly around each other. Dr. Prince is right. Kissing Randy wasn't the first time I felt like I was cheating on Nathan.

"Because I didn't want to graduate without him," I whisper. "I didn't want to go to college without him. It would have been"—I pause to catch my breath—"*wrong* to do all the things we planned to do together alone."

The lump in my throat is growing, but instead of letting it choke me, I start to cry.

"Did you know that when your mother called me, she told me that she was scared you were going to hurt yourself?"

I nod, though I didn't know it before last night.

"Moira, I understand why it feels like cheating on him. Nathan *was* cheated. It's a terrible cheat that a person with all of that potential, with his whole life ahead of him, died so young. A terrible, terrible cheat that you lost someone who might have been your friend for your whole life."

"What if he wasn't?" I ask suddenly, wiping away my tears.

"What do you mean?"

I tuck my hair behind my ears. "What if we didn't get into colleges in the same town? What if we had a fight, or drifted apart the way some people do? Like, my mom used to tell me she wasn't still friends with her best friend from high school." I thought at the time that she was trying to convince me that Nathan wasn't as important as I insisted he was, but now I wonder if she was trying to comfort me. I think about Dr. Prince. Surely when he and his wife got married, they believed they'd be together forever, but their relationship fell apart.

Maybe Nathan and I would've taken our gap year after graduation to backpack through Europe and discovered that our friendship didn't work outside of New York City. Maybe we would've bickered our way across the continent, angry every time one of my library visits interfered with his one of his museum tours.

Maybe in college, he would've fallen in love with a girl who hated me, or maybe we would have fallen in love with each other and had a terrible breakup.

I'll never know, because Nathan is frozen in time, and so is our friendship. It froze while he was still angry at me.

It froze while we still loved each other in a strictly platonic way.

It froze when there was no one who could've come between us.

It froze at a time when I never considered that we'd ever be anything other than best friends.

All I wanted to do was hold on to that friendship exactly the way it was. But it probably would have changed one way or another if he'd lived.

"Even the dearest of relationships fall apart sometimes," Dr. Prince agrees. "It might have happened to you and Nathan. You'll never know what might have been, and there's nothing to be gained by guessing. We will quite literally *never* know. And Moira"—for once, I don't mind the way he says my name, slowly and heavily—"we can't keep the people we love alive by putting our own lives on hold. In fact, we can't put our lives on hold at all. Time marches on, even when we don't want it to.

"Over the past few months, you have moved forward, whether or not you meant to. You've made new friends; you've had an adventure Nathan couldn't join. And sometimes it felt like you were cheating on him, leaving him behind. And sometimes it felt like he was right by your side."

I take a deep breath. "I used to hear his voice in my head. For months, I could hear his commentary on everything I did, but lately… it's just silence. And I know you'll say that's a good thing, a sign that I'm moving on or whatever, but it feels like losing him all over again. Even the fact that I can talk about him now, that I can say his name—does that mean I don't miss him as much as I used to? That I'm not keeping him alive anymore?"

"Moira, you were never keeping him *alive*. You felt connected to him, but in doing so, you disconnected from everything else."

I don't feel like crying anymore. Now I feel like stamping my foot like a bratty little kid. "What's wrong with that, if I could still have him?"

"But you *can't* still have him. Whatever you do, you're doing something he'll never do. Wherever you go, you're going someplace he can't go."

"So I should just let him go. Isn't that what they say? *Let it go.*" The enormous wingback chair suddenly feels tight, as though the armrests could come to life and strap me in like a seat belt.

"No," Dr. Prince counters. "But instead of a voice in your head, one only you can hear, talk *about* him. Share memories of him with your *new* friends. And," he adds gently, "his voice isn't really gone. For the rest of your life, there will be moments when you'll hear him, when you'll know exactly what he would have said if he were standing beside you."

I drop my head and rub my fingers against my scalp in frustration. "So now you're saying I'll never get over losing him?"

"I'm saying that grief doesn't necessarily end, but it does

change. The pain shifts and lessens, becomes dull more often than it is sharp. I don't like terms like *moving on* or *getting over*. I prefer *moving forward*. Accepting Nathan's death doesn't mean letting him go, Moira. But accepting his death does mean letting yourself off the hook for being alive when he is not and allowing yourself to live in the world without him."

I look up. "What about Eleanor?"

"I'm sorry?"

"Should I let myself off the hook for what happened to Eleanor? If I hadn't told you she was planning to run, she wouldn't have hurt herself."

Dr. Prince tilts his head to the side the way he does when he's considering something. His son has the same habit. Finally, he says, "And if you'd told me that you were sneaking out weeks ago, perhaps she wouldn't have hurt herself. And if you'd told me about the broken lock the moment you discovered it, you might never have gone to Castle South to begin with, and Eleanor never would have met Henry and never would've wanted to run away."

I open my mouth to speak, but Dr. Prince keeps talking.

"And if I'd moved faster last night, I'd have been able to stop her from hurting herself. If I'd never instituted bedtimes, you might never have discovered the broken lock. If I'd thought to check all the locks on the windows more regularly...*if, if, if, if*. Do you see where I'm going with this?"

"That saying *if, if, if* all the time will just drive me crazy?"

Dr. Prince smiles, a real smile. He and Randy have the same gap between their bottom front teeth. "Saying *what if* never helped anyone. You can't undo the bad things that have happened. Pain cannot be avoided, but it can be accepted."

"So I should just be in pain forever—about Nathan, about Eleanor?"

"Of course not. But some psychologists believe that resisting pain is what drives the majority of our suffering. When something terrible happens, it's natural to fight it: *This shouldn't have happened! I wish I could go back in time, undo what I did.* But resisting that pain doesn't make it go away. We can't go back in time. We are better served by accepting what happened, allowing it to change us, and working with what is left.

"This is called *radical acceptance*. You cannot change the fact that Nathan got sick and died."

It's the fifth time Dr. Prince has said the word *died* today. "You're not big into euphemisms, huh?"

"What do you mean?"

"You don't say things like *Nathan passed* or *he went to heaven*."

Dr. Prince nods. "The words we use are very powerful," he explains. "Those other terms may sound gentler, and people use them with the best of intentions, but they can be misleading. Nathan is dead, and you cannot change that. Just as you cannot change the fact that Eleanor is sick and hurt herself."

I fold my legs beneath me, sit up a little straighter. "Well, if that's how you feel, then are you saying you don't think Eleanor can be helped? That she's destined to be sick and hurt herself forever? Is that what your ex-wife was talking about when she said you weren't going to fight to keep the schools open? Are you just *radically accepting* Eleanor's parents' lawsuit?" Maybe I don't want to *radically accept* that Nathan's gone.

Dr. Prince shakes his head. "Some circumstances can be changed with the right tools. The world is full of injustices that we must fight to change. And I'll be honest with you, Moira: I don't know if keeping the school open is the right thing to do after all that's happened. But to accept things is not to say they're okay. It is to say: *This is what is.*"

"You said that before. Like, I should just say *it is what it is* about my best friend's death. Didn't they teach you to be a little more sensitive than that in medical school?" I press my hands into my chair. The velvety fabric feels scratchy, not smooth, beneath my palms.

"I didn't say *it is what it is*," he corrects gently. "I said, *this is what is.*"

"What's the difference?"

"You're worried about your roommate. Allow yourself to feel that worry. You're grieving your best friend. Allow yourself to feel that grief. Trying to resist what has happened leads to further suffering. It doesn't mean that you're *okay* with the fact that Nathan is gone any more than denial means you *forgot* he died. But this is what is, what will be, no matter how hard you try to fight it."

"*This is what is,*" I echo. "It's not as simple as it sounds."

"It is incredibly difficult," Dr. Prince agrees, nodding. "It's a practice, like yoga or meditation. Honestly, I believe everything in life is a practice. I practice medicine, I practice parenting, I practice teaching, and I practice radical acceptance. Everything I hope to improve at, I practice. I'd be lying if I told you I always succeed at accepting what is, if I didn't admit that sometimes I feel myself resisting my present circumstances."

Dr. Prince blinks once, twice, and looks out the window. I wonder if he ever wishes that he and Maura Prince hadn't divorced. Or maybe that he hadn't let his ex-wife work with their son. Or that he'd stuck to studying neurology and had never became a teacher at all, never set eyes on the castles.

"So radical acceptance is really difficult, even for an expert like you?"

"Yes."

"But I should try anyway?"

"Yes."

Here goes:

Nathan is dead.

Eleanor is in the hospital.

Randy is moving to New York.

The Castle Schools—both of them—might be closed.

My mother and I are very different people.

*This is what is.*

The hurt, the grief, the anger, the fear, the excitement, the joy.

They are all what is.

Accepting that is probably the most radical thing I could do.

# *forty-seven*

About a week later (without visits to Castle South or updates from Eleanor, I lose track of the days, and surprisingly, I don't mind), I hear my roommate's voice, loud enough that I can make out what she's saying behind the closed door of our room from all the way down the hall.

"Mom! I can do it myself."

I consider turning around and hiding somewhere downstairs. Eleanor is surely still furious with me. She can't possibly want to see me.

But I want to see her.

When Nathan refused to see me, I suppose I could have barged into his hospital room. He was practically strapped to his bed with tubes and wires—he couldn't have stopped me. Maybe the hospital staff would have made me leave, but not before I got to see him, say something to him.

But I didn't even try. I thought I had no right to try to force him to forgive me—he was going through enough. And I believed, at the time, that I was in the wrong, that it was my fault he was in the hospital, the last place he wanted to be.

But today, *now*, I open the door.

A man I assume is Eleanor's dad is sitting on my bed while Eleanor uses her one good arm—her right arm is in a sling—to fill her suitcase. Eleanor's mother stands inches away from her, hands outstretched, like she's having a hard time stopping herself from folding her daughter's clothes for her.

"If you keep this up, we'll be here all day," her mother says. "Why don't you let me—" But Eleanor shifts so that she's standing between her mother and her suitcase.

"Maybe that's your plan?" Eleanor's father growls. "Keep us here long enough that we leave you alone so you can you sneak off to see that boy—"

"I'm not sneaking off." Eleanor's wavy hair falls across her face. She's even paler than usual; I can see that folding her clothes takes enormous effort. "And I can do this *myself*."

Eleanor's parents notice me hovering in the doorway. Mrs. Edwards crosses the room and holds out her hand. "You must be Moira." She smiles. "We're so grateful to you."

"Grateful?" I echo, and Eleanor snorts, though she doesn't look up from her folding.

"Haven't you heard, Moira? You saved my life."

I shake my head and pull my hand from her mother's grasp. "I didn't save her life."

"If it weren't for you, she'd have run away, and we might never have seen her again."

I step inside and sit on the edge of my bed. Her father jumps up. Half of our window is covered with plywood while it awaits repairs.

"You're leaving?" I say to my roommate's back as she slowly places a turtleneck, then a cardigan into her suitcase.

"Of *course* she's leaving," Mrs. Edwards answers. "And I'm sure your parents will want to come get you from this place as soon as they hear what happened."

Now Eleanor spins around. "It's not the Prince's fault," she says, and I'm surprised by the ferocity in her voice.

"Well, the place you're going specializes in girls with problems like yours," Mrs. Edwards continues. "No more of this new age nonsense." I swallow a laugh, remembering Dr. Prince's reaction when I called him new age in our first private session.

"Are you really suing the school?" I ask, and Eleanor's mother nods vigorously.

"Oh, yes. We can't in good conscience allow this place to remain open. Imagine if some other girl..." Eleanor's mother presses her fist to her mouth and shakes her head.

"If some other girl is actually helped by Dr. Prince's approach?" Eleanor asks, and when she turns around, I see that underneath her cardigan, she's wearing one of my T-shirts with a low V-neck. Her injured arm is bandaged tightly, held close to her chest by the sling.

"Could you give us a few minutes alone?" I ask Eleanor's

350

mom, who hesitates. "You can leave the door open," I add. "I just want to say goodbye. You'll be right outside." I don't mention that I was right outside when Eleanor hurt herself.

"Only for a minute," Mrs. Edwards agrees, and I think I see a hint of relief in her eyes. Maybe she needs a break from Eleanor's withering stares; maybe she's happy to let me bear the brunt of Eleanor's anger for a change. Is that how I looked at my mom after Nathan died? And for a long time before that?

When Eleanor and I have the room to ourselves, I say, "I know you must hate me."

"Yeah, well." Eleanor turns back to her clothes.

"Let me help with that," I offer.

"I can do it myself."

"I know you can," I say, but I cross the room and fold the rest of her clothes—the bulky sweaters, the long-sleeved shirts— and pile them neatly into her suitcase. Eleanor sits on her bed, kicks her duck boots against each other, then folds her legs up beneath her.

"They're sending me for inpatient treatment," she says. "In Boston. A place that won't release me at the end of the school year. I don't know how long they'll make me stay. There'll be locks on the doors, bars on the windows."

"This place has bars on the windows."

"You know what I mean."

I nod, remembering what Dr. Prince said about some applicants needing a more controlled environment. "I'm sorry."

"I thought they might let me come home." Eleanor sounds

351

almost as wistful as she did when she talked about running away with Henry. "But I was wrong."

"I think you scared them." She shrugs, the motion lopsided with her right arm in the sling. "You scared me," I continue. "I'd never seen that much blood."

"People get too freaked out by blood. What's the big deal? We all have it."

"Yeah, but most of us try to keep as much of it as possible *inside* of us." Eleanor almost smiles. "Maybe that place they're sending you... maybe it'll be good for you."

"*This* place was good for me."

I nod. "I know. But maybe the people there will be able to see how much progress you've already made."

"You mean up until I smashed a window?"

"Did you smash it because you were trying to hurt yourself or because you were scared of being trapped here?"

Eleanor hesitates. "I'm not actually sure. They're kind of the same thing for me. Sometimes I think I started cutting because I felt trapped in my skin, you know?"

I shake my head. There were times when I saw one of Eleanor's scars and thought it was kind of like me getting my tattoo—it hurt, but it was also a relief. But I could never have done what she did to herself the other night. I didn't get my tattoo *because* it hurt.

"I don't know," I answer finally. "I mean, I know about feeling stuck and trapped. But not about wanting to hurt myself."

"Most people don't. Most people think there are easier ways to ask for help than cutting their skin."

"Is that why you do it? It's your way of asking for help?"

"That's what the shrink at the hospital said. That instead of telling the people around me that I'm in pain—you know, *emotional* pain—and asking for help, cutting myself is a way of *showing* them that I'm in pain. Which, I'm sorry, makes absolutely no sense, because I always hid it from everyone, but my parents seemed to think she knew what she was talking about. Not that they actually tried talking about it with *me*—they were too busy calling an attorney to sue Dr. Prince—but whatever."

I think about the way Eleanor started wearing short sleeves and V-necks over the past few months. She believed it was the magic of Castle South, but maybe she was trying to show us—Henry, Dr. Prince, me—her scars because she felt like she could let us see all that pain. Maybe she trusted us in a way she'd never trusted her family, her previous doctors or friends. Like how Raina confided in group therapy a story she'd never told her friends and family back home. Is that what Dr. Prince meant in his brochure when he talked about creating an environment for girls to bond and feel safe?

"Maybe the girls at the new place will understand, even if your parents don't."

"They don't encourage you to make friends at inpatient."

"How do you know that?"

"Alice told me, from when she was in some special ED place. The doctors think it distracts from your own healing when you get too invested in other people."

"Maybe wherever you're going won't be like that," I offer, and

Eleanor shrugs her lopsided shrug again. "Dr. Prince wanted us to make friends."

"All the more reason to think they won't want me to make friends wherever they're sending me next. My parents wanted to find a place as different from here as humanly possible."

I recall that Daniel said once, in between dances, that he didn't come here to make friends, but it's not like there was anything else to do. I think Dr. Prince—well, *our* Dr. Prince here at Castle North, at least—made it that way on purpose.

I think about the girls at my old school who offered me their condolences after Nathan died. Was I wrong to reject them, to judge them as fake, because they'd been unfriendly in middle school? Were they trying to offer me their friendship? Will I be better at recognizing when people do that now?

"Will you and Henry be able to stay in touch?" I ask finally.

"My parents don't want us to."

"Yeah, but—texting, email, whatever. You'll be able to keep in touch somehow, right?"

Eleanor fingers the tips of her hair. "Yeah. They can't stop us. Not forever, anyway."

She doesn't sound panicked, like an addict looking for her next fix, the way she did a few nights ago.

I never knew how to *be*, how to *girl*, without Nathan. Even before he died, going to school without him by my side, whether it was because he was home with a cold or recovering from his latest round of treatments, made me nervous.

Maybe I'll always feel just slightly out of step with everyone.

Who else looks up trivia for fun? Does anyone else dream about libraries instead of adventures when she imagines backpacking through Europe? Maybe I'll never meet anyone else with whom I feel quite as in sync as I did with Nathan. But now I know that there are people who will be my friends, even when I'm out of step.

At least, I hope so.

"What about me?" I ask softly. "Will you stay in touch with me?"

"You think I want to talk to the girl who got me sent off to inpatient? Who kept me from Henry?"

"I'm sorry." I take a deep breath. "I'm so, so sorry you got hurt. But I'm not sorry I kept you from running away. I was scared of what would happen to you."

"You and my parents think I'm some kind of helpless baby, don't you?" She picks at her jeans, and I see a small scar on the tip of her left pointer finger, not much bigger than a pinprick.

I shake my head fiercely. "That's not what I think at all."

I don't know how to explain that I think she's brave to have been ready to go out into the world on her own, to have loved Henry so completely. But I also think she isn't *ready* to be out there on her own. I'm also worried about what might have happened, how badly she could still be hurt.

Nathan would have understood without my having to say a word. Nathan always understood everything about me.

And then something occurs to me: If Nathan always understood me, he also understood why I told his mother he fell, why I wouldn't cover for him to keep him out of the hospital. He might have been angry that he was taken from his home, but that doesn't necessarily mean he was angry at *me*.

Maybe *anger* isn't the reason he wouldn't let me see him in the end.

But then, why?

My soon-to-be-former roommate zips her suitcase shut, bringing me back to the present.

"*I'm* going to keep in touch," I say. "Give me your phone number. I'll text you, once I have my phone back."

She rolls her eyes at me like she's never met anyone so naive. "Yeah, but I probably still won't have my phone. It might be weeks or months before I get any of your messages."

"Will that stop Henry?" I ask.

"Of course not," Eleanor snaps.

"Well, it's not going to stop me, either. And I know you might not want to write back at first. Maybe not for a long time. But I'll wait until you're ready."

"Until I'm ready for what?"

"Ready to be my friend again."

It feels strange to say the words *my friend* out loud and have them not be about Nathan. Strange, but not bad.

From the doorway, Eleanor's mother clears her throat. "Eleanor," she says, "it's time to go."

Eleanor uses her good arm to slide her suitcase onto the floor. The bag thumps against the scratchy carpet, and she bends to pick it up.

"Well," she says, "have a good life, Moira."

"You too."

She turns to the door, dragging her suitcase behind her. She doesn't look back, but something in me is certain that this won't be the last time I see her.

Maybe two people can't share an adventure like ours and never see each other again.

# *forty-eight*

I head up the familiar stairs, open the heavy wooden door, sit in the soft wingback chair.

"So," Dr. Prince begins, "our last session."

I nod. It's been weeks since Eleanor left, and my parents are coming to pick me up tomorrow.

This may be one of Dr. Prince's last sessions ever—at least, here in this room, in the Castle.

"How's the lawsuit going?" Randy's mom stormed in this morning to say that she'd been served with papers, so I assume Dr. Prince has, too. "Do you think you'll have to close?"

"We might. But perhaps it's time to move on."

"I thought you didn't believe in that expression."

Dr. Prince smiles, the real thing. "You're right, Moira. Move forward."

I sink into my chair. All the things I thought were creepy

about Dr. Prince—the smile that didn't reach his eyes; his perfect posture; the way he speaks so slowly, enunciating even his contractions; his refusal to talk about Randy or the other castle—now I think they were all his way of being a blank slate. He was letting me set the tone for our therapy. I didn't exactly set the most optimistic of tones, and some days I barely engaged at all, but he knew—at least, I think he knew—that if he pressed me too soon, I'd close off completely. He was waiting for me to open up, however long it took.

He was being a good therapist.

"When did this chair get so comfortable?" I ask.

"Perhaps you simply got used to it."

The chair isn't the only thing. I've gotten used to the sound of the other girls in the hall outside my room each morning. To eating breakfast at a table full of chatter. To talking with Dr. Prince every other day.

By comparison, my apartment back in New York will be terribly quiet, the opposite of the culture shock I warned Randy about.

I tuck my hair behind my ears, finger the spot on my neck where I know there's a tiny white scar on Eleanor's. "I'm nervous," I begin, "about going home."

"It'll be a big change."

"Shouldn't it feel like going back to normal?"

"The word *normal* can be problematic."

"Okay, well, going back to the way things were before, then."

"Do you want to go back to the way things were before?"

I consider it. My mother's shouts, and my long silences. Sneaking out to visit Nathan's grave. Avoiding eye contact with the other girls at school.

And before that—cutting class to visit Nathan in the hospital, sleeping on the uncomfortable chair next to his bed.

And before that—meals at Nathan's apartment, the two of us doing our homework together, arguing with Mom about spending Thanksgiving (or Hanukkah, or Passover, or New Year's Eve) with Nathan's family instead of mine.

And before that—arguing with Dad at the dinner table, spilling flour when Mom and I baked together, squirming out of her lap, wiping her lipstick off my cheek when she kissed me.

Finally, I answer, "That's a trick question."

"Oh?"

"You want me to say that there is no going back to the way things were before. That's what *was*, not what *is*."

Dr. Prince smiles again. "Very good, Moira."

I don't know how things will be between my mother and me now. We've talked on the phone a few times since the night Eleanor got hurt, and we're always polite. Careful.

"I was angry at her for a long time," I say. "My mom."

"Are you angry at her still?"

I remember the sound of her voice when she answered the phone the night Eleanor hurt herself. She was scared. "I don't know."

He nods. "Almost all parents try their best, and every single parent still makes terrible mistakes."

"So I have to forgive her because she was trying her best?" I think of how weightless I felt when I danced at Castle South. I always thought it was missing Nathan that was holding me down. But maybe it was my anger, like a weight strapped around my belly.

And not just anger at my mother. Anger at myself, because I believed it was my fault Nathan had died in the hospital. At cancer, for invading my best friend's body and turning it toxic. At science, for not being able to cure him. At the doctors, for not being able to ease his pain. At my classmates, who lived through the day Nathan died without knowing the world had changed forever. At my teachers, for thinking I should still care about grades and college applications afterward.

At Nathan, for leaving me all alone.

Dr. Prince shakes his head. "You don't *have* to do anything. But forgiveness certainly might go a long way toward repairing your relationship. As they say, resentment is a poison you drink and wait for the other person to die."

I laugh, and Dr. Prince continues, "But there's a choice other than forgiveness."

"I can stay angry?"

"You can accept what happened, accept the decisions your mother made, accept *her*—flaws and mistakes and all."

"This is radical acceptance, too?" Dr. Prince nods, and I sigh heavily. "Isn't it enough that I have to accept that my best friend died?"

In the last days before Nathan died, he was on a lot of

painkillers. His mother told me that he was drifting in and out of consciousness, never entirely aware of what was happening.

But his mother also told me that he didn't want to see me. How did she know if he was so out of it?

Maybe, even if I'd gone to the hospital the morning before Nathan died, *his* mother would have kept me from him, because according to her, he didn't want me to come inside. Even when he was so medicated that he might not have known I was there.

And suddenly, *finally*, I understand.

Nathan didn't want me to see him like that.

He must have made his mother promise—maybe the day he got admitted to the hospital for the last time, or maybe weeks or months before that—that once it was clear the end was coming, she wouldn't let me in.

He didn't want me to see him die.

In fact, even if he'd been at home—if everything had gone to plan, with home care and hospice and all the rest—maybe I still would have been kept out of his room. In all of our discussions about his end-of-life plan, we never actually talked about where *I* would be at the end.

Nathan made a decision all on his own, without me: he didn't want his best friend to see him breathe his last breath. He didn't want me walking around with a picture of his death in my head for the rest of my life.

I thought I knew everything about him. But it's taken me so long to understand *this*.

Nathan was trying to do the right thing by keeping me away.

Just like Cass was when she broke up with Virginia. Just like my mom was when she sent me here. Just like I was when I told Dr. Prince about Eleanor and Henry. When I told Nathan's mother that he'd fallen.

Who's to say what was right? Would it have been better if I'd had a chance to say goodbye, or was it actually better for me this way? I'll never know.

Maybe there is no better, no right thing. Maybe there's only the effort of trying to get it right.

"Did I ever tell you that this wasn't the tattoo I wanted?" I gesture to my upper left arm.

Dr. Prince shakes his head.

"I wanted a ring around my left pointer finger. I wanted a line from my finger to my heart. My grandmother told me that's why she wore her wedding band on this finger." I hold up my left hand and point.

"Why did you want to mimic a wedding band?"

"I wanted to show that someone had made his way into my heart once."

"You were scared you would forget?"

I shake my head. "I could never forget."

"Perhaps you wanted to show the world that your heart was closed."

"What do you mean?"

"In some respects, that's what a wedding band is for. To show the world that you're taken."

I consider the way I felt not just kissing Randy but comforting

Virginia. "I guess I thought I owed that kind of allegiance to Nathan." I pause, tasting his name. "I know it's stupid. We weren't married. We weren't even in love."

"Maybe you were, in a way."

I nod and stare out the window in the silence that follows. Eventually, Dr. Prince says, "A lot of people have trouble taking their wedding rings off after their husbands or wives die. Some people never stop wearing them."

"Are those people alone forever?"

"Perhaps. Perhaps they remain devoted to a life that doesn't exist anymore."

"Acceptance again?" I ask.

"Yes, Moira, acceptance again."

My eyelids feel heavy, like I could sleep for a thousand years. "I'm so tired."

"Tired of what?"

Of missing my best friend.

Of being angry at my mother.

Of wondering if I did the right thing.

Finally I say, "I'm tired of fighting against what is." I let my hair fall across my face, then tuck it behind my ears. "I'm going to miss these girls. I'm going to miss Randy. I lost my only friend, and now I'm losing the only other friends I've ever had."

"You won't lose them," Dr. Prince begins, but I wave his trite response away.

"You know what I mean. I saw Nathan every day, and then I didn't. I saw these girls every day, and now I won't."

Dr. Prince nods. "It will be an adjustment."

"Is missing them not accepting what is?" Another F to add to my transcript: failure at radical acceptance.

"Of course not. We miss the people we care about when they're not with us. Accepting their absence doesn't mean we don't have feelings about it."

I press my feet to the floor and sit up every bit as straight as Dr. Prince.

"So, this is what is," I begin. "I'm going to miss Nathan every day for the rest of my life. And some days it'll hurt so much I can't stand it, and some days it'll just be a dull ache, but it will probably always be there."

"What else?"

"I'm going to feel like I'm leaving him behind, like I'm cheating on him, when I have new experiences without him, because he *did* get cheated by having such a short life, like you said."

"What else?"

"I'll never know if we would have stayed friends forever or if we would have grown apart."

"What else?"

"I'm not to blame for the way he died." I feel tears spring to my eyes, but I don't brush them away, and I don't feel like I'm choking.

"I'm going to have to repeat my senior year of high school. Eleanor isn't returning my emails"—Dr. Prince granted me internet privileges a couple weeks ago, and he gave me Eleanor's email address—"and I don't know if it's because she isn't getting them or because she's still angry at me. My mother and I won't always see eye to eye."

"What else?"

"I'll miss Eleanor, and Randy, and Virginia, and Cass…"

"Yes."

I feel myself begin to slouch just a little bit. "And you're saying there's nothing I can do about any of this but accept it?"

"Acceptance *is* doing something about it."

"But *how* do I accept it?"

"You talk about it. With me. With your mother. With your therapist back home—I've already referred you to someone. Acknowledging is the first step toward accepting."

"So that I can move not on, but forward."

"Indeed."

# *forty-nine*

"Let's take a walk."

I look up from the book I'm supposed to be reading for Shelly's last "class" to find Randy standing above me. He's wearing jeans and a hoodie, along with his ever-present sneakers.

I'm sitting on the couch in the drawing room; Cass is leaning against the armrest beside me, her feet tucked under my thigh to keep warm, though it's not actually that cold in here today. She raises an eyebrow at me, but she doesn't say anything as I get up and follow Randy outside.

It's late May. Now that I have internet access, it's easier to keep track of the days, though I haven't been paying very close attention. I guess Dr. Prince would say that's progress, not needing to know the date and time to feel oriented. I could counter that it's still a good idea to have a general idea of the date and time so you don't end up wearing a bikini in February or sleeping all day and staying awake all night, but maybe he'd say that people should *radically accept* the weather and their circadian rhythms.

Or maybe he'd say people should sleep when they're tired, wake up when they're rested, and wear what feels comfortable. After all, whether or not I knew it was February, I wouldn't wear a bikini in the cold.

Anyhow, it's May, and it feels like spring. The afternoon sunlight is bright between the trees, the leaves casting shadows as we walk into the woods. There's no snow on the ground, no ice to slip on, though the leaves at our feet—left to pile up over years and years of autumns—are wet and slick after last night's rain.

"Isn't it supposed to be *April* showers?" I ask as I lose my footing for what seems like the hundredth time. Randy reaches out to steady me, and I feel the warmth of his fingers through my clothes. I'm not wearing a jacket or coat. It's warmer outside than it was inside the castle. I take off my sweatshirt and tie it around my waist.

"There." Randy points at a patch of ground a few feet from us. "Some May flowers."

"Crocuses," I say. "They bloom in spring." In New York, south of here, they'll have already bloomed and died.

"Surprised a city girl knows that."

I don't tell Randy that I saw crocuses blooming in a tiny community garden a few blocks from my apartment last spring and looked them up online, which led to a research rabbit hole about which flowers bloom in spring, in summer, in fall, about perennials and annuals and which plants thrive in sunlight or shade.

"Actually," Randy continues, "did you know there are flowers that bloom all through the winter? Snowdrops—I passed them so many times when I was running that I finally had to look up what they were."

"You looked it up?" I echo, smiling shyly.

"Sure," Randy says. "What do you do when you're curious about something?" He reaches out to steady me again as I slip on another patch of leaves and laughs. "Jeez, how did you make it back and forth all those nights without hurting yourself?"

I laugh, too, but the truth is—I usually leaned on Eleanor.

"Isn't this against the rules?" The question has become a running joke between us.

"Which part?" Randy counts off our current violations on his fingers. "We're alone together. You're out of the castle without permission. You're wandering through the woods."

"Not wandering," I correct. There's nothing aimless about this walk. I know exactly where Randy is taking me.

Randy nods in agreement, and we walk in silence until there it is: Castle South. We stop about as far from it as Eleanor and I were that first night when we saw the lights in the distance, the open door.

Today, the door is open again, and a few boys are in the driveway outside, tossing a football between them.

"Do you want to go inside?" Randy asks.

"Do you?"

Randy shrugs. "Only if you do."

"Have you and your mom talked since she last came to Castle North?"

"We text. You know—*how are you, I'm good, me too*—that kind of thing. Nothing important."

"Do you think you'll ever be close?"

"Close?" Randy echoes. "I don't know. Right now we're just working on getting along, you know?"

I nod. "My mom and I are working on that, too." Even after all of our polite phone conversations these past few weeks, I can't imagine that my mother and I will stop arguing entirely. We're too different, or maybe we're too similar. But there's one thing I'm certain of: things between us feel different than they did before.

The first time I saw Castle South, I thought it looked so different from the castle my parents had sent me to. I thought the moonlight hit this place differently, thought the woods here weren't nearly as thick, thought the air was warmer. Eleanor thought there was something magical about this place; I thought there was something sinister.

Either way, I was certain there was something *off* about it. I believed it was the *place* that made the burden of missing Nathan, of being angry at my mother, a little bit lighter. I believed that if I felt better, it wasn't *progress*, but the result of some elaborate, cruel trick played on me by two unethical doctors.

But now, Castle South merely looks like a copy of Castle North. It wasn't magic. It wasn't a trick. It was a distraction.

Dr. Prince would say that distracting myself from Nathan's death was another way of denying it. That even though the lump in my throat was smaller when I danced the nights away at Castle South, I still hadn't accepted what had happened. Here, I referred to Nathan, to his favorite song, in the present tense. Here, where no one knew Nathan, I could pretend he had never died.

When I emailed Eleanor this morning, I told her the real reason why my parents sent me to the Castle School. I thought it might be easy because I wouldn't have to say it out loud, because she might never receive my email or might refuse to read it. Much to my surprise, it was just as hard to type the words *my best friend died* as it was to say them.

But just a few months ago, I couldn't do either.

I remember a line from the brochure: *At Castle, we believe that something magical happens when young people are given a safe space in which to build a community and the freedom to share their problems without judgment.*

Maybe there is such a thing as magic after all. Just not the kind of magic Eleanor had in mind.

I look up at the windows of Castle South, wondering where exactly Daniel is, and Henry, and Dr. Maura Prince. It's hard to believe that I really climbed down from a second-floor window in the middle of the night, that I snuck through the woods in the ice and snow and slush night after night. What were we thinking? How did we go so long without getting caught? Why did we keep coming back here night after night for so long?

Castle South wasn't only a distraction from Nathan another

way of denying that he was gone. It was also an adventure I had without him—an adventure I would never have had *with* him. And not only because my parents wouldn't have sent me here if Nathan had lived, but also because Nathan and I weren't the sort of friends who would have scaled a building together. We sat inside and studied. Even when we planned to backpack across Europe, our dream was to go from museum to museum and library to library.

Maybe Dr. Prince and my mother are right: Nathan made my world smaller. That wasn't necessarily a bad thing—I was happy in our little world together—but now that he's gone, I have to let more of the big world in. Maybe without Nathan, I'm more adventurous. The first night Eleanor and I stepped inside Castle South, I thought, *The worst thing that's ever going to happen to me has already happened; no need to be cautious.* But even before that night, I was taking risks I'd never taken when Nathan was alive: I lied about my age to get a tattoo; I took two subways and walked a mile to visit a cemetery in the middle of the night. I thought I was doing those things because nothing else mattered to me. But maybe I was seeking out new adventures even then.

"Can you believe some rich idiot actually built *two* of these places a hundred years ago?" Randy asks, breaking the silence.

"Your parents bought them," I point out.

"I never said they weren't idiots, too."

I smile. "Where do you think your dad will go if they close the school?"

Randy shrugs. "He said something about setting up a private

practice somewhere. You know, in a town or city where patients would have easy access to him."

"Patients," I echo. "He always insisted on calling us his students."

Randy nods. "He considers himself a teacher first."

"He's a good teacher," I say. "He explains things without making it seem like he's lecturing."

"I know," Randy agrees. "It's impossible to have an argument with him. He never raises his voice, just tries to understand where everyone else is coming from. It drove my mom crazy. Sometimes it drives *me* crazy."

I smile, thinking of the way my mother used to yell at me, the way Randy's mother stormed into Castle North and then out again.

"Like when?" I ask.

"Huh?"

"When does it drive you crazy, the way your dad argues?"

"Like when he says I shouldn't get involved with one of his students. When he tells me it's not entirely ethical and that it puts him in a difficult position."

"I'm not going to be his student for very much longer," I point out.

Randy grins. "How do you think I got his permission to take you on a walk?"

"Wait, so we're not even breaking the rules right now? This is a totally sanctioned activity?"

"Totally sanctioned."

"Aw, man." I feign disappointment. "I think it's the first time we've been together without breaking any rules."

It's so warm that I feel sweat on the back of my neck. The night I arrived at the Castle School, I thought I'd never feel warm again. I couldn't imagine the school in bright sunlight with flowers blooming at my feet.

Randy offers me his hand on the walk back, and I take it. "Can't have you slipping and falling," he says. "That's definitely against Dad's rules."

If Nathan heard that, he'd laugh out loud and point out that Randy's not holding my hand because he's worried about my safety. And Eleanor would sigh wistfully; she never particularly liked Randy, but she's a sucker for romance. I smile.

As we walk, Randy rubs his thumb back and forth across my knuckles. I squeeze his fingers in return.

# MOIRA

Moira liked to finish things.

Finished that homework assignment. *Check.*

Cleaned her room. *Check.*

Took the SAT. *Check.*

At least, she thought, her friendship with Nathan would have a precise end date, a day when it was finished, complete, kaput.

*Check.*

When Moira was told that her best friend had died, she didn't cry or shout, but she was certain her heart stopped beating. She silently focused on the sensation of her blood coming to a standstill in her veins.

Her blood, she didn't doubt, was turning into a viscous sludge, sticking like gum to her veins and arteries. Should she happen to fall on something sharp, or step on broken glass, or let a knife slip between her fingers, she was sure the blood that seeped out from beneath her skin would have the consistency and color of hot fudge.

Much to Moira's surprise, her relationship with Nathan didn't end when he died. It became more one-sided, perhaps, but it continued. *Dead*, Moira discovered, wasn't the same thing as *gone*. You could still visit dead people: Visit their graves. You could still talk to them: Talk to your ceiling at night as though the room weren't empty. You could feel them upon your skin: Get a tattoo to mark the time you'd spent together. You could still smell them, still pick up the phone to call them, still love them every bit as much as you had when they were alive.

*It's a lie*, she thought, *when people say* loved *in the past tense.*

Moira hadn't known that there was a type of crying that didn't involve tears or hiccupped breaths. There was a type of crying that happened on the inside, in your chest, underneath your heart, that rose up into your throat until it choked you. A type of crying that could happen constantly as you went about your day: went to school (or didn't), did your homework (or not), visited your best friend's grave (which you now referred to as visiting your best friend), ate (or skipped) your dinner, went to sleep (or lay awake all night). There was a type of crying that was invisible, that happened beneath the surface.

Drinking water pushed the lump in her throat down deeper, back into her chest. But each gulp was only a momentary relief. The lump always came back, stronger than before.

Moira never knew that her parents were aware of how much time she spent at Nathan's grave. Never knew that her mother stayed up at night, listening to the sound of her daughter's one-sided conversations. Never knew that her mother watched carefully to see how much weight Moira had lost and listened for the click of her daughter's key in the door on the nights when she stayed late at Nathan's grave, so late that the city was asleep by the time she got home. They fought, her mother's shouts so loud that one night, the neighbors called the police.

*Don't stay out so late, Moira.*

*Eat something, Moira.*

*Stop cutting class, Moira.*

When she got her tattoo, Moira's blood was bright red. The brightness of it surprised her, and Moira thought that maybe it was only when the needle touched her arm that her heart started beating again.

*If my mother knew*, she thought, *that getting the tattoo jump-started my heart like cables attached to a car battery, maybe she wouldn't have screamed when she saw it. Maybe she would have been comforted by it.*

Moira didn't know that when her mother screamed upon seeing her tattoo, it wasn't only the arrow that made her yell but also her daughter's face: dark circles under her eyes, skin two shades too pale.

Moira would have been utterly surprised by the catalogs from the Castle School, had she paid enough attention to know what they were. She would have been surprised to hear her mother on the phone with Dr. Prince, the choked sound of *her* voice as she cried without tears, a lump lodged in *her* throat.

Moira would have been surprised to discover that she and her mother could cry in exactly the same way.

# *fifty*

My bag feels lighter than it did when I got here. I think of the shirts I folded for Eleanor—a few of my T-shirts were mixed in with her long sleeves and turtlenecks. I don't mind.

I head downstairs to the dining room. Carol is at the head of the table, distributing the items she confiscated on our first days. She hands me my phone, the battery completely dead. I slip it in my backpack.

Only eight girls are sitting at the table.

"Where's Cass?" I ask.

Virginia answers. "Her parents picked her up first thing this morning. And a bus came to take Halsey and Beth to the airport already."

I nod. No one asks where Eleanor is, of course.

I wonder what we'll remember about this place a year from

now. Will we remember the drafty hall, the wood-paneled dining room, the ugly fluorescent lights?

Two years from now, will I remember the stone floor beneath the carpet in my room?

Twenty years from now, will I remember that this is where I learned the word *wainscoting*?

And what will we remember about Castle South? Will we remember the thrill of sneaking out for the first time? Will we look back and shake our heads at how dangerous it was, climbing down those metal bars in the dark? Will we remember how Castle South seemed so much warmer and brighter than our school, at least at first?

Perhaps we'll only remember a boys' school where we went to dance that year our parents sent us to that special school to ride out our rough patches.

◇◇◇◇

I stand in the driveway outside the Castle. The van Randy drove me here in—the one Dr. Prince drove Eleanor to the hospital in—is parked a few feet away. I wonder if the upholstery inside is stained with Eleanor's blood.

When Nathan was first diagnosed, it wasn't all doom and gloom. We both knew people who'd had cancer—my great-aunt, Nathan's family friend—people who'd had treatment and got better. We thought it would be like that—a lost year, maybe, or a few years. It would be awful, we agreed. He'd lose his hair, throw up, hurt, be sick. But we didn't consider at first that he might die. That he was going to die.

A silver SUV comes up the drive. My father is behind the wheel, my mother in the passenger seat, struggling to fold a map. We're so far off the grid here that GPS must not be of much use.

My father hasn't even turned the engine off before my mother gets out of the car and runs to me. She throws her arms around me. I can't remember the last time she hugged me like this. She smells like vanilla.

"I think you've grown. Honey"—she lets go of me and turns to my father, now making his way toward us—"don't you think she's grown?"

"Mom, I stopped growing ages ago."

She shakes her head and looks at me carefully. I saw this expression on her face at Nathan's funeral. I sat up front with his family, but I turned around a few times to look at my parents in the back.

"Hey, Mom," I say. "Thanks for the strawberry shortcake."

"What? Oh, honey, I'm sorry, I didn't make any. I'll bake you one as soon as we get home."

"No, I mean the one you brought to Nathan's shiva. Thank you for doing that. It meant a lot to me."

Mom blinks, and I think she's going to cry, but instead she asks, "Where are your things?"

I gesture in the direction of the Castle behind me. My mother looks up, inhaling sharply as she takes in the stone walls, the turret where Dr. Prince's office is, the eaves hanging over the uppermost windows.

"Ooh," she breathes. "A real castle."

My parents follow me inside. Those of us who haven't left yet are scattered about; I can hear Alice and Reva laughing as we pass the dining room.

Dr. Prince and Carol are in the drawing room, where they've spent the morning greeting parents and wishing students well. Dr. Prince shakes my father's hand with a firm grip, placing his other hand above my father's elbow like a politician.

My parents follow me upstairs. Shelly walks down the hallway toward us, glancing into the bedrooms, still running checks. I smile at her as she passes us, the scent of stale cigarettes coming from her sweater.

"Goodbye, Shelly," I say. "Thank you for everything."

"Best of luck, Moira." She holds out her hand for me to shake. Her grip is soft, gentle. She smiles without showing her teeth and then walks past, nodding at my parents.

Ahead of us, Raina is hugging a slightly smaller carbon copy of herself; her sister, I guess. She sees me and holds up her phone. I nod. "I'll text you," I say. I haven't been able to program any of my new friends' numbers into my phone—dead battery— but we all shared our numbers on paper last night, saying our goodbyes early since we knew we might not have time today. It didn't feel like betraying Nathan, writing down my number and hoping to hear from these girls. In fact, I think Nathan would like my new friends.

There are hundreds—thousands—of books, essays, articles, movies, quotes, and platitudes about grief. Everyone knows it has five stages, although Dr. Prince told me most therapists now believe that grief actually exists on a continuum, that it's not a set of stages a person can work through and "get over."

Grief is often compared to other, more common—maybe more manageable—emotions: fear, anger, sadness, denial. While Nathan was sick, I had lots of time to anticipate grief. But nothing could have prepared me for just how *strange* it turned out to be. A person is there, and then they're not there. Maybe it's someone you've known your whole life—a parent, a grandparent. You literally haven't ever been on the planet without them, and then suddenly, they leave you. Or maybe it's someone you barely knew, or a celebrity you admired.

Or maybe it's someone you've talked to every single day for years.

And maybe you've forgotten how to *be* without that person. Maybe you don't entirely believe that you *can* be without that person.

Your brain knows they're gone, but it takes a while for your emotions to catch up. You can still hear their voice, still worry about hurting their feelings, disappointing them, letting them down. You still love them.

And I'm not sure any of that will ever go away, not entirely. But I'm getting used to it. It's becoming a part of my life—but just a *part*, not my *whole* life.

I slide my suitcase off my bed and drag it down the stairs, through the hall, and down the driveway toward my parents' rented SUV.

"Hey," a voice says, and I turn around. "You weren't going to leave without saying goodbye to me, were you?"

I grin at Randy and introduce him to my parents. It's breezy and foggy—maybe fifty or sixty degrees—but Randy's wearing shorts and a T-shirt, obviously about to go for a run. My mother looks confused—*this place is all girls, isn't it?*—but she doesn't protest when I say I'll be right back. Randy and I follow the curve of the driveway until we're out of sight.

He holds up his phone. "Put your number in." When he hands the phone to me, our fingertips touch, and I feel a rush of butterflies in my belly. Randy doesn't feel like home the way Nathan did. Randy feels like someplace new. Someplace I'm curious to visit.

"You'll be my first call when I get to New York," he promises. I can feel his breath when he talks. I think for a second that he's going to kiss me, but instead he folds me into a warm, tight hug. "See ya," he says.

"See ya," I echo, and I watch him run off into the woods for the last time.

My father huffs and puffs as he lifts my suitcase into the car. I smile, remembering how easily Randy lifted it my first night here.

My father fits my bag between two others in the trunk. "What are those?" I ask.

"Our bags," my mom says. "We thought we might drive over to the coast. Stay at one of those pretty little inns on the beach. You know—Maine, lobster, hiking. That kind of thing."

"That sounds really nice." Mom gives me another squeeze

384

before I climb into the back seat. She keeps her eye on me in the rearview mirror, but I don't mind.

Before we pull away, Mom looks up at the Castle, eyeing the turret and the etched glass windows. "This place really is straight out of a fairy tale." She twists in her seat to hand me a bottle of water.

"Thought you might need this," she offers shyly.

"Thanks." I take the bottle, but I don't open it.

Someday, I might not be able to recall the exact sound of Nathan's voice. Someday, the sweatshirt I borrowed from him and never gave back won't smell like him anymore. Someday, I'll say his name to someone who never met him, and it won't feel like those two syllables are enough to stop the world from turning.

But some days, it'll hurt to think that every new person I meet is another person who doesn't know Nathan ever existed. Some days, I'll cry—or at least feel a lump in my throat—because I loved him, and I lost him.

That's the never-ending strangeness of grief: Even after you accept it, it doesn't go away. In fact, I think accepting it means acknowledging that it may never go away.

The rental car has a phone charger, and I plug in my phone. When it turns on, I see two text messages waiting for me.

For just a moment, I expect the messages to be from Nathan. After all, for a long time, he was the only person who texted me regularly. In that moment, I feel a familiar jolt of joy at the thought of messages from my best friend. But then I remember that of course the messages can't be from him.

The first text is from Randy: **This is Randy—wanted to make sure you had my number. See you in New York.** I feel something else—not joy, exactly, but a happy warmth in my cheeks. I hold my phone a little closer and save Randy's number to my contacts.

The other message reads: **Hey, it's me. Pretty sure today is your last day at Castle, right? They finally let me have my phone and there were, like, a zillion emails from you. Seriously, who emails anymore? So I thought I would give you my number. Now we can communicate like normal people.**

She doesn't say her name, but I know it's Eleanor. I smile and type, **We're not normal people.**

After a minute, she responds. **What's so great about normal?**

I write: **Dr. Prince would say we shouldn't use that word. He'd say there's no such thing as normal.**

**Well, what does he know? If we were normal, we never would've met.**

I want to ask how she's feeling. I want to ask if the people are nice at her new place, if the doctors are any good, if she has a roommate and whether she's cool. But instead, I write: **Normal is overrated.**

**Amen to that,** she writes.

I can't keep myself from sharing a bit of trivia, even though I know it'll make Eleanor roll her eyes.

**Did you know that amen is Hebrew for "it is so"?**

It occurs to me that I've had internet access for a while now, but I haven't looked up a single new piece of trivia.

Not that there's anything wrong with wanting to know definitions and histories and etymologies. There will always be things I want to know, and I'll look them up from time to time. But I haven't felt the need to fill every empty space with facts and figures.

There's a difference between being interested and needing a distraction.

**Does anyone but you know that?** Eleanor writes back.

No one will love me quite the way Nathan did, just as I'll never love anyone exactly the way I loved him.

But Eleanor will tolerate my facts and figures, and Randy will look up facts of his own and send butterflies across my belly, and that's a kind of love, too.

My mom said the Castle School was like a fairy tale. Fairy tales require evil witches and powerful sorcerers, but neither Dr. Prince is either of those things.

Maybe the characters in fairy tales aren't *really* evil witches or powerful sorcerers. Maybe Snow White's stepmother wasn't wicked but terrified of losing her place as *the fairest of them all* for fear she'd be cast aside. Maybe the fairy who cursed Sleeping Beauty did it not out of rage but hurt. Maybe Cinderella's stepmother wasn't evil but worried for her own daughters' futures. Maybe the twelve dancing princesses snuck out to dance every night not because they were frivolous girls who wanted to dance, but because their father kept them under lock and key and they were searching for a place that made them feel free.

Every fairy tale ends with the same words: *They lived happily*

387

*ever after.* We all know those words are nonsense. Cinderella probably grew bored of living as a princess. Snow White might have developed the same anxieties about losing her beauty as the evil queen did before her. Sleeping Beauty may have been disappointed with reality after so many years spent dreaming.

I thought I'd never be happy after Nathan died, but maybe *happily ever after* means that I can go on loving him for the rest of my life. Maybe *happily ever after* means giggling at Eleanor's eye-rolls and holding Randy's hand. Maybe *happily ever after* means accepting what is, remembering what was, and looking forward to whatever is coming next.

Maybe I can live *happily ever after* after all.

# acknowledgments

Many thanks to the team at Sourcebooks: my editor, Eliza Swift, and Chris Bauerle, Sarah Cardillo, Margaret Coffee, Christa Desir, Steve Geck, Tim Golden, Stephanie Graham, Cassie Gutman, Ashley Holstrom, Nicole Hower, Sarah Kasman, Ashlyn Keil, Kelly Lawler, Lizzie Lewandowski, Sean Murray, Beth Oleniczak, Valerie Pierce, William Preston, Dominique Raccah, Jillian Rahn, Sophia Ramos, Stefani Sloma, Todd Stocke, Sierra Stovall, and Cristina Wilson. Thanks to Amanda Hudson and Faceout Studio for the beautiful cover.

Thank you Mollie Glick, and thanks to Berni Barta and Austin Denesuk, and to Lola Bellier, Adi Mehr, Jamie Stockton, Claire Youngerman, and the entire team at CAA.

Thank you for reading, Nicole Banholzer, Rachel Feld, and Mindy Ferraraccio. Thanks to my lovely writing group and to all my wonderful writing friends (and to my non-writing friends, too!).

Thank you to my family and my teachers.
And once again, thank you JP Gravitt, for everything.

What would the world be like without
music or rivers or the green and tender
grass? What would this world be like
without dogs?
—MARY OLIVER, "THE SUMMER BEACH"

# about the author

© JP Gravitt

Alyssa Sheinmel is the *New York Times* bestselling author of several novels for young adults, including *What Kind of Girl, A Danger to Herself and Others,* and *Faceless.* Alyssa grew up in Northern California and New York and currently lives and writes in New York. Follow Alyssa on Instagram @alyssasheinmel or visit her online at alyssasheinmel.com.

# FIREreads

## #getbooklit

**Your hub for the hottest young adult books!**

Visit us online and sign up for our
newsletter at FIREreads.com

 @sourcebooksfire

 sourcebooksfire

 firereads.tumblr.com